DRAGON'S MEN:
SWAMP COVERED SHIELDS

Don't miss any of Doc Ephraim Bates'
exciting comedic action thrillers

* * *

Boom!!...Killers. Series
Chasing Black Ice
Chasing Revenge
Chasing Liberation
Chasing Redemption

* * *

Dragon's Men Standalone Thriller Series

DRAGON'S MEN:
SWAMP COVERED SHIELDS

Doc Ephraim Bates

Golden Alley Press
Emmaus, Pennsylvania

Dragon's Men: Swamp Covered Shields is a work of fiction. Everything contained in these pages, including the characters, their names, events, and places are either products of the author's imagination or are used fictitiously. Any resemblance to actual people, places, or events is purely coincidental.

Copyright © 2024 Doc Ephraim Bates

All rights reserved. No part of this publication may be reproduced without the prior written permission of the publisher, except in the case of brief quotations embodied in critical reviews and certain other noncommercial uses permitted by copyright law. For permission requests, contact the publisher at the address below.

Golden Alley Press
307 N. Oak Street
Lititz, Pennsylvania 17543

www.goldenalleypress.com

Golden Alley Press books may be purchased for educational, business, or sales promotional use. For information please contact the publisher.

Printed in the United States of America

■ 1 3 5 7 9 10 8 6 4 2

Dragon's Men: Swamp Covered Shields / Doc Ephraim Bates.

ISBN 978-1-7373410-1-7 paperback
ISBN 978-1-7373410-2-4 eBook

Back cover photograph of the author ©Michael J. Hoffman

Cover design by Michael Sayre

This book is dedicated to Angela Leone

*To my friend, Angela Leone
Who watches me every night
from the top of the moon.
Said all the world over,
and each time cuts like a knife
From this life
You are gone too soon.*

Prologue:

Who's Who and What's What

in this Series

Welcome to the city of White Pines, the perfect marriage of beauty and money. Especially money.

Over $100 billion is tucked away in the banks here. Not bad for a town of only 33,000 people. The whole place reeks of luxury. It's all about living the good life.

About a thousand doctors practice in White Pines, half of whom are plastic surgeons. It's also home to movie stars and rock stars, millionaires, billionaires, Arab oil magnates, and Japanese tycoons.

White Pines is not, however, home to the workers who make up its fire department, police department, transit system, or local government. They simply cannot afford to live here. It gives one pause to think.

One might also think about the issues that come along with big money.

For one, there's the danger factor. When people have the kind of money that registers in the "untold wealth" category, you can bet your bottom dollar there are plenty of schemers out there angling to get their hands on it. Con artists. Blackmailers. Thieves. Kidnappers. If you live in White Pines, it is pretty much a given that someone is going to target your money sooner or later. And when you are targeted, you need a place to go for help. For protection.

Facing this problem, the overworked, underpaid White Pines Police Department can only do so much.

That is where the Dragon's Men Protection Agency comes in. When the long arm of the law is not nearly long enough, Dragon's Men are able to do a myriad of things to ensure the safety of their clients, their clients' friends and families, and their possessions. Dragon's Men are there to help the people that are in enough of a pickle to be in legitimate danger, but not enough of a pickle for the police to help them.

DRAGON'S MEN

The Dragon's Men Protection Agency is composed of four former Delta Force operatives: John Watkins, Dr. Mercedes Lara, Daniel Sloane, and Samuel Hawkins.

Three years before ending their military careers, the quartet devised the idea of taking their military skills to the civilian world. They pooled their money, obtained a rather large business loan, and purchased a five-story building on the southwest side of White Pines. They turned the first floor into their office space. The second and third floors became reinforced panic rooms and safe-house quarters for their clients, should the need arise. The top two floors were renovated into apartments for the team members.

Sure, Dragon's Men is a bit corny, as names go. But like all good names, there is a story behind it.

JOHN WATKINS

When they were a Delta Force unit, Captain John Watkins was the troop's commanding officer. John was usually as level-headed as they come. But there was one guaranteed way to tell when he was truly getting angry: his habit of breathing forcefully through his nose, like a dragon breathing flames out of its nostrils. This became so much his trademark that whenever the higher-ups wanted to assign John's team to a job, they would simply say, "Put Dragon's men on it."

The name stuck.

So, when John, Merc, Danny, and Sam moved their talents into the private sector, it seemed natural to name the business the Dragon's Men Protection Agency.

John is a natural-born leader. He is the kind of person who can get the maximum amount of results out of someone with a minimal amount of effort. He is quick on his feet, cool under pressure, and always ready with a plan B if plan A somehow goes awry. He is also a great mediator, and when dealing with the expanse of personality traits offered up by Dr. Mercedes Lara, Major Daniel Sloane, and Specialist Samuel Hawkins, those mediation skills get more of a workout than any of his other military skills.

DR. MERCEDES LARA

Even though Dr. Mercedes Lara is a woman, given her twelve years of military service, she is more of a "man" than 80 percent of the male population walking the planet today.

Make no mistake, Merc, as she is known to her friends, is all woman. At 5 feet 7 inches tall, she has long blond hair, porcelain skin, and a body like a Barbie doll. Dr. Lara is both a general surgeon and a military medic, which means that she is able to perform a myriad of medical procedures under all kinds of circumstances. Beyond that, what sets Dr. Lara apart from her contemporaries is her credentials as a bomb tech. She knows how to make a bomb, and she knows how to dismantle one.

Mercedes received her MD and her MBBS from Johns Hopkins University in Baltimore, Maryland. Her specific field of study was trauma and ER procedures.

When a massive terror strike against the U.S. occurred, like many red-blooded Americans, she decided to join the war on terror by bringing her medical skills to the military. After her six-week orientation, she was immediately sent to Afghanistan to patch up wounded soldiers so they could survive transport back to base. Since she would be traveling in the Afghani war fields, she was put through an intensive crash course in the munitions, IEDs, and other explosive devices that she would encounter daily.

Dr. Mercedes Lara has the two things it takes to be both a top-notch surgeon and an effective bomb technician: nerves of blue steel and hands as steady as a rock.

She is also extremely cynical. When God made Dr. Mercedes Lara, He broke the mold for cynical people. John, Daniel, and Sammy are used to her acute cynicism, but she often rubs members of the White Pines Police Department, as well as many of her filthy rich male suitors, the wrong way with her verbal eviscerations.

As beautiful and as smart as she is, Merc rarely keeps a boyfriend for long. Fortunately, she seems to have found a perfect match in a government assassin named Harper Rowe. No doubt one of the attributes that help make this particular relationship work is that Harper lives a good fourteen hours away. Because of their respective schedules, Merc and Harp spend most of their time on the phone. But whenever they have the opportunity to be together, they make the most of it.

DANIEL SLOANE

Major Daniel Sloane is the team's muscle and mechanic – engine mechanic, not hitman-mechanic.

Daniel takes pride in his physique. When time allows, Danny spends four to five hours a day working out. The thing is, Sloane does not have the stereotypical bulging-bodybuilder look. His physique is defined, to be sure, but he is not "swoll" with hulk-like muscles.

It is his ability to pack a punch – as well as take one – that makes him such an asset to the team.

His talent for giving a beatdown is equaled only by his wizardry as a mechanic. If something has an engine – anything from an airplane to a Zamboni machine – Daniel Sloane can take it apart, put it back together, modify or fix it.

However, much like Dr. Mercedes Lara, Daniel Sloane has a bit of a personality flaw: his extremely explosive temper, which he blames on his Carolina Cherokee heritage.

John and Merc have gotten pretty good at learning how to get the big man under control. But with Samuel Hawkins, the final member of Dragon's Men, it is the complete opposite. No one can get under Daniel Sloane's skin quite like Hawk can. If Sloane's temper is gasoline, Samuel Hawkins is the lit match that can – and usually does – set it off.

SAMUEL HAWKINS

Weapons Specialist and Senior Airman Samuel Hawkins is by far the most charismatic individual of the bunch. Hawk is the team's weapons expert, confidence man, and pilot. Blessed with exceptional good looks, the lean, athletic black man is no slouch with the ladies, either.

Hawk is the only member of the team to have come from a military background. His father, Rodney Hawkins, trained snipers at Camp Lejeune in North Carolina. So, while Hawk never had any official military training as a sniper, his father made sure his son would be able to pass both the MARSOC Advanced Sniper Course and the Special Forces Sniper Course. Thanks, Pop.

With his sniper training and deadly accuracy with a blade, Hawk is a stone-cold killer – and he would be the first one to say so, especially to the ladies. His gift of gab and general knowledge of just about anything make him likable and believable. Even if he doesn't have a clue as to what he is talking about.

Before finding a home on the Delta Force team with Watkins, Lara, and Sloane, Samuel Hawkins was an Army pilot, specifically, a Senior Airman. He had hastened his way up through the ranks by undergoing a strict and rigid process known as "Below-the-Zone," which trained him on various jets, planes, and attack choppers. Sam was just about to be promoted to staff sergeant when he was given the option to join the black ops group. And join them, he did.

LATIN JACKSON: ADJUNCT TECH GURU

Dragon's Men's members specialize in many assets except one: they lack a bona fide computer expert.

None of them are able to break through firewalls or security protocols to obtain information crucial to their cases. For jobs such as these, they turn to cyber-criminal mastermind Latin Jackson.

Latin is a short, portly fellow with a jolly face and dark features. Jackson is his adopted surname. Both of his parents were killed in a fiery car crash when he was just four years old. His birth surname was Tsitak. Latin Tsitak.

Latin's adoptive parents, Stanley and Loretta Jackson, worked in the IT departments of their respective employers: Stanley for an international banking firm, Loretta for a major pharmaceutical corporation. With family figureheads such as these, the adopted apple did not fall far from the tree.

It just landed on the wrong side of the law.

By the time Latin hit ninth grade, he could hack into his high school's computer system and change anyone's grades that he wanted. Anyone willing to pay the right amount of cash, that is. He quickly became the school's most popular freshman.

It didn't take Latin long to figure out that this illegal computer shtick wasn't a bad way to make some decent coin. So, he kept at it.

And he was good. Then he was great.

Of course, one doesn't achieve greatness without a few bumps in the road. Latin did get arrested – twice – for Class 1 misdemeanor computer fraud: trespass by computer done unlawfully but not maliciously.

But, boy, if the law had only known at the time what they were sitting on with him.

Now in his mid-thirties, Latin – never hard to spot due to his trademark gray fedora, black suspenders, white button-down shirt, and orange power tie – had built himself quite the computer hacking empire in White Pines. So much so that, truth be told, he was the seventh wealthiest person in White Pines.

On paper, however, he was an independent accountant and tax preparer that barely cleared six figures. He did have fun with it, though, as he advertised himself as "Latin Jackson: Accountant to the Stars."

It wasn't as if people didn't know. Everybody knew. But knowing something and being able to prove it are two different things. Because of this, Latin was always under the investigative eye of some agency or another.

So, when it came to Latin Jackson, there were two schools of thought. One was to steer clear of the guy and remain guilt-free. The other was to take full advantage of his *verboten* ways and hope that you were far enough outside of the blast zone when the eventual fall of the Latin Empire occurred.

For Dragon's Men, the schools of thought were divvied up 3-1. Doc, Danny, and Hawk were of the mind to stay as far away from Mr. Jackson as humanly possible, while the perpetually straight and narrow John Watkins had quite the friendship with the dude. In fact, Latin was the only one to call John by the nickname D.J., short for Dragon John.

Besides his main computer-hacker hustle, Latin Jackson also has a side hustle. He trains dogs.

But not just any dogs. Latin Jackson trains retired police and military dogs to become normal family pets. No dog whisperer, he is a dog re-programmer. And although the work can, at times, be tedious and repetitive, Latin loves every minute of it.

LIEUTENANT JACK THOMPSON

With the kind of services that Dragon's Men offer, they often find themselves in the presence of the White Pines Police Department, as well as the White Pines city council. Since Jack Thompson is a member of both (a lieutenant in the former and the vice-president of the latter), he often serves as a liaison between the city and the protection agency.

Hailing from Tulsa, Oklahoma, Jack is a bit of a cowboy as both a lawman and an individual. He does not take much guff from anyone that runs afoul of the law, and he is a straight shooter when it comes to his personality and communication style. Plus, when he isn't in uniform, he is quite often adorned in a cowboy hat and his favorite gator-skinned cowboy boots.

Married to his wife, Helen, for close to thirty years, Lieutenant Thompson is the father of two twenty-something daughters, Jackqueline and Helene, and grandfather to a set of bouncing triplet boys that Jackie and her husband brought into the world just a few months ago.

Jack has a good working relationship with the protection agency crew, and quite often farms out jobs to them whenever someone approaches the police with a situation that runs outside the confines of help that the police can offer. All-in-all, the lieutenant finds Dragon's Men to be very helpful to the city and its shamelessly wealthy citizens

WHAT'S THE PECKING ORDER?

Ever since the quartet stopped being a government-run Army Delta Force and shadow ops team and started being the Dragon's Men Protection Agency, John Watkins insisted that they were a democracy. He was no longer the team leader, and everyone now had an equal say. But as much as John Watkins tries to tell them that the days of Captain, Medic, Major, and Specialist are over, Merc, Sloane, and Hawk still tend to follow John's lead. After all, he has gotten them through many a perilous situation, both military and paramilitary.

Why change a good thing now?

DRAGON'S MEN:
SWAMP COVERED SHIELDS

1

THE HEAT IS ON

Summer in White Pines was a mixed blessing: the Midwest heat bearing down on the town of incredibly attractive people, causing them to shed their clothing right up to the point of illegality.

The higher the temperature, the lower the items of clothing covering up the gorgeous people of this beautiful town. At times, it could be downright distracting.

What was there not to love?

Well, the intensely uncomfortable heat was what there was not to love, especially on a day like today.

On this particularly blistering hot August afternoon, John Watkins and company were deskbound inside the protection agency, enjoying the refreshing comfort of the office's air conditioning.

John was busy at his computer doing the firm's books.

Daniel Sloane was ordering automotive parts for the company's SUVs.

Samuel Hawkins was at his desk putting in an order for some new weapons and additional ammunition for the agency's war chest.

Dr. Mercedes Lara was reading an article on radical new brain surgery for blind people that would connect the part of the brain that controls a person's sight to certain nerves in one's spine that would act like jumper cables, enabling them to "jump start" the signals that run from the eyes to the brain and vice versa.

Just before three o'clock the agency's main phone line rang.

"Dragon's Men Protection Agency, you're speaking with John Watkins. How may I be of assistance today?"

"Hello?" came the voice of an old woman on the other end of the line. Or somebody doing a very good impersonation of one. "I was trying to reach my grandson, Samuel. Do I have the right number?"

"Yes, ma'am," Watkins answered. "Please hold on for one moment, and the next voice you hear will be his."

John pressed the button to transfer the call to Hawk's line. "Sam," he said, "it's your grandma."

Sam gave Watkins a quizzical look. "Meemaw?"

"If that's what you call her, yes."

* * *

Sam's parents had passed away a few years earlier. Both of his grandfathers and one of his grandmothers had all also passed. His aunts and uncles were all dead, as well. The only relative he had left was a sister that lived in Bangkok–and his ninety-eight-year-old Haitian Creole meemaw, on his father's side.

The other members of Dragon's Men had never met Meemaw, but they all felt like they knew her well just from Sam talking about her so much.

Sam, whose desk sat on the other side of the office, picked up his phone.

"Meemaw, it's Sambo. Are you okay?"

"No, Sambo. I don't think I am," the old lady answered. "Is there any way you and your little friends can come down?"

"What's going on, Meemaw? Take your time, take a breath. Alright?" Sam reached over and hit the speakerphone button.

"Do you remember my friend Dorothy?" Meemaw's voice came out of the speaker.

"You're on speakerphone, Meemaw. We're all listening: my friends, John, Daniel, and Mercedes. And, yes, I remember your friend Dorothy. You call her Dot, don't you?"

"Yes, Sambo. Now, Dot has a beautiful granddaughter named Melissa. She's just a baby, twenty-three years old, but she's married to this evil, evil man named Clint Thoreaux, and he beats the devil out of her, Sambo. He done put her in the hospital four times in the last year."

"Can't someone call the cops on this dirtbag, Meemaw?"

"Well, that's just the problem, see? Clint *is* a policeman." Meemaw was exasperated. "We already wents to see the policemen here, and they just looked the other way."

Meemaw, whose actual name was Sandrine Benoit, began weeping softly "Now, Dot and I tried to get Melissa away from this man, but he won't let her get out of his sight. And when he's at work…he gots other people 'round his house keepin' eyes out for him. And now…the police is hasslin' me and Dot…and I'm scared Sambo. I'm scared, and I don't really know what to do."

"You did the right thing by calling, Meemaw," Sam reassured her.

"Can you and your little Dragon's Friends come down, Sambo?" the old lady cried.

Sam looked at John, who gave him a nod and a "thumbs up." They all knew that Sam was the product of a military family, and that for some semblance of stability he and his brother St. John Hawkins used to spend prolonged periods of time living with Meemaw while their parents were deployed overseas.

"It's Dragon's *Men*, Meemaw, and yeah…we'll pack up our gear, drive down tonight, and be there in time for breakfast tomorrow morning."

"Really?" Sam could hear her smiling on the other end of the phone. "Thank you, thank you, thank you! I'll have the grits and scrapple ready for y'all by the time ya get here."

"Can't wait, Meemaw. You think you'll be okay until we get there?"

"I'll have Dot come stay the night with me. Don'tcha worry a thing about it. You and your team just be safe. I'll pray the Lord's hand of protection be on all v'ya." Sandrine Benoit let out a sigh of relief. "I love you, Sambo."

And then she was gone.

Travel Preparations

It was a simple matter for the team to close up the office for an extended absence. The windows enclosing the agency's foyer were bullet-resistant, so good luck trying to break through them. And the window and door locks were all weaponized and ready to send 450,000 volts of electricity through any poor sap that fiddled with them for more than five seconds.

In addition to all that, once the security system was activated, Kevlar barriers dropped into place behind every window and door, further minimizing the possibility of the building being breached.

Currently, the four members of Dragon's Men were milling around the agency office.

"How long should we pack for?" Sloane asked.

"Hard to say. If we're dealing with dirty cops, that means feds, which means it could be a quick, two-day turnaround...or it could be a week or six," John told them. "So, better to pack it and not need it than to need it and not have it packed."

"I love that saying," Merc said, shutting down her computer and transferring her landline to the agency's answering service. "That's Chaucer, isn't it?"

"Chaucer...John Mandeville...one of those 14th Century authors," John laughed. He looked at Sloane. "Danny, I know you usually load the vehicles when we go on trips, but since we have a quick leave time, you should probably try to get some sleep since you'll be driving. Hawk, same for you. Pack a bag and get a few winks."

"Copy that, Boss," Sloane responded.

"Tell ya this much, boys and girls," Hawk advised, "pack for extreme heat and humidity as well as sauna-quality air. Think it's hot here? Compared to Natchez, Loozeeanna, this is a walk-in freezer."

"They have AC down there, don't they?" Sloane asked.

"They do," Sam sighed, "but my meemaw keeps her AC set at a tropical 83 degrees. She's an old lady; she gets cold when an elephant breaks wind."

"Perchance, does she have any electric fans in her house?"

"If she does, who knows how long it's been since she's used them. My advice would be to pick a few up on the way down."

"It won't matter," Watkins cut in. "We may start out there, but we won't be staying with your grandmother the whole time. Once we get down there, there's a good chance we'll be drawing some heat. It will be best for everybody if we set up shop elsewhere. You should probably let your meemaw know."

"No doubt, John Boy. I'll give her a call on the way down," Sam said. "If I call her now, I'll never get any shut eye before we head out."

"Speaking of *the way down*, are we sure we want to drive down?"

"Yeah, we're sure," John confirmed. "Leaving this time of night, we can probably make it in less than eight hours. If we were to haul everything over to the hangar, load it up, and get a flight plan okayed, that alone could take eight hours."

Watkins' cell phone rang. He recognized the number as that of Latin Jackson, his longtime friend. "What's up, Latin?"

"Not much. Hardly anything. It's finally slowed down enough for me to touch base with you guys. Whaddaya have going on at your end?"

"As it turns out, we're getting ready to head out of town for a few days."

"Oh, yeah? Where ya headed?"

"South to Louisiana," John said. "Natchez, Louisiana, to be exact."

"Ya don't say," Latin remarked. "Can't say that I've ever trekked across that part of the nation. Not a lot of my people down that way."

"Your people? Who's that...hackers? Bookies?"

"Greek Orthodox," Latin said flatly. "So, what's taking the lot of you down to the Pelican state?"

"Sam's grandmother–she's ninety-eight years old–is having trouble with some opprobrious law types. We're closing up shop for a few days and heading down to see if we can't come to some kind of understanding with these knuckleheads."

"You want my help? I just finished training a dog, and I'm not due to start training with another one for about three weeks. And we all know I can do my *other* business affairs any place there's even a hint of a Wi-Fi signal."

"I appreciate the offer," Watkins acknowledged, "but since we're dealing with potentially dirty cops, things could get dicey, and we might need a safety net. That'd be you."

"You know I got you, Dragon John," Jackson assured. "Matter of fact, let's go ahead and put some safety protocols in place now."

"Yeah, let's set up some check-in times. Want to shoot for noon and midnight, central time?" Jackson suggested.

"A lot can happen in twelve hours, Hoss. Maybe we should make it every eight hours."

"Eight hours it is then," John confirmed. "We'll make our first check-in time for eight o'clock tomorrow morning, and we'll go from there. If you don't hear from any of us at those times, you know what to do. Once we get down there and get settled, I'll call you with some coordinates or an address."

"Keep your beacons on."

"Hey, real quick, Jax, can you do a deep dive on the Natchez Police Department, especially an officer named Clint Thoreaux–that's Thoreaux with the Cajun spelling. Pull any news stories, financials, department records, employee records, what kind of educa—"

"D.J., I know how to do a deep dive. This ain't my first swim, ya know."

"Right," Watkins smiled. "We'll be looking to hear from you soon."

"Have a good trip, brother. Give me about two hours, and I'll have a pretty thorough intelligence report for you. We'll talk then." Latin Jackson disconnected the call.

John tucked the phone into the breast pocket of his gray tweed suitcoat. He looked up at the digital clock hanging above the main entrance: 19:39 hours.

"I'm going to retire to my room, pack a bag, and take a nap for a couple of hours," John directed the squad. "Let's have wheels on pavement by twenty-two hundred hours. We'll take the two black SUVs. Danny and I will ride together. Hawk, since you know where you're going, you'll be in the lead vehicle with Merc. It'll take about seven and a half hours, drive time. We'll give ourselves somewhere between forty and sixty minutes of stoppage time."

"I'll do the packing for the trip," Dr. Lara volunteered. "The SUVs will be stocked to capacity come leave time."

3

The Ingredients for a Bad Husband

Melissa Thoreaux had finished preparing an evening meal of pork chops, mashed potatoes, succotash, and a tossed salad. She set the table for two and placed the food neatly upon it. The young housewife was waiting patiently for her husband, Clint, to get home from work. He usually walked into the house around eight o'clock. But tonight, the clock read 8:26, and he still was not home.

Melissa was starting to worry.

She was not worried that something bad had happened to Clint at his job as a Natchez Parish policeman. She was worried that supper was getting cold, and Clint hated coming home to cold food. So, Melissa put the meal back in the oven to heat it up.

The house phone rang.

Melissa looked around the kitchen for the handset, then remembered that she had left it in their bedroom. She retrieved the phone in time to see that her Grandma Dorothy was calling.

"Grandma Dot, hello."

"Good evening, Sugar. Are you alone?" Grandma Dorothy asked.

"I am for the time being, but Clint will be home anytime now."

"Okay, sweetie, I'll be quick then. I talked to my friend, Sandrine, and her grandson's gonna be coming down with some of his friends. They gonna be able to help you, honey."

"Grandma Dot, I told you to stay out of this. I don't want to see you get hurt."

"But these is military men, Missy. They can get you and your baby away from that evil, evil man."

Just then, Melissa heard Clint come through the front door.

"Missy! Where y'at?" she heard him holler.

"Grammy, I gotta go," she whispered and quickly hung up the phone.

"Missy!"

"Back here," she answered, emerging from their bedroom at the back of the house.

"Where's my dinner?" Clint growled.

"I put it in the oven to keep it warm. You're a little later than usual."

"It was a rough day at work. Paperwork kept me over, but I'm here now." Getting right up in Melissa's face, he shouted, "So, get me my supper!"

"Okay, okay" she said. "I was going to get it for you. I'm sorry you had a bad day, but you don't have to take it out on me."

That was apparently the wrong thing to say, as it caused Clint to grab her harshly by the arm. "You think I'm taking my bad day out on you?" He backhanded her across the face. "Now! Now I'm taking it out on you."

Melissa pulled away from him, her eyes welling up with tears. "I'll get your supper."

"And?"

"And...I'm sorry I upset you."

"Get me a beer while you're up," Clint ordered. "And I'll take my supper in the living room. I'll watch some TV while I eat."

"Okay," Melissa said. "We can talk about your day if you want?"

"My day was bad enough already. I don't want to have to relive it by having to talk to you about it. I just wanna be left alone."

Melissa fixed her husband a plate and served it to him in the living room.

Her face was still stinging from Clint's backhand. She had been hoping that now that she was pregnant, he would stop hitting her as much.

He did not.

4

Road Chatter

The Dragon's Men Protection Agency owned nearly enough vehicles to start their own used car lot. Each member had their own ride, but of course they were all registered under the company name so they could use them as a tax write-off. Five additional automobiles were used strictly for company business: two Audi Q4 E-trons (one blue, one silver), two Cadillac Escalades (both black), and one black soft-top Jeep Wrangler.

The Q4s and the Escalades were tricked out to the max with security features. Both the bodies and the windows were bullet resistant, and the tires all had run-flat capability for up to fifty miles. Thanks to Latin Jackson, each vehicle also had one of the best GPS and tracking systems in the world. He had hacked into a U.S. defense satellite and linked it into the agency's GPS system. Latin would often say, "Every site and every system has a back door for emergency purposes." And he knew that, unless someone was looking at the satellite's back door on a computer screen at the very moment he was performing the hack–which was about as likely as winning the lottery twice on the same day–he would not be detected. Upon finishing the operation, Latin cloaked the hack, making it completely untraceable and imperceptible. Then he gave the quartet a tutorial on how to use the satellite, not only for GPS purposes, but also to track traffic patterns and detect police radar along their route of travel. In essence, Latin Jackson had given the team the ability to travel at any rate of speed they deemed necessary. Usually, the foursome drove the speed limit, as the town of White Pines was littered with stop signs, traffic lights, and traffic patterns that made most drives very slow. It was one of the reasons that, when the weather would allow, people walked wherever they needed to go. It was simply quicker than driving.

All of which explains why the two black vehicles were now heading south at just about 120 miles an hour. Samuel Hawkins was behind the wheel in the lead vehicle, with the lovely Dr. Mercedes Lara riding shotgun. The two were engaged in a deep political conversation.

"Does it ever bother you, Doc, that the people making the decisions about a woman's right to choose are mostly old men in suits that have never even had a whiff of an abortion, nor its impact affect their lives?"

"You can look at abortion in one of two ways, Sam. First of all, there is abortion as an act. That would be the actual medical procedure of terminating the fetus before it comes to full term. This is what affects the life of the would-be mother, would-be father, the lives of those around them—what have you. This is what I think you are referring to when you ask me your question about the 'old men in suits', yes?"

"Yes."

"No. What you're talking about is the philosophy of abortion: is it right? Is it wrong? Is it right to do up to a certain point but not after that point? Is it right to do so under certain circumstances? That's what the politicians, religious leaders, and lawmakers are talking about," Mercedes corrected Hawk. "The first—the *act* of abortion—is almost always wrong."

"Really?" Mercedes' statement surprised Hawk.

"Well, sure," Merc said. "And I'm not even talking about the effects an abortion has on a fetus."

"You're not?"

"As you well know, one of the main staples of the Hippocratic Oath, which all doctors take, is to first, do no harm. When an abortion is performed on a woman, there is always the risk of physical harm– infection, hemorrhaging, damage to a myriad of internal organs, etc. And no doctor can say how much damage or how little damage could possibly occur because each case is different. On top of that, there's the potential for a massive amount of mental and emotional scarring. There's no way to measure or document the damage an abortion causes because, here again, in each case it's different. It would be like trying to document how bad a bee sting hurts. For some people, it can kill them. For others, it barely even registers on the one-to-ten pain scale index."

"I see what you're saying," Hawk nodded. "It's real easy to get the act and philosophy mixed up and confused."

"Want to know why it's so confusing? Want to know why we argue so much as Americans over abortion?"

"It's the lawmakers," Hawk said matter of factly.

"Yes, it's the lawmakers," Dr. Lara concurred. "They say that if the mother is pregnant, she has so many weeks until the fetus becomes a viable life. But let's say, the same woman goes strolling down the avenue, and Joe Gunman comes up to her and puts a bullet right in between her eyes. She doesn't even know she's pregnant, but upon doing the autopsy, they discover that she is, indeed, pregnant. Guess what?"

"Joe Gunman gets charged with a double homicide."

"Double homicide, double standard."

"When one standard is more than enough," Hawk said.

"Then you have the states that are set up to allow abortion for women that become pregnant via rape or incest," Merc continued.

"Here's my question, though: what's the standard for determining when it's rape? Or incest?"

"Whaddaya gettin' at, Doc?"

"If we're going to say rape or incest, we need to make it uniform and consistent," Doc said. "When is it officially rape? When a rape kit comes back positive? When an arrest is made? When the D.A. hands out an indictment?"

"I'm not a hundred percent sure even the old men in suits know the answer to that one," Sam grinned.

* * *

Meanwhile, in the trail vehicle, Daniel Sloan drove while he and John Watkins were having a much lighter conversation.

"Latin called before we left. These Natchez policemen are the real deal. Lowest crime rate in the state. Highest conviction rate of any parish in Louisiana."

Daniel let out an impressed whistle. "Well, if all the cops treat the citizens like Thoreaux treats his wife, then it's no wonder there isn't any crime in the parish. Maybe they rule with an iron fist and intimidation."

"We're definitely going to have our work cut out for us," John said, watching the world speed by his passenger window.

"You remember my friend Inky Bob?" Sloane asked.

"Um...maybe?"

"He's got a lot of tats, John."

"You've got a lot of tats."

"I've got *some* tats–thirty-six. Inky Bob has over a hundred."

"I guess that's why they call him *Inky Bob*."

"Well, it sure ain't because he's an octopus," Daniel smiled. He cracked his window about an inch, lit up a cigarette, and continued with his story. "So, Inky Bob changed home security companies."

"Okay."

"With his old security system, when he would accidentally set it off, the security company would still call to make sure everything was okay. The new company, though, they don't even do that."

"I guess the company figures that if the homeowner punches in their code within thirty seconds, everything's okay."

"Except for when a random bad actor comes busting through your front door, puts a gun to your head and tells you to punch in the code or else they're going to blow your brains out all over your kitchen counter." Sloane took a drag on his cigarette before progressing with his rant. "Shoot, for that matter, it's not like a phone call is going to make much of a difference either. If some creep has a gun to your head when the phone call comes in, you're going to say whatever they tell you."

"You make a valid point, Danny."

"Eventually, we'll get too old to be running around shooting at people, giving beatdowns, protecting rich bastards from the crazed nutjobs that come to town with their scams and schemes and misguided dreams. When we do, we'll open a private home security business." Daniel finished up his smoke and tossed it. "And we'll do it right. The way I see it, there's only one way to make sure the homeowner is safe after a false alarm."

"Oh yeah? How's that?"

"What you do is, install a small camera and train it on the alarm pad. Whenever the alarm goes off, falsely or otherwise, the camera comes on. We watch on a monitor at our office to make sure it's the homeowner–or a member of their family–that's punching the code back into the alarm pad. If we see something that looks a bit untoward, one of us will make a call to the home while the other three hightail it over there to investigate the situation."

"I have to say, Dan, that is a brilliant idea," John approved. He hit the lever on the side of his seat and reclined it to a forty-five-degree angle. Crossing his arms over his stomach, he laid back and closed his eyes before saying, "It's also good to know that you have our golden years all planned out for us."

"It just seems like the natural next step. We open an independent home security company right in town. Heck, we've already got the name recognition. We'll be able to charge whatever we want. They say that you can't put a price tag on peace of mind, but I think we'll find a way."

5

Home Again

Having driven through the night at an incredible rate of speed, the quartet of Dragon's Men rolled into the small town of Natchez, Louisiana, just as the sun was cracking the southern skies.

Hawkins reached over and smacked Merc on the arm. "Wake up, Doc. We're just about there."

Mercedes opened her eyes widely and yawned.

"What time is it?"

"It's just about six-thirty," Hawk answered. "Won't be much longer."

"Won't be much longer until it's six-thirty, or it won't be much longer until we get there?"

"Um…both."

The gorgeous blond pushed herself up in her seat. "Man, can't believe I slept the whole way here."

"I can't believe it either, Doc. I mean, daggone, we were chatting it up about the abortion laws, and all of a sudden, I look over and you's passed out." Hawk looked over at her and shook his head pathetically. "I'm just all kinds of ashamed."

"Feel free to be ashamed all you want. I'll be over here feeling all kinds of well-rested," Mercedes said, pulling her hair back into a ponytail and putting on one of her dozen or so Jacksonville Jaguars baseball caps.

"You're a punk, Doc," Hawkins laughed.

"It's only six-thirty?"

"In the morning."

"We made a ten-hour trip in less than eight?"

"You got that right we did," Sam acknowledged as an approving grin came across his face. "And that was stopping twice for gas and snacks."

"Aww, I slept through snacks," Doc repined in disappointment. "You didn't happen to get me any pork rinds, did you?"

"I asked you if you wanted anything, but you just kept sleepin'. I mean, if it weren't for the occasional light snoring, I was going to pull down the rearview mirror an' slide it under your nose for some sorta sign of life. That's how sound you's sleepin'."

Mercedes suddenly noticed that the ride had gone from paved streets through a small town to an unpaved, one lane road in the middle of a wilderness. Within just about three minutes, it was as if they had gone from civilization to the land that time forgot. Bogs and marsh and wetwoods seemed to run endlessly on both sides of the narrow lane that Sam was carefully navigating.

"Did you take a wrong turn or something, Hawk? It looks like we're driving through the set of a bad horror flick."

"I know. It's hard to believe there's an actual town out here in all of this–couple of 'em, actually–but this is home to some of the nicest people you'll ever meet."

"Except for that poor girl's husband that uses her for a punching bag on a routine basis," Mercedes pointed out. "And the rest of the local police, who obviously know what's going on, yet they fail to do anything about it."

"It's been a few years since I've been down this way. But I do remember the last time I was here, the local sheriff–who'd been the sheriff forever, seems like–he died, and they were doing an emergency election. My meemaw, she told me that if the one dude got elected, she wasn't gonna be too happy about it. Said the man was a snake oil salesman. Now, I know my grandma better than just about anyone. For her to say that, those are some pretty strong words to come out of her mouth."

"Did your meemaw ever tell you who won the election?"

"Can't say that she did, and up until just now, I hadn't even thought about it."

"If things were bad, your meemaw would've said something, right?"

Sam focused on his driving for a bit before answering. He was being extremely cautious on the dirt road, which seemed to have eroded and was narrower than he remembered.

"I know two things for sure right now," he began his answer to Merc's question. "The first thing that I know is if my meemaw thought things were in a precarious situation, she would've reached out–much like she's done now. The second thing I know is that if you open the glove box, you'll find a bag of pork rinds just for you."

An excited look shot across Dr. Lara's face as she leaned forward to open the glove compartment. She snagged the bag of pork rinds with her right hand, while reaching over to rub Hawkins' shaved scalp with her left.

"Gee whiz, Doc," Sam protested, pulling away from the woman's touch. "Don't be all up on my head like that when I'm driving. Gonna cause me to put this tin can into the drink and turn us both into gator bait."

"Aww, Sammy, you're the best," Merc said, lighting up the morning with her smile. "I hope I can be just like you when I grow up."

Meanwhile, in the trail car, Daniel was participating in his favorite pastime: complaining as much as humanly possible about his teammate, Sam Hawkins.

"Would you look at this, John? Where is this idiot taking us? He probably doesn't even know where he's going."

"Well, I'm sure it's not his fault," Watkins answered. "I'm sure whoever the good people that Google sent down here to map this place probably got eaten by the local wildlife."

"I know they say that white men can't jump," the menacing brute continued, ignoring Watkins' wisecrackery, "but Hawk is a lousy driver. I mean, that dude couldn't drive his way off a golf course. My sister drives better than he does."

"And, if you follow that argument all the way through to its logical conclusion, you'll hear somebody, somewhere say…you don't have a sister, Daniel."

Sloane cocked his head and shot a look over at Watkins. "I know I don't have a sister, John. I don't need you to tell me I don't have a sister. I already know I don't have a sister. That's not my point."

"I hear you," John coaxed his cohort. "We do seem to be more than just a few clicks off the beaten path." He reached down into the center console to fetch a two-way radio and hailed the lead car. "Can I get a pick up on Radio Two, over?"

Within seconds John heard Merc's voice crackle back, "Good morning, Boss."

"Aurora, is that you?" Watkins chided, referencing the little known first name of Sleeping Beauty. "We were just wondering if we could get an ETA to our destination."

"Less than ten minutes, Johnny," Hawk answered. "Won't be long now."

"Roger that, Airman. Watkins over and out."

With that, the former Delta Force Captain returned the radio back to the console. Looking out his window, he took in the scenery and sighed. "Won't be long now."

And it wasn't. Barely ten minutes later, the protection agency members had driven out of the swamp and into the small town of Natchez, Louisiana.

The very small town of Natchez, Louisiana, population 489.

* * *

As they drove through the parish, Mercedes could not help but notice the happy look that adorned Samuel Hawkins' face.

"So? What do you think?" the doctor asked. "Has it changed much since your last visit?"

"Not really," Hawk shook his head. "Everything still looks just about the same…extreme poverty. Still, it's good to be home again."

Meeting Meemaw

It was a little past seven in the morning when the foursome arrived at Sandrine Benoit's residence. Daniel and Sam parked their vehicles next to each other in the wide driveway. John Watkins was the first to get out and experience the heat and humidity of the bayou smacking him and his three-piece suit right in the face. By the time the rest of the team joined him, Daniel and Mercedes were already complaining.

"Good gosh. It's hotter than the devil's underpants on taco night down here," Merc griped. "How do these people live in this mess? I think my toenails are even sweating."

"Is it always this miserable, Sam?" Sloane asked.

"In the summer, yeah. And I hate to tell you this, but this is kinda mild compared to what we'll be feelin' come this afternoon."

Sam's comment was met with a band of groans.

"Come on, y'all. I know it feels uncomfortable now, but you'll get used to it after a day or so," Sam consoled.

"Right," Mercedes said incredulously. "I think that's the same line they feed to the newbies in Hell. 'Buck up, little camper, you'll get used to the bazillion degree-temperature here eventually. You only have all eternity to do it.' I feel like I'm wearing a body-sized dripping-wet hot towel."

"This feels as bad as some of our summer jobs in the Middle East," Sloane remarked. "Only worse."

"Okay, okay," John said, putting a stop to all the griping. "Starting now, we are on the clock. Let's stay on our toes, be one-hundred percent vigilant, and watch each other's six." Watkins patted Hawk on the back. "Since this is your homecourt, I'll let you lead the way, my good man."

They followed Sam to a quaint cobblestone walkway that guided them to an outside flight of stairs. The stairs led up to the screened-in porch of an elevated shotgun house. The place appeared to be in good shape for as old as it was; the wood siding displayed a recently added fresh coat of white paint and the blue shutters adorning both sides of the windows were fastened neatly in place.

"Steady as she goes, mates," Hawk warned. "Where we're standin' is *terra firma*, but just a few steps away…" Hawk let his sentence hang as he bent down to pick up a rock. He threw it towards what appeared to be a clump of high weeds, but as it disappeared into the brush, they heard a loud splash. "Bayou, baby. Swamp. Quagmires and marshland. One-hundred percent pure muck…and up we go."

Some fifty yards in the distance, Mercedes could see fan boats filled with gator wranglers. She watched as they slowly moved through the swamp, checking their gator traps, one by one.

Hawk led the team up the wooden steps. At the top, the door slowly opened to reveal the stout little frame of Sandrine Benoit.

"Sambo!" Her frail, aged voice was filled with glee.

"We made it, Meemaw." Hawkins moved across the porch to give his grandmother a hug. It was a portrait in paradox: Sam's tall, athletic frame embracing Sandrine Benoit's short, podgy build.

Mercedes leaned over to John and whispered in his ear, "Meemaw is *so* cute. She's like the perfect grandma size."

"She even has the little grandma specs, too."

"Meemaw," Hawk continued, "these are my friends, co-workers, and people that make my life worth getting up for every morning."

Sam reached for Watkins' arm and guided him over to his grandmother. "This tall drink of water right here is the boss, John Watkins. Although, don't call him *the boss*, as he has been known to take offense at it from time to time."

"It's a pleasure, ma'am," John extended his hand in greeting.

Sam continued his introductions. "Over here, wearing all the muscles, is the real boss of the team: Daniel Sloane."

Meemaw got a bit wide-eyed looking at Sloane. Walking right up to him, she put her grandmotherly hands on his sinewy biceps. "Ooo...I like you," she cooed.

Sloane, taken aback, looked over at Hawkins. "Did you tell her to say that?"

"Meemaw!" Sam said, equally shocked. "What are you doing?"

Sandrine turned to her grandson. "I believe it's called *flirting*. At least, that's what it was called back in my day."

"Oh, I like where this is going," Mercedes chuckled. She stepped toward Sandrine Benoit and introduced herself. "I'm Dr. Mercedes Lara, and I must say what a joy it is to finally meet you."

"Oohh, a doctor," Meemaw said reverently, reaching out to shake Dr. Lara's hand. "Do you hear that, Sambo? She's a doctor."

"Yes, Meemaw," Hawk smiled. "I am aware."

"I'm so glad you and your friends are here, honey bear," Sandrine said to her grandson. "Are you all hungry? I made breakfast."

"I am *starved*," Mercedes said. She stood back as Meemaw moved past her and opened the door to her home. Moving into Meemaw's home, the four were immediately hit with two things. Number one, the wonderful aroma of breakfast food filled the air.

Grits. Scrapple. Sausage. Pancakes. Toast and coffee. If the breakfast tasted half as good as it smelled, they knew that they were in for quite a treat.

The second thing that hit them: the heat. Ms. Benoit's house was even hotter inside than outside.

"Meemaw, I gotta tell ya, everything smells great. But I have to ask." Sam's tone got all soft and quiet. "Do you have any fans that we might be able to put on?"

"Oh, my. Is it too warm in here?" she asked, surprised.

"Yes," all four answered in unison.

"I have a couple of fans in the back room, but my friend, Dot, is asleep in there. She's a pretty heavy sleeper. Oh my, Sambo, the way she snores. If I hadn't been awake with worry, I'd a-never gotten any rest last night. I'll go see what I can do."

Before Sandrine could make a move toward the fans, Daniel Sloane noticed a squad car from the Natchez Police Department pulling into her driveway.

"Expecting company this morning, ma'am?" Danny asked.

Sandrine shuffled over to the window and carefully peered out. "Oh, dear. It's him. It's Clint Thoreaux."

"He's the husband of your friend's granddaughter, right?" Watkins asked.

"Yes, that's him. The devil incarnate." Sandrine's words hung in the air and fear etched her face as she watched Clinton Thoreaux sit in his squad car at the end of the driveway.

7

A Threat by Any Other Name

Everyone gathered at the front window to watch as Thoreaux exited his cruiser and approached the house. Dressed in full police uniform, he took a few moments to give the Dragon's Men's black SUVs a good perusal. It was plain to see that he was familiar with the Benoit residence as he made his way around back to enter instead of using the more obvious front door.

"Do you want one of us to talk to him, Meemaw?" Samuel asked.

Sandrine stood in silence for a moment, a look of apprehension on her face. "Naw, naw. I'll go talk to him," she said.

"I'll come with you." Hawk volunteered.

Sandrine and Hawk moved to the rear door while John, Daniel, and Doc stayed out of sight near the front window.

Sandrine opened the door to the back porch just in time to see the rugged-looking officer make his way up the outside stairs.

"Good morning, Officer Thoreaux," she said with a friendly smile. "What brings you out this way so early like this?"

"Mornin', Miss Benoit," Clint said amiably. He, too, had a very thick creole accent. "I was just on my way into work, and I saw the rather official-looking vehicles in your drive. Thought I'd stop in to make sure everything was *byen*."

"Oh, it shaw 'nuff is." Meemaw opened the screen door to allow the policeman onto the back porch. She gestured to Hawk. "This here's my grandson, Samuel."

"Well, good morning, Samuel," Clinton said, smiling. "It is a real pleasure."

Sam reached out, shook the officer's hand, and asked, "Do you always make it a habit to stop in people's homes whenever you see a car in their driveway that you don't recognize?"

"Not as a habit, I suppose," the officer said, "but Miss Sandrine is one of Natchez' real treasures, and with her advanced age, everyone in town tries to keep a good lookin' out after her. Ain't that right, Ms. Benoit?"

Before Meemaw could answer, Officer Thoreaux made it a point to say, "Now, Sandrine, you didn't tell me you's expectin' company."

Hawk was quickly developing a bad feeling about this cop. Sure, his disposition was nice enough, but it all seemed as fake as a politician's smile.

"Tell me somethin', Samuel," Clint inquired, "did you drive both of those SUVs here?"

"No, sir, sure didn't," Hawk smiled a counterfeit smile of his own. "Some of my friends and I are on our way down to the Keys. Gonna do some deep-sea diving and maybe a bit o' fishin'. But I hadn't seen my meemaw in quite a spell, so I thought I'd take the opportunity to visit for a bit on our way through."

"We's jus' about to sit down and have a nice breakfast. D'ya have time to come in and sit a spell, Clint?" Sandrine invited.

Officer Thoreaux looked at his watch and said, "Ah, I'm gonna be late reportin' to shift as it is. I will take a rain check, though, Ms. Benoit. And, Samuel, why don't you 'n' your friends come by the station later on today. I'll show y'all how we operate law enforcement in this li'l ol' parish of ours."

"Sure thing, officer. Look forward to it," Hawk replied.

"Ms. Benoit," Clinton nodded and then saw himself out.

Sam and his grandmother exchanged looks.

"Yep," he said.

"Mm-hmm," she said.

8

BREAKFAST TABLE TACTICS

Twenty minutes later, everyone, including Sandrine's best friend Dorothy Michaud, was sitting down at Meemaw's long dining room table. It was covered with an agglomeration of breakfast foods, enough for a small army. Yet, for as hungry as everyone was, no one had taken a bite. Instead, everyone was talking about Clint Thoreaux.

"John, what's our plan for this toolbag?" Sloane asked.

"Sandrine, you said when Clint is at work, he has somebody watching his wife at their house?"

"Yes, sweetie. He has someone watching her at the house. And if she goes somewhere, they go somewhere with her."

"So, the same person that watches her at her house follows her if she goes out on an errand?"

"Mm-hmm. That's right, sweetie."

"Then here's what we're going to do," John said. "When we finish this fine breakfast, Ms. Michaud, I would like for you to go over to your granddaughter's place and take her out to lunch. Make sure she leaves the back door unlocked," John emphasized. "While you, your granddaughter, and whomever Clint has watching her are away from the house, we'll sneak into the home and plant cameras in some very well-hidden places. This way, the next time Clint decides to get rough with his wife, we'll have it recorded, documented, and ready to present."

"I understand, and, please, call me *Dot*."

A troubled look appeared on Sandrine's face. "You mean that po' Melissa is gonna have to get beat on yet again?"

"Unfortunately—as much as it pains me to say it—yes. But we'll be watching those cameras, and as soon as we have what we need, we will go into that house, stop him immediately…and it'll be the last time he ever lays a hand on her."

"Well, I sho don't like that at all, what with everything that girl's already been through and being pregnant. But if it's gonna get her away for good from that evil, evil man…"

"This is what we do. We protect people," Sam assured his grandmother and her best friend. "And there isn't anyone better at it than we are."

"There's just one last thing, Dot," John continued. "While you and your granddaughter are out, you absolutely must *not* say anything to Melissa about the cameras."

"Really? But why?"

"Because, Dot," Sam interjected, "when people know that they're being watched, they act differently. We don't want to tip Clint off or even have him suspect that there are cameras in the house. If Melissa knows about the cameras, she'll start acting differently, and that might be all Clint needs to know that something is going on. If he knows something is going on, we might not get what we need."

"Well, now, I don't really feel right lyin' to my *fi* like that," Dot objected.

"Ma'am, nobody's asking you to lie," John said politely. "But sometimes in order to obtain the greater good, certain barriers of deception need to be encountered and, quite often, breached."

"Well," Dorothy nodded in understanding, "as long as it's to obtain the greater good."

"Okay, now that we're all in agreement on that," Merc said, "let's see if we can't get some of this food moving around the table."

Settling In

It was just a little bit past eight o'clock by the time the group had finished their breakfast and Sandrine Benoit had shown everyone the rooms where they would be staying.

The house was laid out with the kitchen and dining room at one end of the dwelling, with both rooms opening into a large TV room spanning the entire width of the house. From there, a long hallway led to the other end of the house and the main bathroom. Sandrine's master suite was the first room on the left. Just across the hall was Sam's bedroom–the very one he had stayed in when he was a boy.

Sam was amazed. His room not only looked and felt the same, it even smelled the same as he remembered: equal parts *Drakkar Noir* and Yankee Candle. A steep staircase in the far-left corner led up to a sleeping loft containing a double bed, an antique dresser, and shelves filled with countless knick-knacks. This would serve as the sleeping quarters for Watkins and Sloane.

Mercedes' room was all the way at the end of the hall on the right, next to the bathroom.

Having unloaded their bags and unpacked their clothes in their respective rooms, the members of the protection agency were now on their phones.

John was checking in with Latin Jackson.

Daniel was talking to his longtime girlfriend, Jenny Main.

Mercedes was on the line with boyfriend and government assassin, Harper Rowe.

Samuel Hawkins was in the kitchen with his meemaw and Dot.

"Now, Sambo, you been drivin' all night. You need to go lay down for a spell and getcha some shut eye," Sandrine admonished Hawkins. "Dottie and I will get these dishes cleared."

"I'm not worried about it, Meemaw. In the military, they teach you how to get by on two-hour naps twice a day."

"Well, my boy, this ain't the military," Sandrine said. "Now git!"

"Meemaw, I'm gonna go lay down, okay? But it's not because you're right or I'm wrong. It's just that we might only be here for a short time, and I don't want to waste any part of it arguing with you."

* * *

In the TV room, John was giving Latin a rundown of the morning's events.

"I'll say this, Jax, if Sam's grandmother keeps feeding us like she did this morning, I'll be six pants sizes bigger by the time I get back. Then again, for as hot and humid as it is down here, I may sweat it all off just by blinking too much."

"Ahhh, summertime in the swamp," Jackson recollected. "Stickier than flypaper in a molasses factory."

"You're not kidding, brother."

"Anything else to report on down there besides the food and the weather?"

"We met the wife-beating husband already," John answered. "We hadn't been here but fifteen minutes before the creep showed up out of nowhere. Said he saw strange vehicles in the driveway and wanted to make sure everything was okay."

"Nice. Be sure to give that guy a gasoline-filled enema for me."

"We'll be making our way over to his place this afternoon to install some hidden cams. Going to try to catch this guy in the act, and from there, we'll have to figure out just where to send the footage."

"Ain't no bigger piece of garbage in this whole world than a half-ape that beats his wife. Except maybe for one that does it to her while she's pregnant."

"If we can't find someone willing to put this guy where he belongs, I'm certainly not going to mind doing the job myself."

* * *

In the loft over Hawk's bedroom, Daniel Sloane was laid out across the double bed where he and John would be sleeping. He had located a fan and had it blowing across his face while he talked on the phone with his girl.

"Tell ya this much, Jenny-baby, only one thing worth doing in weather like this and that's—"

"Oh, don't say it," she cut him off. "It only makes me miss you more."

"I hear ya, lover. We haven't even been apart a day yet, and I'm already missing you like crazy."

"Any idea how long you're going to be down there?"

"Not yet. We've got some things we're planning to do this afternoon, but what kind of results they'll provide or how soon, is anybody's guess."

"Ugh," Jennifer groaned. "Just promise me that you'll be careful, okay?"

"I will, baby," Sloane agreed. "Love you, Jenny Main."

"Love you, too, Daniel."

* * *

Mercedes was sitting at the foot of her bed talking to Harper Rowe about his latest assignment.

"Wow. It is *loud* there. Where are you again?" Mercedes asked.

"Cairo," Harper answered. "At the Pyramisa Suites Hotel."

"Are they doing road work in your room?"

"No, I'm out by the pool."

"Are you swimming with a jackhammer?"

"No, it's just that we're downtown, love. Downtown Cairo is one loud town."

"Who's *we*?"

"Kin, Laurs, me. The big three." The *Kin* and *Laurs* that Harper Rowe was talking about were his best friend, Kinley Devereaux, and Kinley's wife, Laurie Chase. Not long ago, the three of them had shared a globetrotting adventure, the likes of which few would ever know. Dragon's Men had even found themselves drawn into one particular leg of the journey when the seven of them, along with an international arms dealer that went by the name of Big James Gray, had taken out Brazilian drug kingpin Tito del Fuento. This was when Dr. Lara had first met and fallen for government wetwork agent Harper Rowe.

"Wait. The three of you are working a job together?"

"Oh, we're not working, baby. We're vacationing."

"Vacationing? In Cairo? What time is it there?"

"Just a little bit before four in the afternoon…or 1600 hours."

"Well, take some pictures and have a good time," Mercedes sighed. "Miss you."

"We're still good for the second week in September, yes?"

"Yes," she smiled.

"Alright. And, hey, you guys need to try to wrap things up there as soon as you can. You've got some real maneater kind of weather moving your way in a couple of days."

"We do? How do you know that?"

"I always try to know what the weather is where you are. Helps me feel closer to you."

"Aww, Harp," Mercedes said. However, before she could say

anything else, she heard a loud squelch of static followed by dead air. She tried calling back a couple of times, but the calls went straight to Harper's voicemail. On the last attempt, she left a message: "Hey, Harp. Lost your call. Not sure if it was my end or yours. Text me when you can to let me know you're okay. Bye for now, Big Shooter."

As soon as she finished leaving the message, she hit the weather app to see if what her boyfriend had said was accurate. After a few moments of searching, she let out a quiet, "Son of a bitch."

The doctor jumped up off her bed and yelled, "John!"

10

SOMETHING STRANGE ABOUT THE WEATHER

The four members of Dragon's Men were sitting with Sandrine Benoit around the TV room–Daniel in a brown recliner, Hawk and his meemaw on her brown plaid couch, and John and Merc on the matching loveseat. They were watching the local weather channel to learn about the potential emergency that Merc's boyfriend, the government assassin whose love for her caused him to keep track of the weather wherever she was, had alerted them to.

While they waited for the co-anchors to get to the details of the impending storm, the quintet had to sit through some on-air banter.

"So, tell me, Sabrina," the male host began, "how's that new pooch of yours doing? Housebroken yet?"

"Oh, Gordon," Sabrina laughed playfully, "if my kids had been as easy to potty train as Mr. Pugglesworth has been, I may have had more than just Hope and Cody."

"I guess potty training two little girls and a puppy can really leave you feeling…pooped."

At that, the weather hosts produced more fabricated laughter.

"Are these two for real?" Sloane finally sounded off. "I can't tell if I'm watching a weather show or a couple of fifth graders on a really bad first date."

"I like the witty banter," Hawk disagreed. "It's got a certain folksy charm to it."

"I don't know, Sambo," Meemaw shook her head. "I think I'm with your cute friend here. I find those two to be absolutely unbearable. They're about as folksy as toe fungus."

Sloane burst out laughing. "Yes, thank you, Ms. Benoit."

"Please," she smiled. "Call me *Sandrine*.'"

Before anyone could call anyone anything, the two weather broadcasters finished their banter and began delving into the weather forecast for the greater Natchez area.

Sabrina led things off. "Over the next two days and nights, we'll be getting plenty of the three Hs: hazy, hot, and humid. It will be sticky wickets out there, y'all."

"It's not as if we're not used to weather like this, Sabrina," Gordon jumped in. "The problem comes on Friday night when a front moves in from the Gulf. It's going to bring in high winds, the threat of hail, intense rain, and the definite probability of tornadoes."

"Yes, Gordon, it could get quite dangerous here in southern Louisiana at the beginning of the weekend. We'll have gale warnings in effect for all day Friday and Saturday, severe thunderstorm watches in effect along the southern coast late Friday night, and I'm sure we'll be seeing some tornado watches coming into effect, as well."

The team exchanged concerned looks.

"Alright, Meemaw," Samuel said to his grandmother, "we're gonna go rest up for a few. When it gets to be around the eleven o'clock hour, come wake me up. We'll get this plan underway."

11

HEADS UP, CHIEF

Upon entering the Parish of Natchez Police Headquarters some fifteen minutes late, Seargent Clinton Thoreaux was met by his superior, Chief Darryl Briggs. The 67-year-old chief was a barrel-chested, beer-bellied man that sported a bushy white mustache and a pair of John Lennon-type wire-framed spectacles that rode down close to the tip of his nose.

"Well, I do declare, Lieutenant. I believe it's been about a month of Sundays since I last saw you show up late for a shift."

"Yeah, on my way in, I saw some unknown vehicles in old lady Benoit's driveway, and I thought I'd stop in and check it out."

"Anything to be riled about, lieu?" asked patrol officer Anais Arceneaux from behind her desk on the other side of the squad room.

"I don't think so. It's just her grandson and a few of his friends on their way through. They're headed down to the Keys to do some fishing and deep-sea diving. Clean cut crew. They don't look like anything to get our backs up over. Although, I did invite them to come in later and take a tour of this place, so be alert for that."

"*Tout dwa*," Arceneaux said in her native Haitian Creole tongue, meaning "alright."

"Chief, mind if I catch a word with you in private?" the sergeant asked.

"Not at all, Clint. Come on back."

The two officers made their way back to the chief's office, the younger officer walking in first. Chief Briggs shut the door behind them.

"What's up, Clinton?"

"I got the tag numbers off the vehicles in Sandrine Benoit's driveway."

"Her grandson and his friends, yeah. And?"

"Came back to a company in White Pines called the Dragon's Men Protection Agency."

"What the devil is a 'protection agency'?" the chief asked as he moved to the desktop computer on his large oak desk. "Hale, what's a 'Dragon's Man'?"

"Far as I can tell, they're some sort of former military types that kinda work outside of the law to help people that the police can't."

"Hmph," the chief grunted as he pulled up the Dragon's Men website. "Sounds just like the kinda bullshit we don't need. Especially right about now."

"Speaking of that, are we still looking for our next shipment on Friday night? Looks like we might be dealing with some weather, ya know."

"Mr. Lazarus will be getting in touch with you on the burner after hours tonight. During that call you should give him the coordinates of the drop and how much this payload will be. It'll give him some idea about how many people he'll need to load the boat."

"That'll be good. In the meantime, I invited Benoit's grandson and his cronies to come check out our operation here. If they do, I'll get an RFID on both of their vehicles so that we can track their movements while they're here. If they have somehow stumbled onto our operation, we'll know it. Me and the crew will take those *egares* and turn them into gator bait."

"Won't be the first time," Chief Briggs said, chuckling.

12

CRITICAL WARNING

Melissa Thoreaux had just finished mopping the kitchen floor and decided to sack out on her living room couch. Being six months pregnant made every household chore seem like a major undertaking. The minute she was situated on the sofa, her head on a couch pillow at one end and her feet propped on the armrest at the other, her cell phone sounded off.

Seeing it was only eleven forty-five, Melissa was a bit perplexed as to who would be calling her at this time of the day. She grabbed her phone and looked at the readout screen.

"Grams?" she answered.

"Good morning, precious," Dot Michaud said, her words sweet as syrup. "Are you dressed?"

"Well, I'm not sitting here naked, if that's what you mean," Melissa laughed.

"I'm coming to take you out, sweetie. I got us a reservation at the Red Fox at one o'clock this afternoon."

"Grams!" Mel exclaimed. "Red Fox is expensive, and I'm lookin' a sight."

"You're a naturally beautiful girl, Missy. Just put on something nice and run a brush through that nest of yours. You'll be fine," Grams suggested.

"Aww, if only it were that simple."

"Now, Missy, don't you be a diva. I'll be there in fifteen minutes, and I'll expect you to be ready to accompany me to the finest eatin' establishment east of New Orleans, ya hear?"

"But Grams—"

"No *buts*, child. Go on now. I love you, and I will see you in a bit."

Dot disconnected the call, leaving Melissa with no choice but to get her weary self up from the couch and go get ready for lunch with her grandmother.

* * *

Close to twenty minutes later, the call that Dragon's Men had been waiting on came through. Dot Michaud and her granddaughter were on their way to lunch, Clinton Thoreaux's spy was on their way with them, and the Thoreaux residence was ready to be infiltrated.

The four members of the protection agency were once again seated in Sandrine Benoit's kitchen.

"So, what's the play here, Johnny?" Sloane asked.

"Danny, you and Merc are going to head over to the Thoreaux's house and get the cameras installed and set up, while Hawk and I take Clinton up on his kind invitation to visit the Natchez Police Department."

"Oh, please, be careful," Sandrine urged. "While I believe some of those officers is good people–I really do–Clinton and that Chief Briggs are the devil's foot soldiers. They always be up to no good. They run this town with an iron fist and a mighty sword. But they'll smile and talk to you, sweet as watermelon tea, while behind your back, they be bleedin' ya dry."

"I've been told that the Natchez police department has one of the highest conviction rates in the state," John noted.

"Oh, sure." Sandrine gave him a sideways look. "They have

their friends get arrested, then they convict them, but while they're in jail, the Natchez police pay them handsomely so they can afford to keep their families in a comfortable way until they get out."

"Sounds to me like someone is cookin' the books," Daniel said.

"What about actual criminals?" Mercedes asked. "Do they pay them, too?"

"What actual criminals?" Sandrine asked rhetorically. "The only criminals in this parish are the Natchez police department."

"Thank you, Sandrine. We appreciate the heads up," Watkins said sincerely. "We'll definitely be on our toes while we're around them."

"We'll be alright, Meemaw. You can worry if you want to, but there's really no need," Sam coaxed. "The four of us, we've dealt with *move mouns* like this a hundred times before in our line of work," move moun being the creole term for bad men.

"Now, Sambo, you know that since I was just a little girl I've had to encounter so many different kinds o' bad in this world, but this man's different. This Chief Briggs, he has a coldness in his soul and a darkness in his eyes. You got to promise me, *pitit pitit*, that you won't underestimate him, and that you won't turn your back on him. Promise me, Sambo."

Hawkins stood up from his seat at the table and walked over to his meemaw. When he put his arms around her, he could feel her shaking, feel her trembling. "It's okay, Meemaw." Hawk swallowed hard as he looked at his three teammates. "We promise we won't underestimate this man. We will…bring him to his knees."

13

COVERING ALL THE ANGLES

Daniel Sloane and Dr. Mercedes Lara listened intently to their navigation system as it guided them through the streets of Natchez, Louisiana, to 26 Brighton Lane, the home of Clinton and Melissa Thoreaux. The address was located just outside the parish limits in a heavily wooded area that had just two other houses.

"This place looks pretty well isolated from the line of sight of those two other houses," Merc noted as they pulled into the Thoreaux's driveway. "Still, let's stay stealthy."

"Roger that, Doc," Sloane replied, parking the black SUV and shutting off its engine.

Mercedes held up her cell phone and checked it to see what kind of reception it was getting. "Not much of a signal here."

"I'm surprised there's any at all. This is almost third world down here."

The duo exited the vehicle and scanned the property for any pets and security cameras that might be on the premises. They found neither to be present.

"Gloves." Merc chose a pair of black leather gloves for herself and tossed a pair to Danny.

"I'll grab the bag. You go ahead in and start getting the lay of the place," Sloane instructed. They had already been informed by

Dot Michaud that the house contained no sort of security system.

Arriving at the back door, Mercedes was relieved to find it had been left unlocked, as requested. She let herself in and began searching for the best places to install the clandestine surveillance equipment. The one-story home was small, containing just one bedroom, one bathroom, a kitchen and dining area, and a living room. It would take just a few cameras to cover the entire living quarters.

"I'm coming in," she heard Daniel say as he entered through the back door. He carried a large navy-blue duffel bag to the kitchen table and set it down. "Wow. This place is more like a cottage than a house," he said, taking a quick look around.

"I think I already have things pretty well mapped out in here."

"Great," Sloane nodded. "That's good work by you."

Daniel unzipped the duffel and began removing items from it. First, he pulled out a laptop computer, opened it up, and turned it on. While he waited for it to load, he retrieved several small cameras, switched them on, and placed them on the table while they powered up. As he did that, Mercedes began scouting the best location for a camera in the bedroom. Spotting a tall wooden bookshelf in the corner, she reached up and blindly ran her fingertips across the top. She found exactly what she was hoping to: dust, and plenty of it.

"How're we doing out here?" she asked, walking out of the Thoreaux's bedroom.

"Rockin' and rollin'," Daniel replied. "Checking the motion sensors in these things right now." He held the small camera in his right hand, ran his left in front of the lens, and watched as the laptop monitor came to life.

"Beauty." Sloan then reset the camera and computer, placed the minute device on the kitchen table and pointed it at his partner. "Give us a spin, Doc."

Merc placed her hands on her hips and did a little shimmy.

The monitor came back on as the camera focused on the doctor.

"Lookin' good, Merc," the big man laughed. "Okay. How many cameras are you thinking?"

"Four. Maybe five."

"Cool."

Sloane and Lara went through the same routine with four more cameras to make sure all their sensors and lenses were working properly. From there, they strategically hid the cams around the home to make sure they covered all the angles.

Before they left the homestead, Daniel and Merc made sure that they left not a hint or a trace of themselves behind.

As they made their way back to the SUV, Mercedes' phone chirped.

"Well, I guess you're getting some kind of signal on your phone," Sloane said. "Missed call or something?"

When Mercedes looked at her phone, a look of disappointment came across her face Well, sugar, honey, and iced tea."

"That bad?"

"Harper's in Cairo," she explained, "and I was waiting to hear back from him because we got cut off earlier. I guess his call must've gone straight to voicemail."

"Is he the type to leave a message?"

"Oh, geez, is he ever. One time he left a voicemail that was over eight minutes long. His average voicemail length is easily around two and a half minutes."

"Whoa," Sloane said, shaking his head. "If someone I was dating left me messages that long, I'd have to break up with them."

"You've only dated one person in your whole life, Danny. You expect me to believe you'd call it off with Jenny over the length of her voicemails?"

They put the bags into the back seat of the Escalade before Sloane answered. "Since I'll never have to cross that bridge in this lifetime, I'm gonna go ahead and say *yes*."

14

GETTING TO KNOW THE LOCAL EVIL

Clinton Thoreaux was sitting at his desk when his cell phone rang. The call was from Cyprien Guillory, the deputy that Thoreaux had assigned to keep watch on his wife. Clint picked up his phone and answered quietly, "What's the good word, *zanmi*?"

"You didn't tell me that your wife had traveling plans today. Did you know about this?" Cyprien asked.

"Traveling plans? What are you talking about?"

"Yeah, a little after twelve-noon her grandma picked her up and took her out to lunch. They're at the Red Fox Restaurant on Lombard Street. They got here a little bit ago."

"And you're just calling—"

Thoreaux cut his sentence short, as suddenly there were two men standing in front of his desk. He recognized them from his visit to Sandrine Benoit's house earlier in the day. "Cyp, I'm going to have to call you back." Clint ended the call and stood up to greet the two men. "Mr. Hawkins," he said looking at Sam. "And…Mr. Watson, is it?" he asked, looking at John.

"Watkins," John corrected. "John Watkins."

"We thought we'd take you up on your offer to come check out your police station. I'd like to see if it's anything like the one back home." Hawkins said.

"You got it, *mi amigos*," Clint said affably, his creole accent thick as the London fog. "Let me take you back to meet the boss first. His name's Chief Darryl Briggs." As Clint made his way from behind his desk to lead John and Hawk back to Chief Briggs' office, he asked, "Where's the rest of your crew? Not interested in seeing how local law enforcement works?"

"Ah, they were tired from the drive last night," Hawk said.

The door to the chief's office was closed. Clint rapped lightly on it and asked, "Hey, Chief, you got a minute? We've got some visitors."

"It's open!" Briggs roared from behind the office door.

Clint opened it up, and the three men went in.

"Chief, this here's Mr. Hawkins and Mr. Watkins. Mr. Hawkins is the grandson of our beloved Sandrine Benoit."

Chief Briggs stood up and leaned over his desk to shake the two men's hands. "Really good to meet you fellas. Whereabouts y'all from?"

"We hail from up in White Pines," Sam answered. "We're on our way down to the Keys to do some deep-sea diving and some fishing."

Both John and Samuel were sizing up the chief, recalling Sandrine's description of the man as having a coldness in his soul and darkness in his eyes. Despite the chief's best efforts to hide it, the men could see exactly what the elderly woman had meant.

"White Pines? "Well shoot, y'all must be used to a different kind of people from what we have here in our little parish," Briggs smiled. "How long you boys plan on stickin' around our humble little neck of the woods?"

"Couple o' days," Hawkins came back. "It's been some time since I've seen my meemaw. She's gettin' up in years, and I might not have too many more times to see her…this side of Heaven, so I'm hopin' for a nice visit before we head out of here."

"Mm-hmm," the chief said as he, too, was sizing up the two men. "Well, I hear up in White Pines that y'all have a pretty fast and loose way of livin'. Just want you two boys to know that we don't put up with that kind of foolishness down here."

"Well, Chief, you don't have to worry about us," Hawk replied. I'm sure if you haven't looked us up yet, you will, and you'll see that my compatriots and I have seen enough war to last us a lifetime. Anymore we're all about peaceful living–for us and those around us. You won't get any trouble from me and my crew while we're here. Besides, my meemaw made it very clear that you and your officers don't put up with any nonsense from anybody. She said you run a tight ship in this town, and we can certainly appreciate the job that you do." Hawk leaned over the chief's desk and extended his hand toward the burly man. "We're not taking the lieutenant away from any important police business while he shows us around, are we?"

"I'm sure we can spare the sergeant here for a few minutes," Briggs said as he shook Hawk's hand. Then the chief put his other hand on top of Sam's and grasped it tightly. "I hope you and your friends enjoy your stay here in our peaceful little parish, and if y'all need anything while you're here, don't hesitate to give us a call."

Hawk retracted his hand from the chief's firm grip and flexed his fingers a few times.

John Watkins did not bother to offer a handshake. Instead, he simply saluted the man and said, "Chief Briggs, we certainly appreciate your time."

"Mm-hmm," the chief murmured, sitting back down in his chair. "We'll be seeing ya now."

"Thanks, Chief," Clint said, leading Sam and John out of Briggs' office.

The sergeant spent the next twenty minutes giving John and Samuel a tour of the building. He showed them the processing area, followed by the holding area, the officers' break room, the interrogation rooms, and then back to the front of the precinct where the officers' desks and the offices of the department's higher-ups were located. Once the three men were back in Thoreaux's office, Clint took a few minutes to tell John and Sam about how their arrest and conviction rate was the highest in the state, at almost one hundred percent.

"One hundred percent? That's impressive," Watkins admitted. "I think the White Pines rate is somewhere around the sixty percent mark, and they're one of the highest in our state. You'll have to share your secret with me, Lieutenant."

"I guess our secret is Chief Briggs. He came in here about three years ago and really streamlined our whole department. He cut away the officers that were weighing us down, and he put in a whole new operating system."

"Whole new operating system? You mean, in your computers?" Hawk asked.

"Oh, no, no," Clint laughed. "I mean in the way that we do things 'round here. Chief showed us it was okay to break a few eggs to get the necessary end result."

"And just how do you go about *breaking a few eggs*?"

"You know…we do whatever it takes to get the bad guys behind bars. You might think that the chief was being a bit judgmental toward ya, but we're careful whenever any outsiders come to town. Big cities have crime problems, grime problems, and homeless problems. Not here. Not in our little parish. We keep our people in line, and at the first sign of trouble from outsiders, we make life really uncomfortable for 'em. If we have to break a few eggs and a few heads to do it, sobeit. I'm sure in your military days that y'all must've done the same thing. Am I right?"

John looked over at Samuel before answering, "Sure, but we were dealing with terrorists from third world countries that were looking to hurt thousands of people–some of them Americans. We weren't dealing with local townsfolk that are U.S. citizens."

"Right, right," Clint said slowly, "but the principle is still the same, just on a smaller scale."

"Yeah, we understand the concept, Sergeant," Sam replied. "Y'ever get any complaints?"

Clint laughed again. "Complaints? Well, let's just say that after a while people saw what happened when someone tried to file a complaint. We nipped that one in the butt real quick-like."

Sam leaned forward in his chair and said, "Yeah...I bet you did nip that in the *butt* real quick."

"You fellas got any questions for me? I'm afraid I'm gonna have to wrap this up."

John thought for a moment. "No questions from us, Sergeant. I think you've laid out quite nicely for us how things work around here."

15

THE OPERATION BEGINS

By the time John Watkins and Samuel Hawkins returned to Sam's grandmother's house, the team's other black SUV was already sitting in the driveway. Sam pulled in next to it and shut off the motor. When they got out of their ride, both Daniel and Merc were waiting for them by the stairs.

"So, how did show-and-tell go down at the Natchez Police Department?" Sloane was quick to ask, puffing away on a cigarette.

"It was a lot more tellin' than it was showin'," Hawk answered back. "The dopey guy we're here to stop from beatin' his wife, he was just goin' on and on about how the department breaks some eggs to get things done. For a moment there I thought he was just going to tell us *all* the department's secrets."

"Plus, we got to see firsthand what Hawk's grandmother was talking about as far as Chief Briggs is concerned. He certainly lived up to the billing of being a very dangerous wolf dressed in sheep's clothing."

"Yeah," Sam verified, "except this jackhole is more like a villain dressed in police clothing."

"How did things go with you guys?" Watkins asked.

"In and out like a burger," Mercedes spoke up. "The house is incredibly small–gosh, I think my first apartment in Orange Park,

Florida was bigger than that house. So, we were able to set up a minimal amount of cameras and get every inch of the place in view."

"Let's head inside and take a look at your work," John suggested.

"You guys head in. I'm going to finish my smoke."

"Good enough," John said as he, Mercedes, and Samuel began the trek inside.

Left alone outside, Sloane began walking the property just to see what he could see. He walked around the front of the house to see a very nice flower bed made up of ironweed, goldenrod, sunflowers, and asters. The colors of the different plants really stood out against the gray and marshy backdrop of Sandrine Benoit's property.

Suddenly, Daniel heard the sound of a car slowing down on the road behind him. As he slowly turned to see what was going on, he was not at all surprised to see that it was a Natchez Police Department squad car. Walking toward the vehicle, Daniel eyed up the wheelman. He saw the driver well enough to know that it was a female officer, not Clinton Thoreaux.

"Hey!" he yelled. "Can I help you?"

As soon as the driver saw Sloane moving toward her, she peeled out and sped off.

Daniel made sure to get the vehicle's license plate number: A-63.

"See ya soon, sweetie!" Daniel hollered.

Within seconds, Sloane's teammates had rushed out of the house and into the front yard to see what the ruckus was.

"What's going on, Danny?" John asked.

"You out here stirrin' up trouble again, Sloane?" Hawk was the next to inquire.

"Seems like trouble's trying to stir us up. A Natchez patrol car came creeping around. Not sure what they were trying to see."

"Was it Thoreaux?" Mercedes asked.

"No, it was a woman cop," Daniel answered. "I was able to get the plate number. A-63."

"Okay, gang," John said, "let's take a beat and head back inside. We've got the computers up and running. Melissa Thoreaux just got home. I don't think it will be too long before Clinton gets home, too."

When the four members of the protection agency re-entered Sandrine Benoit's home, they saw the tiny woman in the kitchen, slicing fruit on a small cutting board.

"Whatcha doing, Meemaw?'

"What's it look like? she laughed happily. "I'm fixin' to make some pies and some fresh croissants."

"Meemaw, y'ain't gotta go through all this trouble just because we're here. It's not that we don't appr—"

"Now, Samuel Lapè Hawkins, shame on you. I don't know what kind o' host you are up where you live, but down here we treat our house guests with hospitality and kindness. I'm sure with what you and your friends do, y'all don't get pie and croissants very often… if ever. I know you have work to do, so y'all go tend to it. In a little while, there'll be a nice strawberry pie and croissants waitin' for ya. If you don't want the pie, I've never yet had a man nor woman take a pass on my coffee 'n' croissants."

"Well, that is true, Meemaw. It is hard to say no to your *bread-n-brew*," Sam had to admit.

"Thank you, Sandrine," Daniel Sloane said appreciatively. "You heard your meemaw, Sam, let's get to work."

And get to work they did. Sloane had already set up two computers in the sleeping loft. One laptop was set up on the bed, while the other sat on a makeshift table made from two stacked cardboard boxes Hawkins had found in his grandmother's garage.

"Everything looks great, and the microphones on each camera are picking up every little sound," Mercedes reported.

"I wonder how much of the Cleaver's daily life we'll have to surveille until something happens?" Sloane queried.

"I don't think we'll have to wait too long," John answered. "When Sam and I walked into Clint's office this afternoon, he was on the phone with whom I believe was the spy he had set up to watch Melissa. He ended the call as soon as he saw us, but from what I could hear before that, he was none too happy that his wife had gone somewhere without his approval. That's why when he does get home, someone is going to need to be close enough to their house for us to intercede if things start to get out of hand." John turned to Daniel. "Do you mind taking the first watch?"

"And miss Meemaw's bread and brew? Forget that." Daniel's serious look soon turned into a wide smile. "Of course, I'll go. I mean, a chance to put this mope down for the count…I'm all in."

John pulled a pad of paper from the breast pocket of his suit and grabbed a nearby pen. He scribbled an address down and handed it to Sloane. "This is a rental car place about twenty miles north of here. Take an alias with you and rent something inconspicuous."

"You got it, Boss." Danny tucked the address away in his pants pocket and grabbed the box containing the team's ear coms from John's open suitcase. Grabbing one for himself, he set the box on the makeshift table.

"See you in a while, gang."

As Danny headed down the stairs from the loft, Sam called down over the railing. "Hey, don't forget to take the tracker off the SUV. We don't need the cops knowing that you're not here."

Sloane pursed his lips together and nodded. "Copy that, Hawk."

And down the steps he went, out of sight.

16

WHEN PULLING A CAPER, ALWAYS RENT A CAR UNDER A FAKE NAME

Daniel Sloane found a good place to park the SUV where no one would mess with it, about three blocks away from "You Need A Car Rental Cars."

"Okay, who's on the com with me?" he asked as he began double timing it toward his destination. Dusk was just starting to set in across the evening sky.

"We're all on," John answered.

"Any action yet?"

"No," answered Mercedes, "but Clint just got home. Right now the conversation is casual and mundane, but this guy scares me, Danny. He seems like the type that can go from zero to flammable in just a moment's notice."

"Well," Sloane breathed heavily as he raced toward the rental car agency, "I have the car place in sight. I'm going to mute my com for a few so you don't have to listen to me wheezing like an asthmatic dog while I small talk the rental clerk."

"Do you have a disguise?" they asked Sloane.

"Yeah, I'm going to use the one I hate."

"Godspeed, dude," John said.

Sloane muted his com as he pulled a ball cap out of his back pocket and put it on. Next, he removed a Covid mask from his front jeans pocket. He found it preposterous that in this day and age some people still wore the Covid-19 masks even though the pandemic had officially ended ages ago. Plus, from what he had learned, the masks never really did much, if anything at all, to protect people from the disease. Nevertheless, they did serve as a legal way to obscure your face if the need ever arose, and tonight the need had arisen. Daniel's plan was to rent a car, drive to the Thoreaux's house, and if necessary, intervene in the situation. Should that happen, he would need an inconspicuous-looking vehicle. And, if someone were to get his tag number, they would trace it back to You Need A Car Rental Cars. Once they realized that the name of the person that rented the car was a dead-end alias, they would look at the security camera footage to try to I.D. the person that had rented the vehicle. Thanks to the ball cap and the Covid mask, this would prove to be an exercise in futility.

While he was filling out the rental car paperwork, Sloane listened closely to the conversation among his teammates on the other end.

John, Samuel, and Doc were relatively quiet as they listened intently to the conversation between Melissa and Clinton Thoreaux.

"How are your chops?" Melissa asked.

"Good," came Clint's muffled answer in between chews. When he finally swallowed, he asked, "What'd you put on these? It's good."

"I used a chipotle rub and some smoked molasses."

"You'll need to write that one down in that cooking book of yours. Speaking of that book, didn't your Grandma Dot give you that?"

"Yes. Yes, she did. Why…why do you ask?" Melissa found the question to be a bit odd.

"When's the last time you saw your Grandma Dot?"

Melissa hesitated a minute. "I…I saw her…today, actually."

"Today?" Clint asked. "Well, I don't remember you telling me about any plans you had with Grandma Dot. Are you keeping things from me?" Clinton's tone was eerily calm.

"No, Clint, I'm not keeping anything from you," Melissa protested. "She called me this morning with no warning at all. Said she wanted to take me out to lunch. I was in my house clothes and only had about fifteen minutes to make myself presentable. By the time I was ready, she was here and off we went. I swear, Clint, there was no time to call you at all."

"What about a text, Melissa?" Clint stood up from the kitchen table and made his way around to Melissa's chair. He put one hand on the table, the other hand on the back of Melissa's chair, and leaned down to within six inches of her face. "Didn't have time to text me?"

* * *

Watching the scene unfold before them on the two laptop computers, John, Samuel, and Mercedes were all starting to feel the tension build at the Thoreaux household.

"Where y'at, Danny?" John asked.

"The driver's seat of a white Hyundai Elantra, making my way back toward Natchez. Looking at the GPS, it says I'm a little less than twenty minutes away from *casa de Thoreaux*."

"Well, the situation's getting kinda *loco* at *casa de Thoreaux*," Merc noted.

The threesome returned their attention to the computer monitors and the Thoreauxs.

"You're six months pregnant, Melissa," Clint continued berating his wife. "You need to be at home. You don't need to be out there runnin' around on the town with your grandmother."

"We weren't running around, Clint," Melissa snapped back. "We just went out to lunch."

"Don't backtalk me, Melissa," Clint snarled. "Now, get up and get in the bedroom."

"I'm not finished eating yet," she protested.

"I said get up!" Clint grabbed Melissa by the hair and ripped her up from her chair. With his other hand, he grabbed her by the left arm and forcefully guided her back to the bedroom. Once in the bedroom, he tossed her like a rag doll onto the bed. Moving around to the right side of the bed, he lifted his fist into the air with the intention of teaching his wife a powerful lesson. But just then, by some kind of divine providence, his cell phone rang.

Clint reached into his pocket for his phone and saw it was the call he had been expecting from Mr. Lazarus.

"You stay right there, Melissa. You try to get up, and I swear I will put you back in the hospital."

Clint headed back into the kitchen before answering the phone. "Mr. Lazarus?"

"Good evening, Clinton," the voice on the other end replied. "I am calling to verify my order and verify the pick-up location."

"Yes, sir," Clint replied. Opening a drawer in the cabinet, he pulled out a long piece of paper. "I have the shipping manifest right here. Looks like you'll be receiving a hundred forty-four AR-15 rifles, forty-two Heckler and Koch G-36 rifles, another forty Sig SG-550s, and thirty-eight FN SCAR assault rifles. After that, we have you down for thirty-five M203 40mm underbarrel grenade launchers. Add in our time and effort, and the bill comes to four hundred and fifty-five thousand dollars."

"Very good, Sergeant. Now where and when are we going to make the pick-up?"

"It's going to be on the Cane River just outside of Natchitoches at Pier 51. We've got it cleared from twenty-two thirty until twenty-three thirty on Friday night. We'll have six men ready to load you up as soon as you arrive. Just a reminder that the cash will need to be shown before any loading will begin."

"I understand. We will see you Friday night, Sergeant."

"Look forward to doing business with you again. Have a good evening, Mr. Lazarus." Clinton ended the call, replaced the shipping manifest back into the kitchen drawer, and walked back into the bedroom.

* * *

John Watkins looked up from his computer and gave a quizzical look to Sam and Mercedes. "What the heck was that?"

"Well, we only heard one side of the phone call, but it sounds to me like the local police force is doing a little extra-curricular activity."

"We should notify Agent Ritter," Merc suggested. "This may be our chance to get these guys shut down once and for all."

Special Agent Jake Ritter was an ATF agent that the protection agency had worked with on several occasions. He would be the perfect person to bring down this Mr. Lazarus fellow.

Daniel Sloane, who had been listening in on his com while he sped toward the Thoreaux residence, chirped in, "Hey, now. Let's stay focused on why we're here. We're here to get evidence that this meathead is beating his wife like a piñata. And we're here to get her to someplace safe so she can have the baby and live a beating-free life. We're not here to bust up some illegal gun-running ring. That's for somebody else on another day. Besides, we wanna get this done and over with before Friday when those storms move in. That's the assignment, and we need to stick to it. Final answer."

"Ugh," John sighed in disgust. "I hate it when he's right."

"Got that right, I am," Daniel smiled. "Hey, I'm just about there. Is this guy close to smacking his wife around yet?"

"No. After he got off the phone, he went into the bathroom. I think he's taking a shower."

"His wife's still laying on the bed," Hawk said, shaking his head. "No doubt that this woman lives in utter fear of her husband. She's a prisoner in her own house."

Sloane informed them, "I'll be arriving in about two minutes."

"Shi', boy!" Hawk exclaimed. "How fast have you been goin'? I think you just made a twenty-minute trip in about half that time."

"This little car handles nicely. Plus, there's been no one on these back roads. Half of them are dirt…it's like driving in Baja."

"Find a good place to hunker down," John told him. "It looked like we were going to get what we needed, but that phone call came just beforehand. Who knows how long it will be now."

"Tell ya what, kids," Hawk laid back on the bed, "I feel like a real piece of crap sitting here waiting for this woman to take a beating."

"I don't feel real great about it either." John got up from the bed and found a chair in the corner of the loft. "It's unfortunate that these are the circumstances, but we have to stay focused and know that the next time her husband abuses her will be the last."

"Alright. I'm here," Sloane said as he pulled into a cutout on the road behind the Thoreaux's house. By now, the Louisiana sky had turned completely dark, the new moon showing no light whatsoever. Once Daniel turned off his headlights, the area was completely shrouded in darkness. The only visible lights were coming from the Thoreaux's house and a neighbor's house several hundred yards up the road. Staring out into the darkness, Daniel suddenly remembered something that he had forgotten.

"Ah, crap with peanuts!"

"Whoa, what's going on, big man?" Hawk asked.

"I forgot to grab the night-vision goggles. It's as black as a Baccara rose out here. I have my messenger bag of equipment, but the only thing I have in there to use is a little penlight flashlight."

"Well, make it work," John said.

Sloane grumbled as he got out of the rental car. "We've got

millions of dollars in expensive equipment, and here I am having to use this stupid tiny flashlight. This is a lot of bull."

Daniel began heading toward the Thoreaux's house. The berm was flat and level, but as he stepped off the gravel road, he found himself trekking across a grassy area which soon turned into a woods.

"I feel like I'm in Hell's waiting room. It's pitch black and hotter than Hades out here. Somehow, it actually feels hotter now than it did when the sun was out earlier today."

"That's because it is…sorta," began Hawkins. "In the daytime, when the sun is out, it burns away some of the moisture in the air, keeping the humidity at a decent level. However, at night, when the sun's away, the humidity spikes up to insanely uncomfortable levels. That's why it feels worse now than it did today."

"Whatever the reason, I'm out here sweating like a chicken at a KFC."

17

The One Good Thing About Fighting a Naked Man

The work that John and company were doing in the upstairs loft was suddenly interrupted by Meemaw's voice calling from the bottom of the stairs.

"Hello? Samuel?" she called. "I just made a fresh pot of coffee and a sheet full of croissants. Is it okay to come up?"

Hawkins rolled off the bed and peered over the railing in time to see his meemaw slowly ascending the staircase with a coffee pot in one hand and a tray filled with coffee cups, a tub of butter, and fresh croissants in the other.

"Meemaw!" Sam hollered. "What the green green grass of home are you doing?" Hawk quickly made his way down to relieve his grandmother of the tray and coffee pot. "You shouldn't be going up and down these stairs like this, Meemaw," Hawk scolded her. "You shoulda just yelled for us to come down. You're gonna fall and get hurt."

"Balderdash, Sambo!" Sandrine shot back. "I don't need you coming here and treating me like some kind of Tiffany lampshade. I'm not some fragile and frail old woman that needs you telling me what I can and can't do."

"I'm not telling you what you can and can't do," Sam said. "I just don't need you pulling a Ringling Brothers routine while you're climbing up the stairs."

Sam carried the coffee pot and tray upstairs and set it on the bed. When he turned around, his grandmother was taking the last step up to the loft.

"Sandrine, these look fantastic," John said. "Thank you so much for this."

"Well, I do try to be a proper host," Sandrine said with a wide grin. "Where's the big cute one?"

"He is over at your friend's granddaughter's house. When her husband starts getting physical with her again, not only will we have it recorded, but Daniel will be there to stop the fighting and get Melissa to the safety of her grandmother," John answered.

"Oh, I did what you told me to do," Sandrine made a point to say. "I told Dot to go to a hotel, check in under the assumed name of Carol Jenkins, and to pay in cash."

"As soon as Daniel has Melissa safely to transport, we'll have you call your friend Dot," Mercedes explained, grabbing a croissant from the tray. "They'll be safe there until we can figure out some place for them to go. If they don't have a safe place of their own, we can relocate them."

"Relocate them? You mean like that witness relocation program?" Meemaw asked.

"Yes, very similar, except for one difference. When federal agents relocate someone, that has to go through a whole bunch of people. Plus, they are all put into a computer somewhere so there's an electronic record of them. When *we* relocate someone, the only ones that know about it are the four of us and a friend of ours named Latin Jackson. On top of that, we don't put anything about it into a computer. We write it on a piece of paper that goes into a notebook that goes into the most expensive top-of-the-line wall safe made.

It's virtually impenetrable."

"Ohh," Meemaw said, "I see. So, when you relocate people, you relocate them without a trace."

"That's exactly right, Sandrine," John said, his mouth half full of the French roll.

Just then, Daniel Sloane came over the com. "Uh, Hawk?"

"Yeah, buddy," Sam answered.

"Hey, uh…I have a question that I'm hoping you can answer," Sloane said in a hushed tone.

"Okay. Shoot."

"Any idea what the proper protocol would be when you encounter an alligator outside of its natural habitat?"

Hawk burst into laughter.

"Shut up, Hawk. It's not funny," Sloane whispered firmly.

"Okay, okay." Hawk said, sobering up. "First of all, are you sure it's even real? A lot of people down here put fake gators around their yard to keep the varmints out of their garden, their trash cans, et cetera. They look real enough, sure, but they aren't."

"Do the fake ones move?' Danny asked. "Because this one is moving. And it's moving in my direction."

"Then you need to shoot at it, Sloane, because I'll tell you this: ya can't outrun it." Hawk said. "D'you have a gun in your messenger bag."

"Of course, I do, you stooge, but I can't shoot at the stupid thing. It'll give away my position."

"Shoot through your messenger bag, Daniel," Watkins suggested. "It'll muffle your shot."

"Oh, screw that, Johnny. I'm not going to shoot a hole in my dang bag. I've had this since I was a grunt in the army."

However, Sloane's attitude quickly adjusted as he saw the alligator quickly advance toward him.

"No, no, no. Stay!" he commanded the reptile in a loud whisper.

Sloane grabbed his Sig Sauer from his messenger bag, placed his hand on the trigger, and got ready to fire. The gator was just about ten yards from Daniel when it stopped.

"Jee-hosaphat," he said breathlessly.

"You okay, Danny?" Hawk asked.

"For now."

"Oh, geez." Mercedes said from the other side of the bed. "Look at this."

Watkins popped what was left of a croissant into his mouth as he moved back over to the laptop closest to him on the bed. "What do we have?"

"We have Clinton Thoreaux, naked as a jaybird."

"Oh, man, I don't want to see this," Sam complained.

They watched the naked man walk into his bedroom and make his way toward his wife, who was still laying on the bed.

Melissa sat upright when she saw her husband enter the room. "No, Clint," she said, seeing the look on her husband's face. "I don't feel right."

"I don't care how you feel, Melissa," Clint said.

Melissa tried to slide away to the other side of the bed, but Clint grabbed her ankle and pulled her aggressively toward him.

"No!" she objected, trying to push him away. But it was to no avail as Clint grabbed her by the wrists and pinned her down.

"This is happening whether you want it to or not."

"No! Stop it, Clint!" she wriggled like a fish out of water.

※ ※ ※

"Okay," John Watkins said. "I don't care if that's his wife or not. She clearly said *no*, and he is still trying to have his way. Get in there, Danny!"

"Uh, hello, I still have Chance the Snapper nippin' at my shoes."

"Daniel," Watkins said sternly, "shoot the gator and get into the house!"

"Roger that, Captain."

Sloane falteringly maneuvered his messenger bag around to the muzzle of his weapon. He took aim and fired. The bullet landed some six inches to the right of the gator's snout. It was properly effective. The alligator turned tail and took off into the darkness. Sloane gathered himself and began making his way toward the house. As he got closer, he could hear Melissa's screams.

"Heading in the back door," Sloane informed his colleagues.

Daniel hustled up to the same door that he and Mercedes had entered earlier in the day. He was ready to kick it in when he thought to just check the doorknob to see if it was still unlocked.

Indeed, it was.

Sloane reached into his bag, retrieved a black ski mask, and pulled it down over his face. "It's just too hot for this mess," he whispered to himself. Turning the knob on the back door, he let himself in, checked his weapon, then made a beeline to the Thoreaux's bedroom.

Seeing Clint having his way with his wife made his blood boil.

Clint saw Daniel out of the corner of his eye just in time for Sloane to rear back and flatten Thoreaux's nose like a pancake.

"And stay down, ya naked bastard!" Sloane yelled.

He then turned to Melissa, who recoiled away from him in fear.

"It's okay," Daniel put his hands up. "I'll introduce myself in a second."

He then turned his attention back to Clint, who was still reeling from Daniel's first blow to his face.

"How's it feel, jackhole?" Sloane disguised his voice with a German accent. He grabbed Clint by his hair. "Not too good, huh?" Daniel gave a quick knee lift to the cop's sternum, knocking the wind out of him.

"Who are you?" Clinton asked breathlessly.

"I'm the Sandman, and it's time to say 'good night', jerk face."

And with that, Sloane grabbed the back of Thoreaux's head and slammed it into the wooden foot of the bed. The naked man went out like a light.

"You want me to kill 'im?" Sloane asked.

"No!" Melissa cried out.

"Uh, sorry, ma'am. I wasn't talking to you."

"No, don't kill him, Danny," John answered.

"Danny, what's that accent? Did you suddenly join the *Stasi* and not tell us?" Mercedes mocked Sloane's fake accent.

"He's just going to come after us, John."

"That may very well be, hoss, but we don't need a dead cop on our resume, okay?"

"Fine."

"Just get the girl and get yourselves out of there."

"Ya know? I actually prefer fighting a naked man," Danny admitted. "A naked man ain't gonna pull a knife from his boot or a Glock he has hidden in the back of his waistband. The only thing a naked man is gonna pull is his—"

"Yeah, yeah, yeah, we get it," Mercedes said. "You don't have to say it."

* * *

Sloane moved next to the bed. Taking no chances that Clinton Thoreaux might still be somewhat conscious and hear what he was saying, he moved in close to Melissa and spoke very quietly.

"I know you don't know me, but we're friends of your grandmother…Dot."

"Oh, right," Melissa expressed equally quietly. "We had lunch today, and she told me that you were going to come get me. She said that you were going to kidnap me and take me somewhere safe."

"Right. I'm kidnapping you, so make it look good just in case anyone's watching. I've got a car about five hundred yards away from here, give or take. We have to go back through the woods behind your house. Once we make the tree line, you won't need to pretend you're being taken. Ain't nobody gonna be able to see us once we're there."

"Can I get a few things to take with me?" Melissa asked.

Sloane looked at her in disbelief. "Lady," he said, "keep in mind that I'm *kidnapping* you. Why in the world would I let you pack a bag?"

"Right. Sorry."

"Let's move. He's bound to wake up any second now. Once you're with your grandma, she'll take you wherever you need to go to get some things."

Melissa Thoreaux hopped off the bed and did her best impersonation of a kidnapping victim as Daniel Sloane led her out the door.

18

HERE IS WHAT HAPPENED

Clinton Thoreaux had indeed been knocked out cold by Daniel Sloane. When he finally regained consciousness, he had a solid headache. "Melissa," he called out instinctively. "Baby, where are you?"

The officer pulled himself onto his knees, his head still filled with cobwebs. He looked around the bedroom to see that Melissa was not there. A quick check of the clock said it was 10:12 p.m. Clint got up and walked through the small house calling his wife's name, but there was no response. He quickly dialed Darryl Briggs' home number. His boss answered on the second ring.

"Everything okay, Clint?"

"Chief, Melissa's been kidnapped," Thoreaux said in exasperation.

"What?"

"A man in a ski mask. He broke in, knocked me out, and now Melissa's gone!"

"Any idea who it was? Why would someone want to take Melissa?"

"It's gotta be those Dragon's Men jackasses."

"Alright, just calm down, Clint," Chief Briggs said. "If that's what you think, I'll call the station and have everyone get over to

Sandrine Benoit's house, and we can bring them all in for questioning. I just need you to keep a calm head."

"They took my wife, Chief. How calm would you be?"

"I understand, Clint. Just keep your head; we'll get to the bottom of this."

"Tell whoever's on duty that I'll meet them at Sandrine Benoit's place in ten minutes."

* * *

Officers Solange Leblanc and Dorian Dubois were on duty. The duo got the call from Chief Briggs to head over to Sandrine Benoit's residence on suspicion that their sergeant's wife had been kidnapped and she may have been taken there. Briggs instructed them to keep Clint under control and to make sure everything was done by the book. They rode together in a police cruiser to the house, not sure just what to expect. When they arrived, Thoreaux was already there, his temper boiling.

"Let's go," Clint was abrupt. "We need to get in there. They've either got my wife, or they know where she is."

"Got no problem with that, Sarge, but let's make sure we do this by the book," Leblanc said calmly. Her French Cajun accent highlighted every word she said. "Chief's on his way here, and he wants this done right."

Clint opened his car door and popped up out of the front seat. "How's that again?"

"Um…uh," Leblanc stammered.

"Yeah, I thought that's what you said." Clint walked past the two officers. "I'm going to go in. If you two want to stay out here and wait for the chief, be my guest."

Leblanc and Dubois exchanged looks, shrugged, and followed the sergeant toward Sandrine Benoit's house.

"Sarge, why do you think Ms. Benoit knows something about

your wife being taken?" the female officer asked. "She's just a little ol' lady."

"It's not her. It's her grandson and his friends. They showed up here this morning and now, less than twenty-four hours later, my wife is taken. Funny how before they showed up here, my wife had never gone missing once, but now they're here, and boom! Just like that, she's gone. Coincidence? I think not."

Thoreaux made his way up the back steps toward the screened-in back porch. "Natchez Police, Ms. Benoit," he yelled. "Open up, please."

It was not long before the porch light came on, and Sandrine slowly opened the back door. "Clinton Thoreaux, is that you?"

"Yes, ma'am, it is. I'm needin' to talk to yer grandson and his friends."

"Well, Clinton, I'm afraid you just missed them," the sweet little lady said kindly.

"Do you mind if we come in and take a look around?" Officer Leblanc asked.

"No, I don't mind at all." Meemaw shuffled slowly across the porch to the back door. She opened it and let the three members of the Natchez Police Department into her house. "Oh, do you have your body cams on?"

"Body cams on? Why the devil do you—"

"Yes, ma'am," Officer Dubois answered. "We have our body cams on."

Clint gave the officer a dirty look.

"Would you care for a cup of coffee? Slice of pie?' Sandrine asked. "Both?"

"I'd love—"

"We're fine," Clint cut in. "You two, check the house. Make sure we're the only ones here."

"Anything for you, Clint?" Sandrine asked politely.

"Yes. I'll take some coffee, and, oh yeah...Where's my wife, Ms. Benoit?"

"Whatever do you mean, Clinton?"

"I mean that my wife has been kidnapped."

"And you're here to question my grandson and his little friends about *that*?"

"I am, unless *you* know something about it?"

To Clint's surprise, Sandrine answered, "I do."

"Oh? I mean...oh," the officer stammered. "Just what is it that you know?"

"I don't know about your wife, but I do know about my grandson and his friends. They were here with me all evening, and then they went out a few minutes ago. Down to Smitty's for some doughnuts and cider. What you can tell *me* is what's going on with your wife, and why would you even think that Samuel or his friends could possibly know a thing about it?"

"If you don't mind, Ms. Benoit, I'll ask the questions," the sergeant said.

"You can ask all the questions you want, Clint, but until you answer my question, I won't be answering any of yours. What's going on with you and your Missus, and why do you think Samuel and his people have anything to do with it?"

"Because I don't believe in coincidence, ma'am. My wife and I had a perfectly normal and trouble-free life before your grandson and his friends came to town. Your grandson and his friends get to town, and all of a sudden, our perfectly normal and trouble-free life goes bye-bye."

"I'll tell you what I've told my own kids, and grandkids, on several occasions. You might think that you're making sense, and maybe in your own head, you are, but to those of us that don't have the pleasure of living inside of your head, you sound completely *fou*."

"Oh, I sound crazy, do I?"

"Yes, ya do. Now, slow down and explain yourself so that you make some kind of everlovin' sense to the rest of us, Clinton."

Officers Leblanc and Dubois returned to the kitchen. "The house is clear, Sarge. Plus, it looks like the chief just pulled up outside."

"Great," he addressed both officers. "Go walk him in." He turned back to Sandrine. "I need you to get on the phone to your grandson. Have him and his friends meet us down at the station."

"Us?" Sandrine asked.

"Get dressed, Ms. Benoit. I'm taking you in for questioning."

"Am I under arrest?"

"If I have to," Thoreaux snapped.

"Go get the chief," Leblanc said to her fellow officer.

"Yeah," Officer Dubois agreed. "Sarge, you wanna come with me?"

"Now, why would I want to do that?"

"Because you need to calm down, for one. For two, if this is an inquiry about your missing wife, you shouldn't be within ten miles of this investigation."

"Just go get the chief," the sergeant huffed. "I'm sure he'll see things my way."

"Oh, my goodness, Clinton," Sandrine's voice took on a compassionate tone. "Melissa's missing? Okay, okay. I'll call my grandson, and then I'll get dressed, and we'll all meet you down at the station. If anyone can find your wife, it's my grandson and his friends."

"Find her? They're the ones that took her!" Clint exploded.

"That'll be enough, Sergeant." It was Chief Darryl Briggs. "Sandrine, I apologize for the actions of my officer—"

"Apologize? Chief, come on."

"Sergeant, you need to get on back home. We'll take it from here," Chief Briggs instructed his subordinate. The chief then looked at Sandrine. "Ma'am, I am by no means forcing you or your grandson or his friends to come in for questioning, but the sooner we can get this cleared up, the sooner we can move on to the real culprits."

Sandrine played her part perfectly. "I know I speak for everyone on my side of the aisle when I say that we want to help in whatever way we can. I'm going to call my friend, Dot. Melissa's grandmother. She needs to know what's going on here, too."

"I'm going to get my people out of your house, Sandrine. We'll look for you and your grandson down at the station shortly."

"We'll be down forthwith, Chief Briggs."

Meemaw waited for the police officers to leave her home before she called Samuel.

He answered with, "How'd it go, Meemaw?"

"Just like you said it would, Sambo. Just like you scripted it yourself."

19

HERE IS WHAT SAMUEL SAID WOULD HAPPEN

Twenty minutes prior to Sergeant Clinton Thoreaux's arrival…

John Watkins, Dr. Mercedes Lara, Samuel Hawkins, and Sandrine Benoit had just watched Daniel Sloane give Clinton Thoreaux his much-deserved comeuppance for trying to have his way with his very unwilling wife. Sloane had then taken Melissa Thoreaux out of the house, through the woods, and to his rental car.

"Where am I taking her?" Sloane wanted to know.

"Sandrine, where is Dot?" John asked.

"She's at the Best Western in Natchitoches."

"Daniel, she's at the Best Western in Natchitoches. Have her give her grandmother a call," John instructed. "Once you drop her off, hightail it back to town. I'll let you know what the plan is and where to meet us."

Sam walked over to his meemaw. "Okay, Meemaw, pay close attention. Here's what's going to happen. We're going to leave. We're going to go to Smitty's and get some doughnuts and cider. Clinton is going to come here looking for us. When he does, make sure he has other officers with him. If he's by himself, do NOT let him in. Okay?"

"Okay, Sambo. I won't let him in."

"There's a very small chance that will happen. But he'll probably have other officers with him. When you let them in–and this is very important–you make sure they have their body cameras on. That's your insurance that they won't try something stupid, okay?"

"Okay." Meemaw's voice trembled.

"I know you're scared, but I wouldn't be having you do this if I thought there was any chance of you getting hurt. It's going to go just like I'm saying. You just have to make sure that they have their body cams on, okay?"

"Okay, Sambo."

"Now, Clint's going to be upset and irate. He's going to try to bully you. Don't let him," Hawk continued. "Just stick to the story that we were with you all evening until now when we decided to run out to Smitty's."

"For doughnuts and cider," Sandrine said.

"Right. Now, Clint is going to be talking crazy, so be sure not to offer up any details about anything. You make sure that he tells *you* what happened to his wife. Once he does, you be all kinds of compassionate and understanding. You will cooperate, one hundred percent. If they want to look for us, let them. Be polite and hospitable like you are to any other guest that comes here. They'll leave, and as soon as they do, call me. We'll come back here to get you, and we'll all go to the police station to give our statements. Do you have all that?"

"Yes. If it's just Clinton, don't let him in. If it's other officers, let them in but make sure their cameras are on. You were all with me until you went to Smitty's to get doughnuts and cider. Make sure Clinton tells me what happened to his wife; don't offer up any information. Once he explains the situation, I pour on the sympathy and understanding and cooperation. When the police leave, I call you right away."

Sam looked at John.

"I think we're solid, Sam. Your grandma really knows what's what," Watkins smiled. "By the way, what's *Smitty's*?"

"Smitty's is a twenty-four-hour market with security cameras. Between the timestamps that will be on the video and the trackers that they put on our vehicles, we'll have a built-in alibi."

"Nice," Merc smiled. "That being said, let's go to Smitty's."

The trio walked Sandrine downstairs from the loft and to the kitchen.

"You gonna be okay, Meemaw?" Sam asked.

"I'll be fine. I've dealt with bigger and badder than Clinton Thoreaux in my days."

Hawk walked over to his grandma and gave her a very reassuring hug. "You're the coolest woman I know, Meemaw. I've got every faith in you to do this."

Mercedes walked up behind Sandrine and put her arms around her, saying, "I always wondered where Samuel got his cool, smooth persona. Now, I most definitely know."

"Miss Benoit, I will be your safety net," John told her. "I won't be going to Smitty's with them; I'm going to be standing out of sight, across the street. If for any reason, you feel threatened or concerned, just find a way to flick the front porch light on and off, and I'll be in here before the situation has any chance to elevate."

"I appreciate that, Mr. Watkins, but I'll be fine. Y'all need to get a move on, and I'll talk to you in just a short while."

When the trio walked out to the SUV, John said to Sam and Mercedes, "I'm going to grab some binoculars out of the ride and stick around here just the same. I know Sandrine can handle herself, but a back-up plan never hurt anyone."

20

KEEPING THE STORY STRAIGHT

After Daniel Sloane dropped Melissa off to her grandmother at the Best Western in Natchitoches, he dropped the rental car off to You Need A Car Rental Cars, got back into the company's black SUV and, per John's instructions, met up with everyone back at Sandrine Benoit's house.

Everyone was seated around Sandrine's kitchen table, going over their story before they went down to the police station.

"Alright," John began, "here's what's what. As always, just answer their questions; don't volunteer or add any information. We were here with Sandrine, eating croissants, talking about Friday night's incoming weather, our job as a protection agency, and fishing. If they ask about specifics–and you know they will–we talked about what bait to use for catching marlin. Daniel and I said ballyhoo; Merc and Sam agreed upon mackerel."

John took a moment before continuing. "We talked about getting out of here before the storms moved in on Friday. The other specific thing we talked about was the security job we did for sportswriter Dan Wetzel. We went to Norwell, Massachusetts, where we were able to subdue an unsub named Kevin Billings. He took exception to something that Wetzel had written about Steph Curry. So much so that he decided it was a good idea to silence sportswriter Wetzel, once and for all."

In unison, the four members of Dragon's Men all turned to look at Meemaw.

"Now, don't y'all worry yourselves even a tinge. I got it all stowed away right up here in my noggin." She inhaled and began again, "Fishin' for marlin, Mr. Sloane's and Mr. Watkins' bait bein' ballyhoo and Dr. Lara's and Sambo's bait bein' mackerel. Y'all's was protectin' a sportswriter named Dan Wetzel, and y'all went to Norwell, Massachusetts, to protect him. The man who's after him was named Kevin Billings because he was upset about somethin's he had written about Steph Curry. I got it all right here."

"I'm good with that," John said.

"Then let's go to the police station," Merc said, standing up from the table.

"Don't forget to put the tracker back on the SUV that you used tonight," Hawk said to Sloane, and the five of them departed Sandrine's house.

21

MEEMAW AND THE CHIEF

When the quintet walked into the Natchez Police Station, they found Chief Briggs and Officer Dorian Dubois waiting for them.

"Officer Dubois, if you don't mind escorting the two white men, the black fella, and the pretty white lady to the interrogation rooms, I'll take Ms. Benoit to my office and interrogate her there."

As directed, Officer Dubois took the four members of Dragon's Men down the hallway to the interrogation rooms. John had Clinton, Sam had Officer Solange Leblanc, Daniel had Dorian Dubois, and Mercedes drew Officer Anais Arceneaux.

* * *

"Now, Sandrine," Chief Briggs began, taking a seat behind his desk, "I have to ask you to just tell me, in your own words, what happened tonight at your house."

"Sho, Chief," Sandrine sounded tired. "Now where'd you want me to begin?"

"How about after seven o'clock."

"After seven. Okay. The boys and Dr. Lara were upstairs in my loft, so I thought I would take them some after-dinner coffee and croissants. I had made a strawberry pie, but they seemed to have a bit of a penchant for my croissants. They were talkin' 'bout some business matters, so I asked if it would be alright if I stayed. I was so wantin' to hear what my Sambo did for a livin' and all, and they were gracious enough to let me stay."

"Do you remember what it was they were talkin' about, Sandrine?"

"Hmm, let me see," Sandrine took a moment to recall that part of the story. "Yes, they were talking about havin' traveled up north to Massachusetts…Norwalk. No wait, Norwell. Yes, Norwell, Massachusetts. It was a man named Wetzel. He was a sportswriter. He had written about a fella named Steph Curry. Another fella named Kevin Billings had taken some umbrage to what the article had to say about Mr. Curry, so he–the Billings fella–began to stalk and try to kill Mr. Wetzel. I found this so fascinatin' that I was a little upset when they changed the subject to marlin fishin'."

"Do you recall any parts of the conversation? It's okay if you don't. I don't expect you to remember everything," Darryl Briggs said.

"Now, Chief, I do declare, showin' me favoritism like this." Sandrine snapped. "Are your other interrogators going to be as lenient with my grandson and his friends?"

"Okay, okay," the chief put his hands up in a defensive position, "If that's how you want it, that is surely how I will give it to you. Let's get back at it then."

"Yes, let's do that."

"Before we continue, is there anything that you need? I know my people will do *that* with your grandson and his friends. Water, crackers, etc."

"I'm quite sure I'm fine," Sandrine Benoit said rather curtly. "But thank you just the same."

"Okay, I think we were at marlin fishing."

The chief leaned back in his chair and rested his folded arms atop his corpulent belly.

"We were," Sandrine said, crossing her arms across her stomach in a passive-aggressive move of her own.

"Marlin fishing? What in the world was that about?"

"The four of them talked about what's the best bait to use for catchin' marlin. They were divided amongst themselves about what to use."

"And who said what?"

"Hmm." Again, Sandrine took a minute to recollect who had said what. The chief watched her eyes intently. "Sambo and Dr. Lara's thoughts were mackerel, while Mr. Watkins and Mr. Sloane, they's both of the mind that ballyhoo was the better bait."

"Well, I have to agree with Mr. Watkins and Mr. Sloane. Not to slight your grandson, but my opinion is also ballyhoo," the chief said.

"I ain't gonna lie to ya, Chief, about that point, my thoughts began to wander, as I am not much of a fisherman."

"And was that about it?"

"Well, no," Meemaw unfolded her arms and leaned forward in her chair. "Eventually, we started talking about the weather, and the storms that they're predictin' to be movin' in here on Friday. We all agreed that it would be best for them to be gettin' out of here on Thursday."

The chief, knowing what was going to take place on Friday night, breathed a sigh of relief.

"That's what I did, too." Sandrine said.

"I'm sorry, what?"

"I breathed a sigh of relief, too."

"Right, right." Briggs said. "I did see that we're supposed to be getting some nasty weather. So...it sounds like y'all had some deep conversations."

"My Sambo and his friends–I'm tellin' ya, Chief, they don't miss a trick."

"As I am becoming very aware of," Chief Briggs said, trying to hide the tone of concern in his voice. "I have to say, Sandrine, your recall ability seems impeccable, even if your story does sound rehearsed."

"Well, I'm sure you wouldn't know about that, would ya, Darryl?"

"I'm sorry?" Briggs replied. "Just what are you implying?"

Meemaw took the opportunity to go on the offensive. "You think because I'm a little old lady that I don't pay attention to your press conferences. Well, let me tell you, Chief Briggs, that I most certainly do. I see you referrin' to note cards or reading off a teleprompter when you should be speaking from the heart. You're quite the disgrace sometimes, Darryl."

"You better watch your tongue, Ms. Benoit," Briggs warned.

"For example," she continued without missing a beat, "two months ago when that fireman, Luke Dancy, was killed in that house fire over on Juniata Street. You're up there sayin' how tragic the whole thing was, and how much he meant to this town. Truth was, the real tragedy was your press conference when you, apparently, couldn't be bothered to learn the man's name. Had to read it off of a teleprompter. And you still got it wrong! Called the poor fellow Luke *Fancy*!" Sandrine gave a stern look to the chief. "Maybe you should've done a bit of rehearsin' yourself, Chief Briggs."

By this time, Chief Briggs had had more than enough. He regained his composure and tried to close the proceedings. "Anything else about tonight's events that you'd like to say before we wrap this up?"

"As a matter of fact, yes."

"And what would that be?"

"Well, Chief, time had really gotten away from us, so Sambo started talking about goin' to Smitty's to get some doughnuts and cider for tomorrow's breakfast."

"And?" the chief asked impatiently.

"*And* they did. But they hadn't been gone even three minutes when suddenly, the next thing I knew, your officers were showin' up at my door...like they were just waitin' for me to be alone. You want to talk about impeccable? Seems like the timing of your officers showin' up at my door was just a little *too* perfect."

"And what did you do?"

"I let them in, of course." Sandrine smiled. "Told them they could look around; I offered them some coffee and pie. I treated them just like I treat any guests I have in my home."

"Well, Ms. Benoit, you are everyone's favorite grandma in this town," the chief chuckled. "Okay, anything else to add?" Briggs asked.

"Don't think so. Other than that, your officers were just as nice as could be...except for maybe that Clinton Thoreaux."

"Well, did he tell you that his wife has been abducted?" the chief asked.

"He did, so I took that into consideration."

"Well, ma'am, I surely do appreciate your understanding the situation." Chief Briggs stood up from his chair, reached across the desk and gently took Sandrine's hand. "And I just want to thank you for your complete cooperation about all this."

"You're welcome, Chief Briggs," she smiled.

"I'll walk you out to our waiting area, Sandrine. You can wait for your grandson and his friends there. I'm sure it won't be long now."

"Aww, Chief Briggs, you are such a gentleman," Meemaw said to him. However, in her head, she thought, "*Enjoy your freedom now, ya fat clown.*"

22

Q & A: Samuel Hawkins

"**My name is Officer** Solange Leblanc. I will be interviewing you about last night's events that led to the kidnapping of Melissa Thoreaux. I will also be video recording the interview," the female officer informed Samuel. "Do you understand?"

"Wasn't too much in there that was all that confusing, so, yeah." Then Sam added, "By the way, I could listen to your accent all day."

"I will now turn on the recorder," Solange said, ignoring Hawk's comment. "My name is Officer Solange Leblanc. It is 12:21 a.m. on August 27th. I will be questioning Mr. Samuel Hawkins about the events that took place on the evening of August 26th.

Q: Will you please state your name for the record?

A: Samuel Lape Hawkins the first–and if you believe 23 and Me–the only.

Q: And what is your occupation?

A: I work with an elite group of former Delta Force members called Dragon's Men Protection Agency. What we do is help people that are in danger, but the police are handcuffed by societal laws and unable to offer the much-required help that people need.

Q: So, is it accurate to say that you work outside of the law?

A: No, we work within the law. We're just not governed by the same rules which the police are.

Q: Where were you last night between the hours of 7 p.m. and 10 p.m.?

A: I was at my meemaw's–Sandrine Benoit's–house. I was there with four other people. A little after ten, John Watkins, Daniel Sloan, Dr. Mercedes Lara, and I went to Smitty's twenty-four-hour market. Got some cider and doughnuts. Oddly enough, while we're gone, your police department comes to my meemaw's house and starts harassing and brutalizing her.

Q: Do you know why we were there?

A: Yeah, because one of your officers thought my ninety-eight-year-old grandmother had something to do with the kidnapping of his wife. Y'ask me, that's plain ignorance. My meemaw has been nothing but an upstandin' citizen in this community for decades. Not years. Decades!

Q: We'll check the security footage at Smitty's, and we'll run your alibi against those that were with you. If it all syncs up, you'll be good to go. Is there anything you'd like to add?

A: No. That's my testimony.

* * *

Sam could not believe that was all she asked. He waited for her to turn off the video camera before he asked her, "How long have you been on the job?"

"About six months. Why?"

"Do you like it?"

"It's a bit of a boy's club sometimes, but for the most part, it's pretty good."

"Solange, is it?"

"Officer Leblanc," she answered sternly.

Samuel Hawkins sensed an opening.

"Well, you run a heck of an interview, Officer Leblanc. Good stuff."

"Oh...thank you," she said, somewhat taken aback.

"Hey, can I ask you something?" Sam leaned in close to the officer. "This officer who's accusing us of knowing something about the disappearance of his wife, what's his deal? I mean, obviously we didn't do it. I'm just here visiting my meemaw while my friends and I are passing through on our way to the Keys to do some fishing. We don't even know this guy. Ya feelin' what I'm saying?"

"I do, Mr. Hawkins. You're wondering why our sergeant is pointing a finger at you and your friends when you don't even know him, much less would want to kidnap his wife."

"Exactly." Hawk moved in even closer and whispered, "Does the dude have a lot of enemies?"

"Mr. Hawkins—"

"Sam. Please. You say *Mr. Hawkins*, and I look around for my father. On top of that, if I actually saw him, the sitch would hit da fan. Things would escalate dramatically, real quick and in a hurry."

"Why? Do you not get along well with your father?"

"Uh, no. He's been dead for over a decade," Sam said seriously.

"Look, Sam, I'm sure once they check your stories, you'll be cleared of any wrongdoing." Then Leblanc whispered. "And then you guys should leave town as soon as you can."

Hawkins said barely loud enough to be audible, "Are they listening now?"

"The interview is over, Sam."

"Okie dokey."

"I'll need you to stick around while we verify your alibi. We've got someone at Smitty's checking the security footage there. Shouldn't be very long."

"Do you have a vending machine on the premises? I could use something to snack on while I wait."

"Yeah, I'll walk you to it, if you don't mind the company?"

"No, I don't mind at all."

Sam opened the door to the interrogation room and let Officer Leblanc lead the way. The vending machines were at the end of a hallway near the front of the building, well isolated from the desks and offices and interrogation rooms.

"Can I trust you, Sam?" Solange asked.

"Yeah, of course. Is that why you came with me to the vending machines?"

"We can talk here and not have to worry about being overheard."

"Okay," Hawk said, "what is it that you want to trust me with that's so important that you would trust a perfect stranger with it?"

"The cops here are dirty. Plus," she continued, "I was there when they went into your grandmother's house. Our sergeant is sure that you and your friends had something to do with his wife's disappearance. When the evidence proves that you didn't, I'm afraid he and the other officers will harass your grandmother until she admits to knowing something."

Sam's cheerful expression was suddenly replaced by one of concern and uneasiness.

"If you know the cops are dirty, why haven't you said anything to someone?"

"Because we have the highest conviction rate in the entire state. To all the higher-ups and supervisors, the Natchez Police Department is the golden child of Louisiana." Officer Leblanc swallowed hard. "And if I were to try and blow the whistle on these guys, and it didn't work...I'd be as good as dead."

"What about the FBI? Have you thought about contacting them?"

"I've thought about it," she said, "but I'm too scared. I just know that it would get back to Chief Briggs, and that would be it for me." Solange put her hand on Hawkins' shoulder and looked him in the eyes. "You said that you and your friends help people that can't be helped by the police. Well...I'm the police, and I need your help."

Sam took one of his business cards out of his wallet and handed it to Solange. "Give me a call when you can talk. I can't make any promises," Hawk said. "You know how that is. Cops and doctors... never make promises."

"Whatever it is that you do, can you please keep my name out of it? I'm trusting you with my life."

And having said that, she turned and walked away.

23

THE INTERVIEW OF DR. MERCEDES LARA

Mercedes drew Anais Arceneaux. Anais had beautiful brown skin, tightly rolled cornrows, and wore an officer's button-down shirt that was about two sizes too small, which accentuated her ample bosom.

"Hey, if you want to switch with one of my other co-workers…" Mercedes let her words hang in the air.

"Why would I want to do that?"

"Just a hunch," Mercedes shrugged.

"What about Samuel Hawkins? What's he like? More importantly, is he single?"

"Let me tell you this about Samuel Hawkins–he lives to be single. He loves to date, he loves women. I think he'd be great for you."

"And he's black, too," Arceneaux beamed.

"Does that matter?" Mercedes asked.

"In these parts? Yes. Yes, it does," the female officer said regretfully.

"Off the record?"

"Of course," Anais answered, moving closer to Dr. Lara.

"I think that most of the racism in this country is brought on by politicians. I mean, they say on the TV that this country is racist.

Yet, if you go out and talk to the people in your community, you'll find that almost–if not everybody–gets along very well. I figure that my community is the rule and not the exception. Have you experienced that?"

Officer Arceneaux's mouth was agape. "You and I think exactly alike, Mercedes. Is it alright to call you Mercedes?"

"You most certainly may. If you want to interview me you can, or you can interview Samuel Hawkins. You can call him Hawk."

"I don't actually have a choice, and even if I did, I still don't think I would. I think I would be too distracted," Anais answered. "But I've been given an order by our boss, and when Chief Briggs says to do something, you do it."

"I certainly understand," Mercedes answered warmly, reaching across the table to shake Officer Arceneaux's hand. "I'm excited to work with you."

"Okay, if it's alright with you, I will now turn on the camera which will record our conversation."

"I am very ready."

Officer Arceneaux reached up and turned on a small video camera that was mounted on a tripod and began her interview.

Her style of interrogation was less Q & A and more of a conversational approach.

"This is Officer Anais Arceneaux of the Natchez Police Department. Today, we are live with Dr. Mercedes Lara. It is 12:17 a.m. on August 27th, and we will be talking about the events of August 26th, specifically regarding the disappearance of Melissa Thoreaux. My first question to you, Dr. Lara is… where were you tonight between 7 p.m. and 10 p.m.?"

"Before I begin," Mercedes said, "I'd like to say thank you for being so nice and accommodating to me. So, to get into my story, I and my teammates, Sam Hawkins, Daniel Sloane, and John Watkins, were at the residence of Sam's meemaw, Sandrine Benoit, and we had a wonderful supper. After that, we cleaned up the dishes and the kitchen. From there, Mr. Watkins, Mr. Sloane, Mr. Hawkins, and I went up to the loft and relaxed for a bit."

"And how long was this relaxation period?" Anais asked.

"Well...we were talking shop–the four of us–and probably after twenty minutes, give or take, Sam's meemaw came up to where we were, and she brought with her a tray of croissants and a pot of coffee."

Officer Arceneaux let out a little chuckle. "Sandrine Benoit never met a person that she didn't want to fatten up."

A smiling Mercedes nodded her head. "And of this, there is no doubt." Mercedes was finding this woman's interrogation style completely refreshing. She did, however, have in the back of her mind that the officer could turn on her at any time, so she kept her guard up.

"Anyway, when Sandrine came up to the loft, we were talking about a job that we had recently finished."

"Can you tell me about the job, Dr. Lara?"

"Sure. We had been contacted by a sportswriter Dan Wetzel—"

"Oh, my gosh! I love that guy!" the interrogating officer interrupted. "I read his column all the time."

"Sweet. Hey, by any chance do you remember the piece he wrote on Steph Curry a couple of weeks back? Apparently, it was a pretty critical story," Mercedes explained. "Does any of that ring a bell?"

"Heck, yeah, it does. Like I said before, I read Wetzel's column religiously."

"Religiously? You mean you only read it on Sunday?"

"Ha, ha, that's a good one. No, I read it every day. I remember that particular article. He had some really scathing things to say about Curry. Said he was a ball hog and a real chucker."

"Wow, you really know your stuff, ma'am."

"Tell me more, Dr. Lara," Anais requested.

"I will tell you more on one condition: please call me Mercedes."

"Right, right. So, tell me more about your conversation, Mercedes."

Merc took a moment to gather her thoughts before beginning again. "So, Wetzel began to notice that a lot of things were going on–phone calls at all hours of the night, someone was messing with his car, he got *swatted* more than a few times–things like that. And with every occurrence, the danger level increased. It got pretty intense, so Wetzel came to see us. It took about fifteen minutes for us to make the decision to bring him on as a client."

"Can I ask who the stalker was?"

"This recording will be used for court proceedings only, right?" Mercedes asked. "This isn't going to be leaked to TMZ or some organization like that."

"No, ma'am," Anais answered. "I can assure you that the only one that will hear this recording is the judge himself."

"I don't know why, but there's just something about you that makes me trust you," Merc said. What she thought was, "*I trust you about as far as I can throw you…which is probably somewhere between the moon and New Jack City.*"

"So, you'll tell me who the stalker was?"

"I will," Dr. Lara agreed.

"Right now?"

"It's not a name anyone would know. The unsub was a man named Kevin Billings."

"And may I ask how you caught him?" the officer asked.

"You may, but I'm not going to answer that. It was my understanding that this interview was about the evening of August 26th. While we did discuss the case last night, we certainly didn't have Mr. Billings or Mr. Wetzel in the loft with us re-enacting the takedown."

"Yes, you are correct. I was out of line asking that question. We'll have that stricken from the record. My apologies, Dr. Lara."

Merc was somewhat caught off guard by the tone of the officer's apology. Despite being caught in an obvious interviewing faux pas, her demeanor never changed. Always the consummate cynic, Mercedes was just not buying Arceneaux's shtick. Still, there was always the chance that Officer Arceneaux's bubbly personality was not a façade. "May I ask you a question?"

"Sure, Dr. Lara. Ask away."

"In my line of work, I've been interrogated by people from federal investigators to international negotiators to small town constables to the world's worst thugs. You, Officer Arceneaux, have to be the most laid-back and congenial and friendliest interrogator I have ever had the privilege of meeting."

"Well, bless your heart, Doctor—"

"Please–again–call me Mercedes."

"Okay, *Mercedes*, it's like the old saying goes, 'You catch more bees with honey than you do with vinegar.' Some of the menfolk around here, they like to be all kinds of macho–get in perps' faces, pound their fists on the desk, yell false threats. And it has its place, I'm sure. It's just not for me. I like to talk. Have a conversation. As much as I despise what suspects may have done, I try to treat them just like any other person."

"I have to say that you are exceptional."

"Thank you. Now, while I appreciate all the accolades and compliments, I think we should be getting back to what happened earlier tonight."

"Okay, so after we finished talking about Mr. Wetzel and Mr. Billings, we started talking about our trip to Key West. That's where we're headed once we leave here. Going to the Keys to do some deep-sea fishing, and we'll also be doing some snorkeling. We talked about that for a while."

The conversation was interrupted by Officer Arceneaux's phone. It was a text message from Sergeant Thoreaux.

"Pardon me while I read this real quick." Anais reached up and paused the video recording.

After taking about thirty seconds to read the text, Arceneaux looked up at Mercedes.

"Is there a problem?"

"No problem a'tall," Arceneaux answered in her sweet Cajun accent. She reached up and turned the video camera back on. "Let's get back to the fishing trip. Are you much of a fisherman?"

"I do all right. I can certainly hold my own against the boys on the team," Mercedes smiled. "What about you? Ever get a chance to put a line in the water?"

"Not nearly as much as I'd like to. My father used to take me fishing all the time when I was a little girl, and I just fell in love with it. My dad is up in years now, but he'll still get out there with me when time allows."

"That's sweet," Mercedes said sincerely. "A chance to make some memories to hold on to when he does pass…which hopefully won't be for a while. How old is your father, if you don't mind me asking," Mercedes asked.

"He'll be eighty-eight on his next birthday." Anais flipped through papers she had on her desk. "Do you know how long you talked about fishing?"

"Sorry, I really don't remember."

"Was there a clock in the room?"

"I don't remember if there was or if there wasn't. I don't pay attention to the time unless I have to. I have an internal clock that does a wonderful job for me. Plus, for a backup, I wear a watch."

"And does anyone else wear a watch?"

"Well, yes. Sam. Always."

Anais wrote something down in her notebook. She looked up toward Mercedes and asked, "What happened next?"

"We did talk some more, seemed like it was a while."

"What else did you talk about?" Arceneaux asked.

"As cliché as it may sound, we talked about the weather. Specifically, we talked about the storms that are supposed to be moving in on Friday. Which means that we'll be needing to get out of here on Thursday. We think if we leave Thursday, we'll be able to get down to the Keys and skate past whatever weather that might be making its way here on Friday." Mercedes thought for a moment. "I think that was about it. After that, Samuel said he wanted to go to some grocery store to get some cider and doughnuts for breakfast."

"And do you recall what time that was? Roughly?"

"I'd say it was roughly ten o'clock, give or take."

"And did you all go to the store together?" Anais asked.

"We did, yes."

"I do appreciate your patience and cooperation, Mercedes," Anais said. "Just a couple more questions, and we can wrap this up."

"Okay, fire away whenever you're ready."

"Do you or any of your friends know anything about the disappearance of Melissa Thoreaux?" Anais asked point blank.

"No, I sure don't," Doc lied like a rug. "Can I ask you a question real quick?"

"Um, yeah, sure."

"You know that my friends and I are former Delta Force, right?"

"Really?" Arceneaux asked, somewhat surprised. "No, I was not aware of that."

"I'm sure if your chief wanted us to, we certainly wouldn't mind putting our plans on hold and sticking around for a few days to help with the search."

Officer Arceneaux's mind immediately went to the operation in which she and her fellow officers were about to be partaking. She knew that the last thing that any of them would want was a group of former Delta Force members snooping around where they were not wanted.

"Oh, goodness, Mercedes, that is an incredible gesture, but I think we'll be handling the investigation. Should we need any extra hands for the job, we'll just reach out to the state police. But that is just so kind of you to offer like that."

"Think nothing of it," Dr. Lara smiled. "I just can't imagine what you and your fellow officers are going through."

"Okay, one last question," Arceneaux let the beautiful doctor know, "do you swear that what you've told me in this interview is true to the best of your knowledge?"

"Absolutely. The truth, the whole truth and nothing but the truth." Mercedes attested.

Arceneaux wrote something else in her notebook. She looked back up at Mercedes, "That concludes my interrogation. Before I turn the recorder off, is there anything else you would like to add?"

"Just that I'm praying for the missing woman. And even though I'm not sure that there is much we can do, like I said before, please let us know if there's anything we can do to help out with the search."

"Thank you for that, and, again, thank you for your cooperation during this interrogation." With that, Officer Arceneaux reached up and turned off the video recorder.

"I must say"—the officer sat back in her chair—"you are a real delight, doctor. I would love to spend an evening with you while you're in town."

Mercedes was surprised by the proposition. It took her a moment, but she finally said, "I didn't know an officer could get involved with a potential suspect in an ongoing investigation."

Anais began to laugh. "Believe me, just between the two of us, I think you're about as much of a suspect as the person that cleans my pool."

Although Dr. Lara did not condone Arceneaux's lifestyle, kissing up to the police officer that was investigating her definitely seemed like a good idea.

"That's good to know," Merc smiled, "but I have a wonderful boyfriend and if I went out with you, it would just break his heart. So, I am going to have to respectfully decline. Although, if I were so inclined, I would certainly be camped out on your doorstep."

24

Q & A: Daniel Sloane

The interrogation room that Daniel Sloane was led to smelled oddly of fish and body odor. When Officer Dorian Dubois entered the room and sat down across the table from him, Sloane mentioned the smell.

"Officer, do you guys have any Glade or some sort of aerosol air freshener? This place is a bit malodorous."

"Is it?" Dorian asked, not really giving a darn.

"It smells like a locker room for a basketball team of catfish."

"You'll get used to it," Dorian replied.

Daniel began to cough and retch. "Do you have a bucket or something?"

"No. Are you ready for the interrogation?"

"Can we go to a different room?"

"No."

Daniel kept coughing until he brought something up, then he puked all over the floor.

"How 'bout now?" he asked Dubois. "Do you smell anything now?"

"Aww, you little dick!" Dubois slammed his hands on the table and jumped up from his chair. "Let's go," he ordered Daniel as he led him out into the hallway.

"Don't be calling me names, Slick. I told you it smelled bad there. I have a very sensitive stomach."

Officer Dubois took Sloane to the bathroom. You've got three minutes, and then I'm coming in.

"Thank you, officer," Daniel said. "You're a good man."

Sloane went into the bathroom. What nobody knew–not even his fellow teammates–was that before he left Clinton Thoreaux's house with Melissa, he had gathered all the tiny cameras that he and Merc had placed around the Thoreaux's house. Then, before he left Sandrine Benoit's house, he had sneaked one into his pocket. Now, alone in the police station bathroom, he attached the camera in the most inconspicuous spot he could think of: up in the corner, just below the ceiling, by the bathroom door. He made sure the camera was securely in place.

Having cleaned the spittle off his face and straightened his attire, he came out of the bathroom looking a good deal better.

"Sorry about that," he said to Dorian. "I'm okay. Think we can get a different interrogation room though?"

"Yeah, I think we will. Sorry I didn't believe you."

"It's just a thing. Let's go do this."

Officer Dubois led Daniel to a fresh interrogation room, where some of the other employees were setting up the video equipment for the interview. After about ten minutes, it was time to begin the interrogation.

"Are you ready to do this?" Dubois asked.

"Born ready, for whatever that means, because I was born naked, too, and I sure enough ain't that."

"I like that," Dubois smiled. "Don't do it during the interview."

"Copy that."

"Turning on the recorder in 3...2...1." Dubois hit the record button.

"This is Officer Dorian Dubois. I am here with Daniel Sloane to question him about the August 26th disappearance of Melissa Thoreaux."

Q: Could you say your complete name, sir?

A: Daniel Matthew Sloane

Q: What is your occupation?

A: I kick ass and take names at Dragon's Men Protection Agency

Q: Could you please refrain from swearing during the interview?

A: Probably not

Dorian gave Daniel a stern look and shook his head emphatically.

Q: Where were you between seven o'clock and ten o'clock tonight?

A: I don't know the address, but I was at Hawk's meemaw's house.

Q: Were you alone?

A: No, sir, I was with Sandrine Benoit, John Watkins, Mercedes Lara, and Sam Hawkins.

Q: What were you doing?

A: Do you mean me specifically, or do you mean all of us as a whole?

Q: Were you doing something different from the rest of the group?

A: Nope.

Q: Then why ask the question, Mr. Sloane?

A: I thought the question deserved an answer.

Officer Dubois shook his head back-and-forth like a dog shaking water from its fur. "Mr. Sloane, if you're not going to take this interrogation seriously, I'm going to have to place you under arrest for hindering an investigation. Is that what you want?"

"Nooo..." Sloane said in a little kid's voice.

Q: What were you doing at Sandrine Benoit's house this evening?

A: We had some coffee and some delightfully tasty croissants. By the way, have you ever had any of Meemaw's croissants? Just heavenly. And we shared some wonderful conversations.

Q. And what time did that occur?

A. It was just about 7:30 in the p.m.

Q. You remember that time, specifically?

A. I wear a watch.

Sloane held up his arm to display his watch.

Q: What did you talk about?

A: Generally or specifically?

Q: Specifically.

A: Specifically, we talked about the weather moving in on Friday, and how we'd need to get on down to the Keys on Thursday to miss all that mess. We also talked about fishing for Marlin and the best bait to use for that, ballyhoo or mackerel. Umm, Hawk's meemaw, Sandrine Benoit, wanted to know a little bit about what it is we do as a protection agency, so we told her about our last case.

Q: Which was what?

A: A stalker case.

Q: Specifically?

A: Sportswriter stalked by a disgruntled reader.

Q: Were the topics in that order: weather, fishing, work?

A: No idea.

Q: You don't remember the order of conversation that you had just a few hours ago?

A: I might put a little effort into it on one condition.

Q: That being?

A: You tell me the two kinds of Marlin bait that I mentioned a few seconds ago.

Officer Dorian Dubois thought for a moment. "This ends the interrogation of Daniel Sloane."

The policeman turned off the video recorder.

25

Q & A: JOHN WATKINS

Since the Natchez police department owned only one mobile video cam, Clinton Thoreaux had to use a recorder and microphone for his session with John Watkins. Of course, the interrogation would be captured by the cameras that were installed in each of the interrogation rooms.

Clinton hit the record button on his recorder. "Please, speak into the microphone, sir."

"Absolutely," John said, sliding the microphone closer to his mouth.

"This is Sergeant Clinton Thoreaux. It is 12:17 a.m. on August 27th. I will be interviewing John Watkins about the events of August 26th, specifically, between the hours of 7 and 10 p.m. last night."

Q: What is your full name, sir?

A: Saint John Watkins.

Q: Really? That is your full legal name?

A: It *really* is.

Q: What is your job, sir?

A: I work for the Dragon's Men Protection Agency.

Q: In regard to the events that took place on the evening of August 26th, can you recall for me, in detail, what happened?

A: I will do my honest best.

Q: Beginning at seven o'clock, would you please go through the events of the evening, allowing for me to interrupt for follow-up questions on the specific details?

A: I will adhere to that, yes.

Q: Okay, you may begin.

A: It was roughly about that time that I and all of my cohorts were upstairs in the loft of Miss Sandrine Benoit's home. She came up just a short while later with some coffee and croissants. We were talking about a job that we had recently performed.

Q: And what was that job?

A: It was a job for a sportswriter named Dan Wetzel. He was being stalked by a man named Kevin Billings.

Q: Real quick, going back to what you said earlier about Sandrine Benoit coming up to the loft, did she come upstairs on her own, or did any of you help her?

A: Her grandson, Samuel Hawkins—who she calls Sambo—went down to help her.

Q: Thank you. Please continue.

A: Miss Benoit, being interested in learning more about what her grandson did for a living, asked if she could stay to listen. We, of course, said that she could.

Q: So the five of you were in the upstairs loft?

A: Correct.

Q: Can you walk me through the details of what happened next?

A: Sandrine stayed. We went on with the story.

Q: Didn't this violate some sort of client protection privilege?

A: Sadly, we do not have that sort of privilege afforded to us under the law. We can throw it out there in hopes that the person inquiring about the information does not know the law, but legally speaking, we do not have any such clientele anonymity privileges. Anyway, we went on with the story. We talked about that for a while.

Q: How long is a while?

A: I don't know. A clock may have been in the room. At this moment in time, I do not recall.

Q: Okay. So, what else did you talk about?

A: From there I believe we talked about a couple of other things. I'm not sure of the order in which we talked about the other topics, but we talked about two more items: the weather and marlin fishing. What to best use as bait for marlin fishing and the weather, specifically, when to leave out from here–which was Thursday, for the record.

John watched Clint's face closely and listened to his breathing to see which of the two, if either, changed. As it turned out, both of them did.

Q: And why was that? Why did you decide to leave on Thursday?

A: I just told you. Because of the weather. Lousy storms are moving in. Leaving Thursday gives us plenty of time to make it out of harm's way.

Q: Who was it that gave you a heads up about the lousy weather?

A: Sandrine Benoit. She loves the weather.

Q: So, anything else about the weather?

A: Not that I recall.

Q: Did you talk about anything else?

A: Yes, we realized the lateness of the hour, so Sam, Mercedes, Daniel, and I went out to get some apple cider and doughnuts for breakfast.

Q: You just said that you didn't recall if there was a clock in the room or not, so how did y'all realize that the hour was getting late?

A: A clock may have been in the room. A clock may not have been in the room. *I do not recall* speaks for itself. I can tell you this much, Sam wears a watch all the time. Just as much chance stands that he told us the time because he realized the lateness of the hour.

Q: If I walked into the interrogation room where Sam is right now, would he have on a watch?

A: Without a doubt. He always wears a watch to keep track of when his dates with different women are. He has two alarms: one for when it's time to start getting ready; two for when it's getting close to time to leave.

Q: So, you can remember all that, but you can't remember if there was a clock in the loft?

A: Is what I am saying to you.

"At this time, I will be pausing the interview and turning the recorder off."

"Is it because you're sending a message to Mr. Hawkins' interviewer to ask him about the watch?"

Clint turned the recording off and then answered, "Yes, that's exactly what I'm doing."

"I figured as much," John said, showing no change in his emotion.

"And why is that? Please, tell me."

"Because I know you're going to taint these interview recordings however you can."

"You're too smart for your own good, Mr. Watkins."

"You're right, Sergeant Thoreaux. That's why you should stop right now with this nonsense. You won't get away with it, and you're too blind to see it."

"I get away with whatever I want. All of us do."

"There's no way you should be involved in an investigation about your own wife. You'll get a recording expert to go back through, edit you out, and put another officer in."

"You bet your ass we will," he said, looking up from his text long enough to give John a sly grin.

"I guess you have us by the short and curlies," John said. "May as well finish the interview."

"Oh, don't you worry. We will just as soon as I finish this text."

"Clinton, I don't like you, but I'm going to give you a head's up."

"And what might that be?"

"These cameras that you have in every interrogation room... everything they record goes to *the cloud*."

"Well, I hope you won't be too offended when I say that I don't believe a word you say." Clinton rolled his eyes at John. "Sincerely, you're a great liar, and I'm almost compelled to believe you. But I don't."

"I don't mind that you don't believe me," Watkins said. "I'm just disappointed that we'll be leaving town before we have a chance to bring you all to your knees."

"The only one that will be brought to their knees is you and your friends," Clinton scoffed.

"So, my friends and I, are we under arrest or are we free to go?"

"We're going to need you and your friends to stick around for a while, John."

"Oh, good. We're on a first name basis now."

Comparing Notes

Officer Cyprien Guillory had been given the task of going to Smitty's grocery store and retrieving the security footage from the previous night. It took a little longer than anyone had figured, but around 3 a.m. Officer Guillory came strolling in with the much-anticipated footage.

"So?" Sergeant Thoreaux asked. "Are they on the tape, or aren't they?"

"Keep your pants on, Sarge. Let's all go to the media room so we can watch it together, and we can form our own opinions."

"What is that supposed to mean? *Form our own opinions?*" Dorian Dubois asked.

"It means everybody get yourselves into the media room so we can clear these fine people of any wrongdoing, and they can be on their way," Chief Briggs bellowed.

For as much as Clinton Thoreaux wanted Dragon's Men to be the ones responsible for the disappearance of his wife, Darryl Briggs needed the members of the protection agency to be free and clear of any wrongdoing so they could be on their way before Mr. Lazarus, the gunrunner, came to town on Friday night.

"We need to get into the media room anyway," Officer Dubois

made it known. "We have to watch and compare all their statements."

At this, all griping stopped and the group of officers got up and reassembled in the media room.

Cyprien Guillory played the security footage from Smitty's first. The video was time stamped, and it did, indeed, show Samuel Hawkins and Dr. Mercedes Lara walking into the market at just a few minutes past ten o'clock. Hawkins got cider and doughnuts, and Mercedes got four energy drinks from the cooler. The video also had sound. As Mercedes was getting the energy drinks, he could clearly be heard asking Sam:

"Did Daniel say he wanted peach or mango?"

"It was my job to get the cider and doughnuts. It was your job to get the energy drinks. If you've dropped the ball on your assignment, don't count on me to bail you out."

"I would just like to remind you that it's going to be a long ride back to Ms. Benoit's house if I get them the wrong flavor, and I'm going to blame you, Hawk."

"Fine. Get him wild berry."

"I'll get him mango," Mercedes responded.

Guillory stopped the video. "So, as you can see, there's only two of them in the store, but they definitely are talking like the other members of their crew are out in the car. The woman is buying four drinks. I mean, it could be an elaborate hoax, but what are the chances that these guys kidnapped Sarge's wife, and then decided to stop off at the market for drinks and doughnuts?"

"I'm with Officer Guillory," the chief concurred. "In my interview with Sandrine Benoit, she said that they went to Smitty's for cider and doughnuts right around ten o'clock."

"Yeah," Anais Arceneaux chimed in, "I've known Sandrine Benoit since I was old enough to remember. She ain't never even jaywalked or run a yellow light. She's the sweetest little old lady

I know. Heck, most of us think of her as our own grandma. In my wildest dreams I could not see her being part of a kidnapping plot or whatever this is."

"What do you mean *whatever this is?*" Clint shot up out of his chair. "It's a kidnapping, and these Dragon's Men a-holes did it!"

"Clint, sit yer ass down and be quiet," Chief Briggs ordered him. "Let's pull up the interviews and see if we can get anything from them."

"Hey, real quick," Officer Pascal Moreau said. It was Moreau who had taken Clint's statement about the whole kidnapping incident when Clint finally decided to sit down and say what happened. "Did anyone of y'all interview someone that had a German accent?"

"A German accent?" All of the officers looked at each other. "Why are you asking that, Pascal?"

"Because when Clint was giving me his statement, he told me that the guy that attacked him had a German accent."

"No," came the collective response from the officers.

"Alright. I have the interview videos ready to go," Officer Arceneaux announced. "Let's get this show on the road, ladies and gentlemen."

"There's no need to get any show on the road," Chief Briggs said. "I watched the interviews from my office. I don't think these people had anything to do with Melissa's kidnapping."

"But Chief!" Thoreaux yelled. "These guys are guilty as sin. Why am I the only one that sees it?"

"Because you're blinded by rage, Clint." The chief reached out and grabbed Clinton firmly by both shoulders. "Sergeant, you need to go home and get your head on straight. We'll find Melissa, she'll turn up, and your life will be back to the way it was. But for now, our focus needs to be on tomorrow night."

"You can't be serious, Chief," Thoreaux uttered.

"I've never been more serious in my life." Briggs made it very clear to Sergeant Thoreaux that the subject was not up for debate.

"Tomorrow night is our big payday, the one we've been waiting for. However, right now, your mind is not in the game. You need to go home and do whatever it is you have to do."

"So, my wife means nothing? It's all about the money and the guns, isn't it?"

"Clint, we're going to turn the investigation over to the Natchitoches police department. They'll handle things from here, and we'll work hand-in-hand with them. We'll find Melissa, but for cripes sake, that interview you did with John Watkins—you pretty much told him we were dirty."

"I just wanted him to know that I knew that they were behind my wife being taken," Clint tried to make his point.

Unfortunately for him, his protest fell on deaf ears.

"Let's go around the room," Chief Briggs suggested. "Who among you think those five people in the holding room had anything to do with the disappearance—"

"Kidnapping!" Clint snapped.

"Right...kidnapping of Melissa Thoreaux?"

Though they wouldn't have dared say it aloud, some of the officers wouldn't have been surprised to learn that Melissa had arranged the whole thing herself to escape her abusive husband.

"They're each other's alibi," Anais Arceneaux offered, "and their stories seem legitimate."

"Plus, we had the trackers on their vehicles, and neither vehicle left the house until they went to Smitty's," Briggs pointed out.

"The video footage at Smitty's syncs up with their story, too," Officer Leblanc said, adding her point of view.

"And none of them have a German accent," Dorian added.

"Anyone could have faked a German accent," Clint muttered.

"Clint, you're the one that said the kidnapper was German," Dorian Dubois blasted him. "Now you're saying that he wasn't a German?"

The chief walked over to the sergeant and put his arm around his shoulder. "Clint, you know I love you like a son, but you need to go. Go talk to the police shrink. Go see a friend, go home and do some drinkin'. But, son, you need to get out of here."

"I'm fine, Chief," Thoreaux objected.

"You're not fine," Chief Briggs said gruffly. "You went and told that Watkins fella that we do what we want, when we want, and that we get away with it. To me, that's not fine."

Clinton hung his head. "I guess you're right, Boss. I'll go ahead and go."

27

Looks Like We're Staying

The four members of Dragon's Men plus Sandrine Benoit were seated at one end of a long table in a holding room. John was seated at the head of the table, with Sam and his grandmother to his left and Daniel and Mercedes to his right.

John motioned for everyone to lean in closely so that they could speak in hushed tones in case the holding room was bugged

"So how did everyone do? In hindsight, do you feel like you made any mistakes, added something you shouldn't have added, left out something you shouldn't have?"

Sam was bursting to tell his news about Solange Leblanc, but he was waiting to see if anyone else had something to say first.

Mercedes went first. "Mine could not have gone better. When the interviewer is basically throwing herself at you, it makes for a pretty pleasant conversation."

"Officer Arceneaux is gay?" Sloane asked.

"Well, she's a switch-hitter, but don't think for one moment that I didn't play into that. I was flirtatious and kind as could be. Made the interview great. She didn't get into any of the specifics like we talked about. Maybe just a little bit. One thing," Merc noted. "She did ask me about Sam wearing his watch. I found that odd."

"Hey, they asked me that, too," Daniel said.

"They asked that because I told them I knew the time that we left to go to Smitty's, but I didn't see a clock in the room," John explained. "I told them that I got the time from Sam's watch because I know he always wears one. Here's the thing: there is no way that any legitimate police station would have allowed Clint to be anywhere near this investigation. So, I just asked him flat out if he was going to doctor our interviews to make it look like we kidnapped his wife."

"You keep talking about the recording equipment," Sandrine said quietly. "The chief didn't use any sort of recording equipment for our interview. He didn't even have a tape recorder going or anything. He just asked me questions and would occasionally write some things down on a yellow legal pad."

"Interesting," John said, nodding his head. He then looked at Hawkins. John could tell by his body language that he had something to say about his interview. "Alright, Hawk, spill it. What happened at your interview that has you champing at the bit like a racehorse at the starting gate at Pimlico?"

"I put a camera in the men's bathroom," Daniel jumped in, his face beaming with pride. "And it's right where they'll never see it, too."

"You did what?" John asked.

"Why on earth would you do that, Daniel?" asked Mercedes Lara.

"What do you mean, why? The men's room is where all the cops talk about the private things going on in their lives. I thought it would be a good opportunity to get some intel that we wouldn't be privy to otherwise."

John lowered his head. He moved his hand up and grabbed the bridge of his nose with his index finger and his thumb and massaged his nose ever so slightly. "I won't say it was a bad idea, Daniel. It was just kind of a stupid one."

"You want me to go pull it down?"

"Once they come in here and tell us that we're free to leave, you can go grab it then," John said.

"Copy that."

"Now go ahead, Sam."

"My interviewer's name was Solange Leblanc," Hawkins began. "She's been working here for about six months." He moved a little closer to the middle of the table so everyone could hear him as he whispered. "She knows that everyone here is dirty. Thing is, she's afraid to blow the whistle because the Natchez Police Department has the highest conviction rate of any police precinct in the whole state. The higher ups treat these guys like they be the golden children of the police gods. If she blows the whistle, and she loses…she feels like she'd be a marked woman."

"We can help her out if she would be willing to meet with us," John suggested.

"Yeah, well there's one other thing she told me. She said if we get exonerated about any involvement in Thoreaux's missin' wife, once we leave, they gonna harass, hassle, and harangue Meemaw until she admits to something. They'll arrest her, seize her property, she'll lose the only house she ever lived in. It'll be pretty much just enough to kill her.

"So, yeah, I know that we talked about just getting the girl and her grandmother and gettin' them someplace safe and gettin' out, but I can't leave. I know we can call the FBI and the ATF, and they can do their thing, but I have to make sure that these Natchez police jackholes get what they got comin' to them and are removed from power. You guys ain't gotta stay, but I have to. I have to take care of my meemaw."

"Well, if you're staying, I'm staying," Daniel said.

"We'll all stay. Plus, if we can take down these dirty cops, we may not even have to relocate Melissa or her grandmother."

"The problem is this," Mercedes said. "How do we explain to

Agent Jake Ritter how we got the information about this weapons buy?"

"I know exactly how we're going to explain it." John said.

"You do?" asked Sloane.

Before John could explain how he was going to make something that was one-hundred percent illegal look completely legitimate, Chief Darryl Briggs came to bring them news.

"Well, after much deliberation, the preponderance of the evidence, and just good old-fashioned police work, we have come to the decision that you had nothing to do with the disappearance of Clinton Thoreaux's wife. You are all free to go."

On his way out the door, the chief stopped to make one last comment. "I just want to say how sorry I am, and on behalf of the Natchez Police Department, how much we regret what we've put y'all through. If there's any way that we can make some sort of amends for what has happened, please, just let us know. I'd like to wish you all safe travels and a good time of fishing while you're in the Keys. I just could not be more sorry for the circumstances—"

"Chief," John interrupted him and walked over to the burly man. Shaking Briggs' hand, he said, "On behalf of my team, apology accepted. We realize that things happen that are out of our hands. No need to spend one more second worrying about our feelings. You need to go find that woman and bring her safely home. Heck, I just wish we weren't leaving so soon, or we would stick around and lend a hand ourselves trying to find her."

"I appreciate that, Mr. Watkins," Chief Briggs said. "It's late. Our manpower is tired, so we're going to put a call in to the FBI and see if we can't get a little bit of help from some of Uncle Sam's finest."

"That sounds like the right thing to do," John agreed. We're going to go home, get some much-needed sleep, and when we wake up, we're going to pack our things, have some cider and doughnuts, and head out before that storm heads in."

Everyone got up from the table and made a point to shake the chief's hand as they headed out into the hallway. When Sandrine got to the chief, she made no secret about how she felt. "My grandson and his friends might have been quick to forgive you, sir, but I ain't them. We've known each other a long time, Darryl, and for you to have the nerve to think that me or anyone I know would be in on some kind of plot to kidnap or whatever Clinton's wife is just preposterous. You ruined my visit with my Sambo. To boot, you tried to make them look like common criminals. I'm ashamed of you, and you should be ashamed of yourself. Shame, shame, shame!"

She did not shake the chief's hand, and when she left the room, the tiny woman slammed the door aggressively, leaving the chief standing all by himself.

28

CALLING IN THE BIG GUNS

After being released from the police station, Dragon's Men and Sandrine Benoit made their way back to Sandrine's house. Once they pulled into the driveway, they had to come up with a way of ditching the transponders on the vehicles.

"How you wanna play this one, Boss?" Sam wanted to know.

John looked at Sandrine, "Is there a mall near here?"

"There isn't a typical mall, so to speak, but there is a place in Natchitoches that has a bunch o' stores. It's called the Louisiana Purchase."

"Okay," John nodded. "It's late. We should call it a night. We'll get some sleep, and then in the morning, Daniel, you and I will take one of the SUVs to the Louisiana Purchase and park it there. We'll call a cab and head over to see Melissa and Dot."

"I don't know about y'all," Sandrine said, "but I am about as tired as a girl can get."

* * *

Eight o'clock the next morning found Daniel Sloane opening his eyes to see John Watkins sitting next to him tapping away on his laptop. Whatever it was, Sloane did not care. What Sloane did care about was the wonderful aroma penetrating his olfactory senses.

"What is that heavenly smell?" the groggy tough guy asked.

"I think it's banana pancakes and scrapple."

"Is there no end to the goodness of this woman?"

"I think there's sausage gravy and biscuits, too," John said. "If you don't like sausage gravy on your biscuits, there's homemade blueberry jam."

"I'll see you in about an hour," Sloane said, rolling out of bed.

"Take your time. I'm getting ready to call Agent Ritter in a few. Right now, I'm checking the bus schedule in Natchitoches. Looks like the bus headed to Miami will be coming through around noon."

"Ah, yes, the bus to Miami," Sloane said. "Good call."

As Daniel headed downstairs, John thumbed through the contacts on his phone to find ATF Agent Jake Ritter's phone number. Upon finding it, he dialed his old friend.

Ritter answered immediately. "Well, it must be a slow day in Beverly Hills."

"You know it's White Pines, ya smug jackass."

"Right, right. White Pines–the Beverly Hills of the Midwest," Ritter laughed. "What's goin' on, Captain?"

"Know anything about a gunrunner named Lazarus? Or Mr. Lazarus?"

"Josiah Lazarus?"

"I'm going to go out on a limb and take that as a *yes*."

"Shoot, yeah. He's one of the biggest gun runners in Central America. What's got you barkin' that tree's name?"

"Oh, cos maybe I know where he's going to be tomorrow night between 10:30 and 11:30 Central Time."

"No," Ritter said in disbelief.

"Yes," John said.

"I mean, *no*, as in half my guys are in a training program about new rules and regs. About seventy percent of the guys that I have left are on a job that I'm not running, which means I can't re-assign them to anything. That leaves me a handful of men that I would have to assemble and bring up to speed and put a plan of attack together and get down there."

"So...?"

"I've been after Josiah Lazarus for years, John. Years!"

"If it helps, my team and I will put together a plan of attack. We're here, we can do the recon work, and have something ready to go in a few hours."

"Are you and your team still on top of their game?"

"We're tighter than ever, Jake. I stake my life on it," Watkins promised.

"Let me ask you this, Dragon John: How did you happen to get this intel on Lazarus and how dependable is it?"

"It's gonna sound crazy, but it fell right into our laps. We are in a small town called Natchez, Louisiana. We came down here for what we thought would be just a simple relocation job. We have a woman that is taking a daily beating from her husband–a dirty cop who's part of an entire police force of dirty cops–so we put cameras in the woman's house so we could watch her and when the husband started beating her, we would have it recorded. Well, lo and behold, while we're watching them, the dirty cop husband gets a phone call on a burner phone he has, and it's this Lazarus guy. The cop proceeds to set up a huge gun buy–the where, the when, the payload, everything. I've got the whole thing on a file that I'm going to send to you.

"Yes, that'll be great, because I'll have to be able to verify this to my superiors before I can even think about requisitioning any people for this job." Ritter started laughing. "You aren't kidding, though, this really did just fall right into your lap. All right, big boy, send me that file. I will call you soon to let you know what kind of manpower

I can scrounge together, and we'll set up a rendezvous point."

"Good enough, Jake. Talk to you soon."

Of course, before John Watkins sent the file, he made sure it only contained the phone call between Josiah Lazarus and Clinton Thoreaux. He had edited out the part where Daniel Sloane made an appearance just in the nick of time.

29

John's Plan for the Cameras

John and Daniel drove the company SUV to the Louisiana Purchase, the place Hawk's grandma had told them about. Once there, they ditched their ride and called for a cab to the Best Western.

Melissa and her grandmother, Dot, were in Room 312, registered under the name of Carol Jenkins. Daniel gave the secret knock, and a few moments later Melissa opened the door and let Sloane and Watkins in. She had apparently just gotten out of the shower as her long brown hair was still very damp, and she was wearing a white hotel bathrobe.

"How's everybody doing this morning?" John asked, entering with his laptop in hand.

"Oh, we's doin' real good," Dot answered. "This one here slept till after ten o'clock."

"It felt good to sleep without gnawing fear for the first time in years," Melissa confessed.

"Come on boys, have a seat on the couch," Dot offered. She took the TV remote off the coffee table and muted the television.

Dorothy Michaud was a thin black woman in her mid-80s, but her age was only given away by her full head of gray hair and the pair of readers that she wore on the tip of her nose. Her overall attitude was upbeat and quite contagious.

John and Daniel took a seat on the couch. John, attired in his usual three-piece suit–today's color was turquoise–on the left end, and Daniel, in a black muscle shirt and tight blue jeans, on the right.

"How are our relocation plans coming?" Melissa asked.

"Pretty well, and while we will have them ready for you by tomorrow morning, there's an outside chance that we may not have to relocate you at all."

"Really?" Melissa and Dot asked together in excitement.

"How will that work?" Dorothy inquired.

John opened his laptop and pulled up the file that showed Clinton Thoreaux talking to Josiah Lazarus on the phone.

"Melissa, come take a seat over here between Mr. Sloane and me." As John waited for the young lady to move to the couch, he asked her a question. "Did your grandmother explain to you that we put surveillance cameras throughout your home so that we could get a visual record of your husband abusing you?"

"Well, I kind of figured out that there was something like that just based on Mr. Sloane's timely appearance," Melissa said, seating herself between John and Daniel. She patted Daniel on the leg and smiled. "It's good to see you again. I also wanted to let you and Mr. Watkins know that, while I realize there are a lot of battered women that can't resist returning to their abusers–yes, I used to be like that, thinking I couldn't live without him–I can assure you that I am no longer that way. I have had enough of the abuse, both physical and mental. I am more than ready to be as far away from that man as I can possibly get, no matter what I have to do. I have to start thinking for two now."

"That's definitely the right mindset to have," John smiled easily. "I want you to watch this clip."

John played the video clip of Clinton Thoreaux on the phone with Mr. Lazarus. As Melissa watched the video, John watched her face. Her expression told him that she had no idea who Mr. Lazarus was nor that her husband was in the gunrunning business.

"I can't believe this," she said disgustedly. "I knew he was a piece of garbage but never to this level."

"Earlier, you said that you would do whatever you had to do to get away from him."

"Right, and I will," she said.

"Okay, here's what is going to happen: Mr. Sloane and I, along with our other team members Mr. Hawkins and Dr. Lara, will be working in conjunction with the Department of Alcohol, Tobacco, and Firearms to bring down this Mr. Lazarus as well as every member of the Natchez Police Department. If that happens and this does go to court"—John looked her right in the eyes and expressed complete seriousness— "I'm going to need you to lie."

"Sure," she said without hesitation. "What do you need me to lie about?"

"We need you to lie about the cameras in your house. We're going to need you to say that you bought them, paid cash for them, and you're not sure where or when you bought them, but you bought them to get proof of your husband's abuse. When you saw this particular part of the footage, you weren't sure who to give it to or even how to do it. You told your grandmother, who, in turn contacted Miss Benoit, and she contacted us."

"Whatever you need, Mr. Watkins." Just then, a pained look passed across Melissa's face, and she grabbed her pregnant belly. "Ugh, the little bugger must be a river dancer for as much as he kicks." Then she smiled and her big green eyes grew wide.

"Hey," she said with a sly tone in her voice. "Do you have the part of the video where Mr. Sloane gives my soon-to-be ex-husband that incredible beatdown?"

"Um, yeah," John answered. "We're going to have to delete that part of the footage, but, yeah, here ya go." Watkins cued up the video and let her watch Sloane do what he does best: beat, thrash, and pulverize a person into a bloody mess.

Sloane and Watkins watched Melissa take in the video with a look of glee across her face. When she saw Sloane slam Clinton's head into the foot of the bed, Melissa said, "Yeah! Take that, ya little pissant!"

Daniel and John looked at each other and nodded. They both knew that this was, indeed, a woman that was done with her abuser.

"So, when's all this stuff with Mr. Lazarus and the ATF going to take place?" Dot asked.

"Tomorrow night," John answered. "Which is why later on, we'll be stopping by with your new identities and enough cash for you to go anywhere and get started…just in case we don't make it out alive with Mr. Lazarus and his people."

"Oh, no," Melissa said, "you can't think like that."

"We don't, but, in reality, it's always a possibility," Daniel said.

"Anyway, Dot, we'll have you set up as a retired person that will receive a monthly check from the government for twenty-five hundred dollars. I know it isn't much—"

"Aw, hale, it's more than I'm getting now!" Dot exclaimed.

"And Melissa, we heard that you went to college for architecture?"

"Yes, I studied to be a city planner."

"Do you think you remember much of that?" asked John.

"Of course. Honestly, I used to toy around with it while Clinton was at work, but one night Clint came home early and caught me doing it. He beat me so badly that I thought I was going to die. He then dragged me out to our car and drove it headlong into a telephone poll. He claimed a deer ran out in front of our car and when he swerved to miss it, he hit the telephone pole. He said I wasn't wearing my seat belt."

"Well, your new identity will be complete with a sparkling resumé as a city planner. We'll include people as your references that will give you equally sparkling recommendations."

"It sounds like the life I wanted before I met Clint."

"There's just one catch," Daniel said seriously. "You can never reach out to anyone that you know now. Ya just can't do it."

"Not even Sandrine?" Dot asked.

"Not even her. As a matter of fact, she will be coming by in a little while to say her goodbyes."

"I have a question," Melissa sounded worried.

"Okay."

"What if Clint does get arrested? Won't he still be around here? What if he gets bailed out?"

"We have a guy. He's a hacker, and prison records are pretty easy to hack. So, maybe Clint accidentally gets transferred to a federal prison in North Dakota, and then maybe his transfer gets lost, and then maybe his prison record gets changed, and the guy just disappears into prison oblivion…never to be heard from again."

"Hey, don't you worry," said Daniel. "One way or another, we'll make sure your husband gets everything he has coming to him, and you'll never have to worry about him again."

30

THE OLD BUS AND SWITCH ROUTINE

By 11:30 that Thursday morning, the temperature was 92 degrees, with the humidity just a few ticks lower.

Having finished giving Melissa and Grandma Dot the lowdown, Watkins and Sloane stepped out of the hotel to flag down a cab back to Natchitoches. They were already sweating their tails off.

"I swear, this town must've designed its weather to feel just like the outer gates of Hell."

"Yeah, it's stickier than flypaper made of bubble gum out here," Daniel said.

They snagged a cab ride back to the Louisiana Purchase where Sam and Mercedes were waiting just as planned. Now, with the two black SUVs together, Daniel Sloane removed both tracking devices from the undercarriage of the vehicles.

"All right, gang, we've done this trick more than a few times. Daniel drives Vehicle One. We find the bus to Miami. I exit Vehicle One, get on the bus, ask the people on the bus if they've seen my niece. I pull out the picture and hold it up. I've got everyone's attention on the inside of the bus. Mercedes and Sam, you exit Vehicle Two. You both start arguing…then you start fighting by ripping each other's shirts off. This will get everybody's attention that is outside of the bus. With everyone looking at the picture in my hand or the fight between Sam and Mercedes, Daniel will put the trackers under the bus, one in front and one in back. This will make them look like they are far enough apart that they appear to be two different vehicles. Hopefully, whoever's watching the tracker isn't paying close enough attention to notice that the two vehicles keep stopping and starting in perfect synchronicity."

"Get them daggone trackers on that bus in a hurry. I don't want to be fighting Doc in this heat any longer than I have to be. It'll be a sweaty mess after fifteen seconds." Hawk complained.

"Yeah, but at least you'll have everybody's attention," John smiled coyly.

"The station is about fifteen minutes away. We should get going if we're going to catch that Miami bus at noon," Samuel said.

31

LIKE CLOCKWORK

Daniel took the lead as the two vehicles made their way to the Natchitoches bus station.

He and John discussed the potential for danger tomorrow night because of their lack of manpower going up against the small army of goons that would be accompanying Mr. Lazarus. Combined with the eight or ten policemen that would probably also be there, the count was quite lopsided.

"I'm waiting for a call from Agent Ritter to let me know how many men he'll be able to bring. I'm not counting on it being very many, with it being last minute and everything."

"If you had to, do you think you could get Latin to come down?"

"I am already planning to call him as soon as we are finished here at the bus station."

While the conversation in the lead vehicle was about manpower, in Vehicle Two, the conversation between Sam and Mercedes was about the fake fight they would be having. They were planning the choreography, both the verbal and physical aspects of it.

"As soon as we park, we'll get out and make a beeline to the front of the Miami bus," Hawkins said. "On the way, I'll call you a thief and accuse you of stealing a hundred dollars from me."

"Okay, and once we get to the front of the bus, I'll tell you that you're crazy and that you need to get away from me."

"I'll say the hundred dollars is in your pants pocket, and I'll try to reach in there for it. You push me down on the ground and when I get up, you will try to sweep my legs. Once I avoid that, I will take a swing at your head. I'll swing high, but you should still duck. When you do, go for my shirt. Grab it from the back and pull it up over top of my head. It's a loose shirt, so it should come off pretty easily."

"Hopefully, by that time, Danny will have the trackers in place, but if he doesn't, don't hesitate to go for my shirt, too. I've got a sports bra on, so we're cool."

"Sounds good to me," Hawk said. "This is the bus station up here on the left."

Upon arrival, they realized that at noon on a Thursday in late August, the Natchitoches bus depot was just shy of being dead. Only ten or twelve cars were parked in the parking lot. Three buses were parked perpendicular to the front of the station, with the Miami bus first in line.

Daniel pulled the black SUV up along the driver's side of the bus. After waiting a few brief moments to give Sam and Mercedes time to park, John grabbed the black and white 8x10 of Jenny Main–the picture of Daniel Sloane's girlfriend that he took with him whenever he traveled–and quickly got out of the vehicle.

"I'll use this picture to show people, pretend she's my niece."

"Roger that." Sloane grabbed the two trackers and got ready to install them on the bus bound for Miami.

Like the gears inside a clock, the four members of Dragon's Men moved perfectly together to execute the plan without a single hitch.

John, the frantic uncle looking for his niece, did a perfect job of holding the attention of the passengers on the bus. Some people even swore that they had seen Jenny Main inside the bus station.

Sam and Mercedes were very convincing as the couple arguing over a hundred dollars. Their fight was so realistic that bystanders came up to pull them away from each other.

No one noticed Daniel Sloane putting the trackers underneath the very front and very back of the 45-foot-long coach. The whole operation took less than a minute.

Then, just like that, the foursome were in their vehicles and headed back to the Best Western, where they planned to stay. Returning to Natchez would have been foolish, since their big SUVs would certainly have been spotted in the small town.

As far as the Natchez Police Department knew, the four members of Dragon's Men were safely on their way to Miami, Florida.

32

A NEED FOR REINFORCEMENTS

Agent Jake Ritter was reviewing the video file that John Watkins had sent of Clinton Thoreaux speaking on the phone with Mr. Lazarus. Unable to believe his eyes–or ears, he immediately took it to his supervisor, Deputy Director Marvin Gayle.

"Sir, you're not going to believe this, but I've got very credible intel on Josiah Lazarus and a group of dirty cops in Natchez, Louisiana. I've sent you a video file of one of the police sergeants talking directly to Lazarus, setting up a weapons buy in Natchitoches, Louisiana for tomorrow night."

Deputy Director Gayle may have been a man of few words, but he was definitely a man of action.

"Alright," he said. "Let's take a look." He pulled up the file and opened it up. "How in the world did you get this?"

"It's a bizarre story, Boss."

"Bizarre is fine. Illegal is not, so lay it on me."

Jake Ritter took a seat and began explaining. "There's a group of former Delta Force members that now work in the civilian world. They are doing a job where a woman is being abused and apparently beaten by her husband on a daily basis. Anyway, these guys–they go by the name of Dragon's Men–they told her to set up some video cameras to catch the guy in the process. And this is what they got."

The two men watched the video clip of Clinton Thoreaux talking to Josiah Lazarus. As soon as it was over, Deputy Director Gayle sighed. "I'm sorry, Jake. We can't move on this."

"What? Why not?"

"Aw, c'mon, man. Put yourself in my position. I can't pull guys off a job that we know is solid to put them on something that we have no idea about."

"No idea about? Did you just watch the same video I did?" Ritter asked.

"It's a video of some guy on the phone with goodness only knows who. The video hasn't been authenticated. We don't have any solid intel. We don't have any agents in the area. You want me to pull agents off another assignment based on some tip from some Dungeons and Dragons guys that you say used to be former Delta Force operatives."

"It's Josiah Lazarus, sir."

"And that's another thing," Deputy Director Gayle said. "We can't possibly set up an operation big enough to take down Lazarus on just twenty-four hours' notice. The guy's got a small army that he takes with him wherever he goes."

"Then just give me three guys, Boss. I can coordinate with these guys, Dragon's Men. They're already in place and doing the recon work."

"Jake, I can't let you do that. How many of these Dragon's Men are there?"

Agent Ritter hesitated for a moment. "Four of them."

"That's a suicide mission! I can't let you do it," the Deputy Director said. "You'd need, at the very least, twenty to thirty men to take out a guy like Lazarus. And that's not even accounting for the dirty cops."

"Then I'll go off-book."

"Look, Jake, I understand your frustration. I'm frustrated, too.

Listen, see if this Dragon's Men crew can get close enough to get pictures of the weapons sale. If they can, then in a few days, we'll get a team together and go down there and bring these dirty cops to justice. At least, it's something."

"Okay, but I'm going down there. I'll make sure we get the evidence we need to bust the dirty cops then."

Marvin Gayle looked at Ritter for a good ten seconds. "Okay. You go down strictly on an evidentiary mission, and that's it. Do we have an understanding?"

"Yes, sir. I understand."

"I'll sign off on it, and you can leave tonight."

33

SHORT ON TIME, SHORT ON PEOPLE

At 1:20 p.m. on Thursday afternoon, Ritter made the call to John Watkins. He was dreading the news he was going to have to deliver.

John was quick to answer the call. "What's the good word, Jake?"

"The good word is I'm coming, but it's not to take down Josiah Lazarus."

"Then what are you coming for?" John asked.

"The Deputy Director has signed off on me to come down there and assist you in doing recon on the gun deal. He wants us to take pictures of the weapons deal, and then when he can assemble a proper team, we'll take down that entire police department."

"Well, that was certainly not what I was hoping to hear," John said. "Still, if that's what we have to do then that's what we'll have to do."

"I wish I had better news for you, my friend."

"I don't guess you have any *friends* that would want to come with you and work off-book, do ya?"

"Even if I did, I would risk losing my job if things went south. I'm afraid it's just going to be me, and we're just going to take pictures and get what we need to take down those dirty cops, and we'll have even more evidence against Lazarus when we can finally get him."

"Okay." John's voice was sullen and flat. "Well, we're going to be staying at the Best Western on University Parkway in Natchitoches."

"Sounds good. I'll be leaving as soon as the Deputy Director signs off on the paperwork. I'll text you my ETA once I'm underway."

"Looking forward to seeing you, Jake."

John disconnected the call.

He and Daniel were sitting in their room in the Best Western, where they had just checked in. Mercedes was also with them, as Samuel was in a cab on his way back to get his meemaw so she could come to see her friend Dot for what may very well be the last time.

Daniel was sprawled out on one of the room's two double beds. Mercedes was on the other, flipping through the channels trying to find something to watch.

Watkins was lying on the couch. Daniel and Merc could both tell that he was not happy with the phone call that he had just wrapped up.

"Bad news, Chief?"

"Certainly not what I was hoping to hear," John sighed, moving to sit upright. "That was Agent Jake Ritter, and the help that I was hoping to get from the ATF isn't coming. There's just not enough time for them to get a team together. Instead, all he could get his boss to sign off on was for him to come down to take pictures of the deal going down. Once they get a team together, they'll send them down here to take care of the Natchez police."

"Oh, what a bunch of rabbit turds that is," Mercedes expressed. "Talk about government bureaucracy at its best. They've got a legitimate shot at getting one of the world's most notorious gun runners, and they're just letting it go by the wayside because they can't get a few guys together on a day's notice? Good Lord."

"So, what does that mean for us and our plans?" Sloane asked.

"Nothing. I'm still assembling a plan in my head," John

answered. "Just because the government can't get its act together in twenty-four hours doesn't mean that we're going to sit on our thumbs and miss a golden opportunity to rid the world of some much-unwanted garbage."

"You going to call Latin?"

"I am. But before I do, I am thinking about taking a drive down to the river for a look at Pier 51 to see what's going on around it. That will give me a much better idea as to what kind of plan will be possible, and what we'll need to make that plan work."

"I'll come with you," Merc said. "Ain't jack on TV"

34

Trying to Maintain Focus

Clinton Thoreaux was sitting in Chief Briggs' office, slowly going crazy over his missing wife. He kept checking his phone, waiting for a call of some sort from whomever it was that had taken his wife.

"I don't get it, Chief," the sergeant steamed. "Why hasn't anyone called with ransom demands or something?"

"I don't know, Clint. It just doesn't make any sense."

"I'm telling ya, those Dragon's Men jackasses have something to do with this."

"And I'm tellin' you, Clint, that dog just don't hunt. We questioned them, and their stories were all straight. Plus, the trackers that we had on their vehicles showed that they never moved from Sandrine Benoit's house except for when they said they did. They said they went to Smitty's to get cider and doughnuts, and the tracker showed that's just what they did." The chief looked at the tracking readout device. "And now according to this thing, they're on their way down to Florida just like they said they would be."

"I don't understand. I'm hardly ever wrong about these things."

"We've got officers at the bus station, the train station, and we've been going through the CCTV footage from all over town. There's just been no sign of her."

"I'm going back home," Clint said. "I don't want to miss—"

"Miss what, Sergeant?" The chief cut him off. "We've got people watching your house. We've got your phone being forwarded to here if anyone calls."

"I know," said a frustrated Thoreaux.

"Know what? You should go home," Briggs said. "You should go home and get some sleep. I know you're worried, but I don't need to remind you how important it is for you to stay focused on what's going down tomorrow night. Mr. Lazarus is going to be coming to town, and we need to have all our attention on making sure there's no mistakes made there. We certainly don't need any screw-ups as far as that goes."

"I know, Chief. I know."

"Go get some rest, Sergeant. If we hear or see anything, you know you're my first call."

35

THE CANE RIVER

The Cane River was absolutely picturesque. A thirty-mile-long offshoot of Lake Pontchartrain, it emptied into the Gulf of Mexico. The river was anywhere from a hundred-fifty yards to a half-mile wide at different parts. The section that ran through the city of Natchitoches was peppered on both sides by beautiful houses and arresting landscapes.

However, just outside the city limits, where Pier 51 was located, both banks were covered with wooded wilderness. State Road 119 ran parallel with the watercourse, with many service roads running down to the river.

John and Mercedes were currently driving slowly along Route 119, looking for the service road that would take them down to Pier 51.

"This heat is starting to get to me, John," Mercedes said. "I tell ya, we find this Pier 51, you just might see me strip down to my skivvies and go jump in the water."

"Well, I certainly can't tell you what to do, but I will ask that you hold off on your water shenanigans until after you've helped me do some recon on the area."

"Hey!" Mercedes shouted. "I think this is our road right here on the left."

John turned the car onto the service road and through a dense patch of trees. In just a few hundred yards, they were where they needed to be.

"Ugh," Merc complained. "I dread getting out." She turned the air conditioning to full blast, put her face in front of the vent, and let the cool air wash over her.

Meanwhile, John crawled into the back seat and pulled out a pair of ankle-high rubber boots. He put them on in place of his wingtip loafers, then rolled up the pants of his turquoise suit.

Crawling back into the driver's seat, John looked over at Dr. Lara, still thoroughly enjoying the stream of cold air. With no empathy whatsoever, he turned off the SUV. Merc shot him a look of great disdain.

"Let's go to work, Merc. The sooner we can figure this out, the sooner we can get back to the hotel and start making a plan."

Mercedes muttered a rather ribald response as they exited the vehicle and began walking through the marshy, shin-high grass.

"This atmosphere is just tragically uncomfortable."

"Come on, Doc. You know we've been through worse. Kandahar, Aleppo, Buenos Aires."

"Yeah, but that was dry heat, John. Here, it feels like the air weighs a hundred pounds."

"The pier is right over there. Let's go check it out."

They slogged their way through the boggy wetlands to discover a wooden pier about eight feet wide, stretching about ten or twelve yards into the river. A good part of the pier had been reinforced with pieces of two-by-six boards to ensure that it would hold the weight of large crates of weapons.

John and Merc stood at the end of the pier looking up and down the river.

"Okay, so that's north," John said, pointing with his right hand. With his left hand, he pointed to the left. "And that's south."

"The water is extremely still," Mercedes noted. "It almost looks like a long, skinny lake."

John was looking south at the long line of sight the view gave him.

"What do you think of that view? How far down do you think we can see the river before it goes around the bend?"

"Maybe a quarter of a mile–a third of a mile, at the most."

"It would definitely give us a chance to pick them off way before they get here, right?" John wanted to know.

"It's something that would give us an advantage."

"We just have to find a way to do that," John replied. "And I think I have an idea."

"If it's to go back to the hotel and sit in the air conditioning, I'm all for it," Mercedes smiled.

"I'm going to run this by you," Watkins said, dismissing her comment. "What if we take the cameras that we employed to catch Clinton Thoreaux and set them up here. We could put two cameras–one in that tree and one in that tree"—John pointed—"and aim them at the pier. That way we have eyes on the pier. We can put another one in that tree over there, and we'll aim it at this service road. Friday night, we can park further up on 119, out of sight of the Natchez Police. When they move the weapons in and onto the pier, we can flank them and take them down."

"When you say *we*, do you mean the four of us and Jake Ritter?"

"I do as of right now."

"Then what? If we take the police, what are we going to do with the weapons?" Mercedes wanted to know. "Are we going to have Jake Ritter take possession of them?"

John gave a mischievous smirk. "Eventually."

"Eventually?"

"Here's what I'm thinking. The police are going to arrive with the weapons long before Mr. Lazarus and his team show up. We take the police down, then I think I have a plan that will lure Mr. Lazarus and his men right into our little mousetrap," John smiled.

"How are you going to do that?" Mercedes asked.

"Things will have to go just right for us, but I have faith."

"And if they don't?" Merc wondered.

"If they don't," John replied, "we can unpack some of those weapons. We watch and wait for Lazarus' boats to come around that bend, and when they do—"

"We'll blast them all the way back to the very first *Fast & Furious* movie," Mercedes finished John's sentence for him.

"That's my plan," John said. "The question we have to ask ourselves is how many guys are the police going to be bringing to the party?"

36

THIS BATHROOM IS A MESS

While John and Mercedes were busy at Pier 51 devising the skeleton of what would soon become an elaborate plan, Samuel Hawkins and his meemaw were visiting with Melissa Thoreaux and Grandma Dot.

"So, I just can't believe that this may be the last time I'll ever see you," Sandrine said, tears welling up in her eyes. "We've seen each other or talked to each other almost every day for the last thirty-some years. I don't know what I'm going to do with myself."

"It'll be okay," consoled Dot. "I'll think of you every day."

"Meemaw," Samuel started, "there's a chance—"

Sam's cell phone went off, interrupting the consolation that he was going to give his grandmother. He did not recognize the number, but he picked it up before his cellphone could reject it as a SPAM call. "Hello?"

"Sam?" a woman's voice asked.

"Yeah. Who's this?"

"Officer Leblanc."

"Oh!" Hawk called out. He looked around to see everyone looking at him. "I gotta take this."

Hawkins walked into the hotel suite's bathroom, which was a complete mess. "Okay, officer, I'm back. Got some privacy now."

"You can call me Solange," she said. "I need to talk to you."

"Well, I'm all yours, Solange. Whatcha got for me?"

"I have some info about what our officers are going to be doing tomorrow night."

Sam Hawkins already knew what the officers would be doing tomorrow night. But he figured if this woman was going to put her life on the line to help them, he was going to let her talk. Besides, she might add information to what he and the rest of the crew had garnered thus far.

"The chief, the sergeant, and the rest of the officers deal in arms trafficking."

"I'm sorry. What?" Sam asked, pretending surprise.

"Yeah, arms trafficking. And they're doing another shipment tomorrow night," Solange explained.

"When you say *the rest of the officers*, are you counting yourself in that, too?"

"Well, yes and no."

"And that means what?"

"It means," started Solange, "that I've been helping them in the past because I really didn't have a choice. Once I found out about what they were doing, I either had to help them, or they would hurt my family."

"Shi', girl, now dat's just straight-up sinister, my friend."

"Well, now that there's someone here to put an end to all this—"

"You've helped them in the past, right?"

"Yes, I just told you that."

"Right. Great. So, how many people are we dealing with, from the police side of things?" Sam asked.

"Sometimes fifteen, sometimes twenty."

"And what about Mr. Lazarus? What kind of manpower is he going to have?"

"He usually has one bigger boat to load the weapons on, plus two or three smaller boats for security. Two or three guys per boat–the smaller ones–and I have no idea how many people he will have on the bigger boat."

"In other words, we could be looking at more than a thirty-five to four lineup discrepancy, is what you're saying?"

"More like thirty-five to five," Solange corrected.

"Oh? You sure you wanna do that?" Sam was concerned that Officer Leblanc may have made the decision to join Dragon's Men on this uncommonly dangerous mission more with her heart than with her head. "I'll tell you the same thing my team tells each other before each mission: 'There's no guarantee that we all come out clean on the other side of this.' And what we mean by *coming out clean*…is surviving."

"I get that, and I appreciate you asking me. But at this point, I have never been more sure of anything in my life. When I think of all the damage I have done to this world with all those guns I helped move, this is my shot at redemption. If I end up getting killed in the process, then that's my penance."

"Hey, Solange, let me ask you something. You said you weren't given a choice because they were threatening your family, right?"

"Yeah."

"Then you've got nothing to feel guilty for," Hawk reminded her.

"Would you feel that way if it were you? That you allowed for the deaths of countless hundreds–maybe thousands–of people, versus the twenty-three people you saved in your family?"

"I see your point," Hawk admitted. "Here's my next question then: Are you the only one of the officers that's being threatened? Maybe there are others."

"No. At first, I was sure that some of the others were being threatened, too. I thought I couldn't be the only one. But I did a thorough investigation. I am the only one."

"Did you take any of the money that was being made?" Hawk asked Officer Leblanc.

"They made me," she answered. "Chief Briggs set up an account in the Cayman Islands in my name. It was made that way so that if I tried to blow the whistle, there was a rock-solid paper trail leading back to me, showing that I made just as much money on this venture as everyone else. But I swear, I have never touched a penny of that money. I swear."

"I believe you, Solange. I do."

"Mr. Hawkins, one other very important thing that you need to know. When they threatened my family, I swore that given half a chance, I would do whatever it took to bring these delinquent monsters down."

"And you see us as your half a chance?"

"I do, indeed," Sam could hear the smile in Officer Leblanc's voice. "You see, Mr. Hawkins, I've done my investigating into y'all, as well. I know all about what happened in Rio de Janeiro. You took down a drug lord and his army of about two hundred thugs. And you did it with just about ten or eleven people."

"Well, there are a few things about that assignment you don't know, the least of which was that we had someone down there for the better part of two years doing amazing recon work on that drug lord and his army of two hundred goons."

"Mr. Hawkins, it's like this. Come tomorrow night when the Natchez Police Department starts moving those guns on to Pier 51, I'm going to be there. I can be there working with you, or I can be there working on my own. It's up to you."

"Now, how do I know that ya not just telling me all this to set me and my friends up? We could be taking you into our confidence, and you could be hanging us out to dry."

"Mr. Hawkins, I swear on my momma's grave that I am being completely straight with you."

For a few moments, Sam pondered whether he should trust this woman. Betrayal was the last thing that he and the team needed right now. However, he remembered from when he was growing up here that when someone swore on their momma's grave, it was the verbal equivalent to swearing on a stack of Bibles. And even though the Bible did not have the same impact in other parts of America, in Cajun country, the Bible and religion still mattered now just as much as they ever did.

After a long pause, Hawkins finally said, "Okay, here's how we're going to do things. Do you know where Fontenot's is on University Avenue in Natchitoches?"

"I do."

"Can you be there in fifteen minutes?" Hawk asked.

"I can, yes."

"Good. Then meet me there in fifteen minutes," Sam instructed. "We're going to switch over to FaceTime, and we're going to continue to talk until we meet in person in Fontenot's parking lot. You good wid dat?"

"Yes."

"Hit me right back on a video call."

Ending the call, he walked out of the bathroom to find Melissa, his meemaw, and Grandma Dot all in tears. He was just a moment away from asking what was wrong when it dawned on him just why they were crying: They were saying goodbye to each other for the last time.

"Hey, y'all, don't mean to interrupt, but I've got to go out and handle some business," Sam informed them. Then, just as he was getting ready to head out the door, he turned and said, "An' y'all need to do somethin' about that bathroom. It's a disgrace."

37

PUTTING THE TEAM TOGETHER

As planned, Sam Hawkins met Officer Solange Leblanc in the parking lot of Fontenot's Cajun Café. Sam had kept Solange on a video call the whole ride there, just to make sure she did not make any calls or send any texts to the Natchez Police Department–or to anyone else, for that matter.

He believed that the officer was telling the truth, to be sure, but he had been fooled by a beautiful woman before. And if he was wrong this time, he'd be getting the whole team into a jackpot, not just himself.

From her police cruiser, Solange rolled down her window as Sam pulled the company SUV up beside her.

"I'm going to guess that you made sure not to be followed?" Sam asked.

"Yeah, we're clean," Leblanc stated. "Right now, they think that I am out looking for the sergeant's wife. We check in about every hour, so I'm good."

Sam got out of his vehicle and moved toward Solange's open window. From his pocket he pulled out what appeared to be a lapel pin in the shape of a U.S. flag. "Pardon me," Sam said politely, leaning in to place the pin on the corner of her uniform collar.

"That there is a camera. Whenever you're with your compatriots, see if you can get them talking about the gun exchange that they'll be doing tomorrow night. Don't force it," Hawkins warned, "but if the door should present itself, by all means, open it up and go on in."

"Will this thing pick up sound?"

"It will," Sam confirmed. "Now, listen, we're just down the road at the Best Western. I want you to follow me there. We won't be long. What time do you have to be back to HQ?"

"End of shift is four o'clock."

"Okay," Hawk looked at the clock in the SUV and thought for a moment. "Follow me."

He drove to the Best Western where the crew was staying. By the time he arrived at the hotel, John and Mercedes had already returned from the Cane River and Pier 51.

Hawk parked the SUV. Solange pulled in right next to him, and they walked side-by-side to the hotel room where John, Daniel, and Mercedes were.

"Haawwk!" Sloane greeted him from the bed on the far side of the room. "Did you bring company?"

Mercedes was lying on the other bed, and John was back on the couch.

"Gang, this here's Officer Solange Leblanc. She's the one good cop on the whole Natchez police force."

John stood up and shook the officer's hand. "Nice to see you again, Officer Leblanc," Watkins said, alluding to when he and Sam had visited the police department yesterday.

"Call me Solange," she said.

"Okay, Solange," Sloane sniped from the far side of the room, "why should we believe you're the one good cop on the whole Natchez police force?"

"Your man Hawkins seems to think I'm okay."

"Well, Sam also thinks rap music is cool. He thinks shining his head up like a disco ball is cool. He thinks wearing tenny pumps with the laces untied is cool—"

"That'll do, Daniel," Watkins shut him down.

"Well, if you're good enough for Sam, you're good enough for us," Dr. Lara said as she got up from the bed to shake Leblanc's hand.

"We kinda need to speed this up, y'all," Sam said. "She needs to be back at HQ at sixteen-hundred hours."

John pulled a com device from a small black leather bag and handed it to Leblanc. "Put this in your ear. We call them coms; they're very sensitive. They'll pick up everything that is being said, and everything that you say. More importantly, you'll be able to hear everything that we're saying to you."

"Will you want me to be with the police tomorrow night, or will you want me to be with you?" Solange asked.

"We're going to want you to be with them. Everything is going to be *status quo* tomorrow night. We don't want anything to tip them off that something might be up. We need Lazarus's boats to be making their way up the Cane River." John put his hand on Leblanc's shoulder to emphasize his next point. "The key phrase is *Go Time*, okay? When we say *Go Time*, you have about three seconds to get clear of the area. After that, we're going to let fly with everything we've got. Feel free to fire away from your position, as well."

"Got it. Key phrase is *Go Time*. Three seconds to clear the area," Solange confirmed.

"Don't forget the earpiece." John reminded her.

"Com." She held it up. "I really need to be going." She pointed at Sam Hawkins. "I've got your number. I'll give you a call later this evening."

"Sounds good."

And with that, Officer Leblanc exited the hotel room.

No sooner had the door closed behind her, than Sloane asked, "Can we trust her?"

"I wholeheartedly believe we can," Sam responded. "But even if we can't, we just won't put her into a position where she can do us any harm. Solange said that there's usually between fifteen and twenty cops that show up for these weapon deals. She also said that Lazarus usually brings a big boat for the weapons and two or three smaller boats with armed gunmen."

Just as Hawk finished his sentence, John's phone rang.

It was Latin Jackson.

"John, it's Latin. I'm returning your call. It wasn't time for you to check in so I didn't have my phone with me. What's going on?"

"Did you not listen to my message?"

"No, I just saw my caller ID and called you back."

"Then why on your answer phone greeting do you say, 'Leave a detailed message'? I left a detailed message, and now because you didn't listen to it, I'm going to have to say it all over again."

"John...because you're my best friend, I'm going to hang up and listen to your detailed message. Just so you know, I wouldn't do this for anyone else, but for you. I'll call you right back."

Latin ended the call and proceeded to listen to John's message. After which, he called John back.

Watkins answered the call with, "So, what do you think?"

"I think it sounds like you guys are really in a jackpot this time. I like your plan, but you're definitely going to need some more help than what you've got right now."

"Think you can come down?"

"I never miss an opportunity to bring down some dirty filthy cops, Johnny. Heck yeah, I'll be there. Do you want me to bring Lou?"

"I don't know. I have a feeling this situation is going to get pretty precarious. Plus, it's about an eight-hour drive."

"Shoot, man," Latin laughed, "Lou would ride in a car twenty-four-seven if I let him. He loves sitting in the back seat and looking out the window and just watching the world go by."

"Then bring the boy on down," John happily agreed. "When do you think you will be able to leave?"

"I'll pack a bag for me. I'll pack some snacks for Lou. We'll be on our way."

Besides being a computer hacker, accountant to the stars, and helper to his best friend John Watkins and Dragon's Men, Latin Jackson had a side job with which he kept himself busy.

Latin trained dogs. But not just any dogs. He fostered bomb squad dogs that were retiring from military or police life. He helped the animals transition from a high-stress life of finding explosive devices to life with an average American family. Latin's job was to turn off the part of the dog that made it a "soldier-officer" and turn on the part that would make it a people-friendly, family-loving pet.

Having done this for years now, Latin had become quite good at it. He had untrained and re-trained many dogs that were now settled into happy lives of retirement as wonderful pets for very deserving families.

However, about two years ago Latin decided to try retraining a dog to live with him in a relaxed environment–while still keeping its bomb-sniffing abilities. His first few attempts were abject failures. Still, Latin kept tinkering with his training methods and looking for just the right dog that would be able to pull off both skills.

Then, one day he was sent a Chocolate Labrador named Louie. Louie was retiring from a career as a bomb-sniffing dog for the City of Detroit Police Department. He had earned a plethora of medals and certificates of valor. The city had even raised a statue in his honor outside of old Tiger Stadium because he had sniffed out a bomb that a whacked-out fan had left in the player's locker room a few years prior.

Louie was the one. Latin's methods finally worked, and Louie became his pride and joy. And even though the brown dog sometimes preferred being a couch potato instead of a bomb detector, for the most part, Louie was everything Latin Jackson had hoped for. He got along well with strangers, especially those of the female persuasion. He made quick friends with other dogs, and he understood when it was time to go back to work–thanks in large part to a special vest that Latin had made for him that said "I'm The Bomb! (sniffing dog)." To date, under Latin's watchful eye, Louie had sniffed out two bombs while enjoying the good life of retirement.

※　※　※

It was time to call Lieutenant Jack Thompson of the White Pines Police Department. Besides Daniel, Dr. Mercedes Lara, and Sam Hawkins, Lieutenant Jack Thompson was probably the closest that John had to a real friend. He knew calling him this late was kind of a Hail Mary, but he also knew if anyone could come through for them, it would be Jack. Lieutenant Thompson had worked with John Watkins and company before, when push came to shove in certain situations. And push was coming to shove.

Back in White Pines, it was a regular Thursday night at the Thompson household. Besides being married to his job, Lieutenant Jack Thompson was also married to his wife of fourteen years, Helen Dalton-Thompson. Helen was a veterinary acupuncture specialist at the White Pines Veterinary Clinic where she had worked since her college days.

Oh, the things that wealthy people would do for their pets.

Tonight, like most nights, Jack and Helen were snuggled up on the couch together watching *Wheel of Fortune*. Like a lot of couples, they were always trying to beat each other–and the contestants–at figuring out the answer to the puzzle.

They were currently on the second puzzle. The riddle had six words and twenty-seven letters, and so far, the only letters that were showing were an *L* and an *F*. Before any of the contestants could guess another letter, the Thompsons' landline rang. Since Helen was lying on top of Jack, she rolled off him and onto the floor. She was up and over to the phone before the fourth ring.

"Hello?"

"Hiya, Helen. It's John Watkins. Is Jack available?"

"He sure is. Hang on one second."

She put the phone down on the kitchen counter. "Baby, it's John Watkins."

Jack was quick to get off the couch and over to the phone.

"Hey, John, how's things down in the bayou?"

"It's not Reykjavik. You got a minute or two to converse in private?"

"Sure. Hang on for a second." Thompson turned to his wife. "Hey, baby, do you mind hanging this up when I pick up in the bedroom?"

Within just a few seconds, Jack said into the receiver, "I got it, baby. Thank you so much, lover."

"You're welcome, sweetie," she said, then hung up the kitchen phone.

"Alright, John, what's going on?" Thompson asked.

"We have ourselves a situation, Lieutenant," John replied. "We have a bunch of dirty cops down here. I tried reporting them to the higher-ups down here, but because they have the highest conviction rate of any department in the entire state, no one wants to hear what I have to say."

"Okay," Jack said slowly. "And where do you think I can be of some help?"

"Well, besides being dirty cops, these chowder brains are also in the gun trafficking business. Tomorrow night they're moving a huge load of weapons with one of the biggest gun runners in the business. We have a plan in place to catch the cops red-handed. We also think that we'll be able to catch the gun trafficker. We have an agent from the ATF coming down. He's a pretty high-ranking official, so we think a call from him to the New Orleans Coast Guard will be effective enough to get them to move off their hind ends and nab this guy before he gets back into the Gulf of Mexico."

"Sounds solid, but what can I do?"

"We need some bodies to help us get the police. They've got fifteen to twenty people, and we have seven. That's counting one of their cops who's on the right side of the law, the ATF guy, and Latin Jackson."

"Ah, good old Latin. I should have known his no-good butt would be participating in this caper."

"Actually, if you want to come down, you could probably catch a ride with him. He's bringing Louie."

"Cheeses Chrysler, John. Why do you always have to make things so hard?"

"Because if things were easy, they'd never work."

Thompson sighed. "Have Latin call me in fifteen minutes."

"Is that how long it's going to take you to talk Helen into letting you go?'

38

THE PLAN FORMULATES

After John got off the phone with Lieutenant Thompson, he signaled for everyone to gather around, which they did. Mercedes and Sloane joined John on the couch, with Hawk in a nearby chair.

"Well, if things go according to plan—" John said.

"Which they never do," interjected Dr. Lara.

"I've got a plan," John continued. "Later on this evening, after it gets dark, we're going to take our little surveillance cameras and set them up in the trees that cover the in-and-out to the Cane River. This way we can keep an eye on the comings and goings of the place. As the time gets closer for the drop, we're going to go find a nice place to hunker down. Once they start moving the weapons on to the pier, that's when we'll make our move."

"Do you have a layout of where we'll be going?"

"Yes. Yes, I do." John got up to pull a piece of paper from the drawer of the nightstand. Sitting down on the floor next to the coffee table, he laid the paper on it and started sketching the layout of the Pier 51 area.

"If Merc and I had gone at night, we would have never found the place," John explained. "When you pull off Route 119 to go to Pier 51, the road is really nothing more than grass, marsh, mud, and dirt."

"You going to be wearing your usual three-piece suit tomorrow night, John?" Sloane asked.

"No, actually, I'm not going to be wearing a three-piece suit tomorrow night," John said, much to everyone's surprise. "I–and Dr. Lara–we will be wearing wetsuits."

"What?" Mercedes asked.

"You're going to be in the river?" Sloane asked.

"Yes, the two of us," John answered.

"Aren't there alligators in that river?" Mercedes asked, a tinge of fear in her voice.

"I wouldn't worry too much about that, Doc," Hawk said coyly.

"Well, of course you wouldn't worry. It's not your ass that's going to be in that river being used as gator bait."

"Hawk's right," John confirmed. "According to a study that was conducted just last month, in the entire thirty-mile stretch of the Cane River, they only found sixteen alligators. Fourteen of those were juveniles, and the two adult alligators were at the end of the river that was closer to Lake Pontchartrain because there are many more food sources near there."

"Well, how big are the juvenile alligators?" Merc wanted to know.

"One to three feet long, and they won't attack anything bigger than they are."

"I guess." Dr. Lara looked skeptical.

"Doc, seriously, sixteen gators in a thirty-mile river? That's just about one every two miles. The amount of the river that you and John will be covering will be about a tenth of a mile. It's like a two percent chance that you'll even encounter one, much less be attacked by one," Hawk said.

Mercedes looked at John, who she knew was a genius with math. "Is he right?"

"He's close," John smiled, "but it's actually less than that. It's more like a half-percent chance that we'll encounter any alligators tomorrow night."

"Alright. Those are numbers I can live with."

John moved back to his drawing of Pier 51. "Sam's going to be back here in these trees. When we return to the combat zone tonight, we'll find a good hide for him so he can have a clear line of sight for Friday. Once we decide it's *Go Time*, Sam will get things started. He'll be the one to kick the whole thing off."

John looked at Hawk and continued. "You know the routine. Once you're confident that you've got three targets you can take down, you'll start the show. From there, Daniel, you and Jack, you'll attack from this tree line here–which is from the west. I'll have Latin and Jake Ritter come in from here," John said, pointing to a specific spot on his scrawled-out map. "Solange Leblanc, I'm going to have her move away from our targets and join up with Daniel and Jack. These cops are going to be so focused on the six of you, they won't be expecting two more of us coming out of the water. We'll be shooting fish in a barrel."

"Quick question: are we shooting to kill or are we just shooting to maim?"

"Shoot to maim, but I have a feeling these knuckleheads think they're indestructible, so they may keep firing even after they are down. I guess what I am saying is that self-preservation comes before courteousness."

"That all sounds like a good plan," Hawk said.

"It's getting dark out. How long do you want to wait until we go to the Cane River?'"

"Let's take a two-hour break. We'll head down there around twenty-one hundred hours."

39

SOLANGE CHECKS IN

Mercedes and Hawk had moved two doors down to Room 326, where Mercedes was now sleeping.

John and Daniel were in their room watching the end of the Orioles-White Sox game at Chicago.

Sam was in Room 312 visiting Meemaw, Melissa Thoreaux, and Grandma Dot. His ear com was activated just in case Solange needed to get in touch with them before her shift began tomorrow morning.

It was a good thing he did. At 10:45 p.m. her voice came through his com.

"Hello? Is anybody there?"

"Yes, I'm right here. It's Sam Hawkins. What's going on?"

"They're going to have us all working double shifts until we find Sergeant Thoreaux's wife," Solange explained. "I had laid down at nine to go to bed for the night, but they just now called to tell me that I need to be in at midnight to start a double."

"That sucks," Hawk sympathized with her.

"Here's the other thing. Sergeant Thoreaux wanted to try to keep the search for his wife *in-house*, but since they've had no success with that, they're putting her picture on TV and spreading out the search area. They're going to have us working with the Natchitoches police checking all the hotels, Airbnbs, bus stations, train stations, and Natchitoches's little airport. Y'all might need to do something because they are looking for Melissa *and* Grandma Dot."

"Okay, we definitely will. Thank you for the heads up."

"I have a question for you. Does this lapel pin record video all the time?"

"No. We were going to wait to hear from you when you pulled into the parking lot at the police station in the morning. We were going to activate it then."

"Okay, good, because I am getting ready to take a shower, and, well…you know."

"No, no, no," Hawk protested. "We ain't like that. None of us are. We'll only have the lapel pin recording when you are at work and that's it. When you are at home, the camera is off, I swear to ya."

"Okay, thank you," Solange said.

"Now, once you get out of the shower, get dressed, etc., when you put the earpiece back in, we'll probably all be on the line. Just lettin' ya know."

"Alright, sounds good. I'll talk to you in just a little while. Taking my earpiece out now."

Sam looked at his meemaw, Melissa, and Dot. "Okay. You three hang tight. Gotta go talk to the team."

"Is everything okay, Sambo?" a worried Meemaw asked.

"It will be," Sam said as he stood to his feet and headed toward the door. "Y'all don't need to worry 'bout a thing."

40

JAKE RITTER TO SAVE THE DAY

Sam scrambled down the hall to Room 322 and knocked loudly on the door. John Watkins opened up within two seconds.

"What's going on, Sam?" John asked, opening the door for Sam to enter.

"We may have a problem," Hawk said, moving to sit on the foot of John's bed. "Solange Leblanc just called to tell me that the Natchez Police Department is widening the search area for Melissa, and Grandma Dot is now officially part of the search. So, it was a good thing we brought her here, too."

"Well, it was just the logical move," John said. "We heard Clinton asking about her, and he knew she was out with Melissa for lunch yesterday."

"Solange also told me that their pictures are now on television. *And* Natchitoches Police are going to be searching the hotels. We may need to do something."

"Okay, hang on." John pulled out his cell phone and dialed a number. He put the phone up to his ear. "Jake, how far out are you?"

"I should be with you in just a little over thirty minutes."

"Great. When you get here, go to the Best Western on University. You're going to check into Room 312. It's under the name of Carol Jenkins. You're her boyfriend."

"Okay, John. Got it."

"In reality, it's where we have the woman who was in need of our relocation services and her grandmother. She's also part of the search now."

"Oh, gotcha. You need me to stay with them?"

"I do. Also, there's an outside shot that the Natchitoches Police Department may knock on your door looking for them."

"And how would you like me to handle that?"

"Answer the door, wearing nothing but a towel. Tell 'em your Carol's boyfriend, and she's driven down to New Orleans for the night. They'll show you the pictures of the woman and her grandmother, you give it the good old college once-over, they'll probably move on."

"And if they don't?"

"You're in luck—"

"Yeah, sounds like it," Ritter muttered under his breath.

"Both of the ladies are very small. The bed in the room has that wooden platform so that you can only put your shoes underneath the bed and not much else. Do you know what I'm talking about?"

"Yes, I believe I do."

"Just lift the bed up a little. It's all hollow inside the wood perimeter there. Those gals will fit underneath, no problem."

"Are you kidding me?"

"No, not kidding. They'll really fit under there," John replied in all seriousness. "I haven't actually done it with those two women, but I have performed that maneuver with other people that were similar in size and had no problem pulling it off."

"I just knew things were going to be a pain in the can when I agreed to come help you guys," Ritter sighed.

"I know what you're saying, Jake. I used to feel the same way, but then...I replaced the words *pain in the can* with the words *a really memorable time*, and my life has been so much better ever since."

"I take it you and your group won't be there when I arrive?"

"We won't," John responded. "We need to get moving on another part of our plan, but we shouldn't be gone long. I won't leave you hanging like that, Jake."

"Alright. Let me make sure I got this right: Best Western on University, Room 312. Carol Jenkins, answer the door in a towel, hide the women under the bed, and…have a really memorable time."

"You, sir, are on the top of your game. I'll see you soon, buddy."

41

UNEXPECTED VISITORS

John had a picture of Jake Ritter on his phone. He forwarded it to Samuel, who, in turn, showed it to Melissa Thoreaux and Dorothy Michaud, a.k.a. Grandma Dot.

"Meemaw, I'm going to put you in a cab and send you home," Hawk said. He then turned to Melissa and Grandma Dot. "I'm forwarding this guy's picture to both your phones. He'll be here in just a few minutes. Until then, keep the lights off and don't answer the door for anyone else except *this* guy," Hawk pointed to the picture on his phone. "His name is Jake Ritter."

* * *

While Samuel Hawkins was squaring away things with Melissa and Dot and putting his meemaw into a cab to take her home, John, Daniel, and Mercedes were gathering up the cameras. The three of them were waiting in the SUV when Sam hopped into the backseat.

"Oh…John's driving."

He said this because Daniel Sloane was the designated driver. Unless the team was driving two vehicles, Daniel drove *everywhere*.

"I'm driving because where we're going isn't on any GPS. Also, the landmarks are few, so I'm sorta driving by faith and not by sight."

"Well, let us be on our way then, James," Hawk said in his best British accent.

"Buckle up for safety, kids," John said, clicking his seatbelt securely in place. He pushed the ignition button and checked the rearview mirror.

That was when he saw them: two Natchitoches City Police cars.

"Huck…Finn."

"What's wrong?" Daniel asked.

"The cops are here already."

Everyone murmured a different expletive and instinctively slid down in their seats.

"No, it's okay," John said calmly. "Just relax, everybody. It's just city cops. No one from Natchez. These officers are not looking for us. So, Mercedes, what I want you to do is, ever so normally, get out, go to the rear entrance of the hotel, go get our ladies, and safely walk them to your room."

"Okay," she acknowledged.

"You have your proper IDs?"

"Yes, I'm checked in as Mykayla McCormick. I have a valid Wisconsin driver's license and a security badge from the chemical company that I work for with my picture on it."

"Get going then. They'll probably start on the first floor and go room to room, so you should have plenty of time to get them and usher them down to your room."

"We're straight. You guys get going. I've got my com on, so if anything happens, you'll hear it when I do."

With that, she matter-of-factly shut the door and walked ever so naturally to the back of the hotel where she disappeared around the corner of the building. John continued talking to her as she walked.

"Mercedes, I want you to stay here with Melissa and Dot. I've been mulling it over, and I just think one of us should be here if there's a problem. Daniel reminded us last night that our main objective for coming down here was to extract and protect Melissa Thoreaux. Her grandmother is now part of that objective, too."

"Why does she get to stay?" Daniel griped. "I'm the strong one. I heard you tell Jake Ritter that he might have to lift the bed and hide Melissa and her grandmother underneath it. Doc ain't gonna be able to lift a queen-sized bed. A single, sure, but not a queen."

"Aww, he's just scared he's gonna see 'nother gator out there," Sam said, mimicking the Cajun accent.

"Well, I was actually thinking more about the heat and humidity. But," Sloane paused, "now that you mention it, the possibility of an alligator rearing its ugly snout doesn't necessarily thrill me, either."

"Mercedes gets to stay because she was there earlier," John answered. "She knows the layout, and I walked her through my plan of attack. You two weren't there earlier, you two don't know the layout, you two have only seen my plan of attack scribbled on a piece of paper. *You two* are going with me." John's tone of voice let Daniel and Samuel know that arguing was pointless. "Besides, I need you"—he turned around and pointed to Sam—"to place the cameras." He then looked at Daniel. "I need you to be there to sync up the monitors with the cameras.

"Isn't it obvious? I'm the driver."

Having said that, John put the vehicle in reverse, backed out of the parking space, looked over to see the Natchitoches City Police still getting their game plan together, then casually drove out of the parking lot.

"Hey, Captain *I Got a Plan for Everything*, you might want to call or text your buddy, Jake Ritter, to, you know, inform him that he doesn't have to answer the door in a towel or lift up a queen size bed to hide two minuscule women. Myself, I'd call him, but since you're driving by faith and not by sight, I guess it's okay to text. We're all buckled in back here."

John looked at Sloane in the rearview mirror. "Man, you are *such* a little bitch when you don't get your way."

"Gimme his number, John. I'll call him and let him know," Samuel suggested.

"Good lord, Hawk," Sloane huffed. "You are such a brown-noser."

"Well, gee, I wonder why that is?" Sam asked cynically. "Could it be because my nose—as well as the rest of me—is brown...ya racist jackass?"

John rattled off the digits to Samuel.

Samuel called Ritter and gave him the update on the situation.

"Hey, he wants to know if you want him to just wait in his car until we get back," Sam asked.

"Yeah, tell him to play a few games of *Wordle*, and we'll be back by then," Watkins replied.

Hawkins relayed the message. A few seconds later, he laughed. "He said 10-4 on the *Wordle*, and that you know him all too well. Then he hung up, so I guess we're all good."

Daniel reached over and slapped Hawk on the elbow. He whispered, "I've seen these people on TV that do stuff by faith, and they're completely blindfolded...and they do it. But you can't talk to them or anything because it completely fouls them all up."

Without taking his eyes off the road, John stated, "Daniel... you are the world's worst whisperer."

42

NIGHTTIME RECON AND OBSCURE FACTS

When John Watkins pulled the SUV off into what seemed like a random cutout on the side of the road, both Daniel and Samuel commented.

"Wow, you weren't kidding. This really is in the middle of nowhere."

"I can't even see the river from here, much less a pier."

"That's because we passed Pier 51 about a quarter of a mile ago," John informed them.

"What?"

"Sometimes I think you do stuff like this to punish us when we irritate you," Sloane said.

"Nonsense. If I wanted to punish you, I would have driven a mile past the situation point," John corrected him. "We have dark clothing and night vision goggles in the back of the vehicle. If I had driven this big SUV up to Pier 51 and we had gotten out with flashlights to carry out this mission, it's highly likely that someone would have seen us, called the police, and it would somehow have gotten back to the Natchez Police. And they would call the whole thing off with Mr. Lazarus."

"He makes a valid point," Sloane admitted.

"Yes, I do, so let's get moving."

The three men moved to the back of the SUV, changed into dark clothes, and donned night-vision goggles.

"Ya know, John, you could have had us change into dark clothes back at the hotel."

"You're right. I should have," John confessed. "That's why you guys *really* shouldn't count on me to always make the best decisions."

"These mosquitoes are eating me up out here," Sloane complained.

"That's funny. They don't seem to be bothering me at all," Hawk said.

"Let me guess," John began. "Sam, you have an AB blood type, and Daniel you have an O blood type."

"Yeah, I am O-positive," Daniel said, impressed.

"And I'm AB-neg," Samuel was mystified. "How in the H-E-double hockey sticks did you know that?"

"I had a deployment in South Africa when I was still a grunt. I did a study of which blood types mosquitoes were most attracted to, so I would know whether to apply a lot of bug spray or just a little. Stuff like that stays with you once you learn it."

"And that, my good man, is why we *really* count on you to make the best decisions," Hawk laughed.

Watkins grabbed a can of bug spray from one of the many compartments in the back of the utility vehicle and flipped it over to Sloane. "Cover yourself in that. It smells like dirty socks, but it'll keep the mosquitoes off you."

John then reached into the back of the SUV and grabbed two backpacks.

He handed one to Daniel Sloane and said, "Here's the bag with your laptops."

He handed the second bag to Hawkins. "Here's the bag with the cameras."

"What are you going to carry?" Sam asked.

"Hey, you all are the ones who constantly call me *boss* and *chief*. So, tonight, I'm the boss. I'll lead the way to where we're going. You two carry the bags." John shook his head and laughed. "It's not like you're carrying twenty-pound dumbbells. It's computer equipment. Grow a pair and let's go."

* * *

Roughly a quarter mile and two minutes later, John, Daniel, and Samuel were standing under the tree where John wanted the first camera placed. Sam made quick work of climbing the tree and crawling out on the limb where John wanted the cam.

"Did you see how fast he got up that tree? He looked a lot like—"

"If you say monkey, I'm gonna climb outta this tree and give you the beating of a lifetime, ya racist jerk!" Hawk hissed at Sloane.

"I was gonna say *squirrel*, ya presumptive jackass!"

"Hey!" Watkins said firmly. "Can you two stop your stupid bickering for ten minutes, so that we can get these cameras placed and get the heck out of here and back to the deluxe accommodations of the Best Western Inn?"

Samuel started laughing. Sloane, too.

"We read ya, Boss," Sam agreed. "Let me know when you got a signal, Danny, and we'll move on to the next tree."

John was not quite finished yet. "This is why I don't put the two of you together in hotel rooms. I'm afraid I'll walk in and the place will look like The Who came through, straight tripping on LSD."

"Johnny," Sloane grimaced, "do you want us to sync up these cameras, or do you want us to spend the next ten minutes trying to figure out what arcane reference you're bringin' up now?"

"Let's sync up these cameras. On the ride back to the hotel, I'll remind you to look up The Who and hotel rooms. My *arcane* reference will make more sense to you then."

"John," Hawk said from his limb up in the tree, "we ain't mad at ya. It's just that you know more obscure facts than Daniel and I know regular facts, combined. So, that puts you four up on the both of us."

"Maybe," John said solemnly, "but I don't know how to sync these laptops with these cameras. And I don't know how to shoot a man between the eyes from a thousand yards out in high winds, so...I'd say that makes us pretty much even."

"This monitor is synced with this camera," Sloane confirmed. "Time to move on to the next tree."

43

Cool Under Pressure

It took less than an hour to place the other three cameras in their respective trees and sync the laptop up to them. Besides talking to each other, John, Daniel, and Sam were in constant contact with Dr. Lara and monitoring her situation with Melissa and Grandma Dot.

The fellas were on their way back to the hotel when Merc let them know that the police had made it to the third floor.

"Sounds like they're about two doors down. I expect they'll be banging on my door any time now," she said.

"The ladies keeping their composure okay?" Sloane asked.

"For the most part," Merc came back. "I'm getting ready to tuck them under the headboard. Unless the cops want to go pulling the bed away from the wall, they'll never see them. Oddly enough, the bed is free from the floor, but the bedside table in between the two beds is bolted down. Oh, and the TV is loose, but the remote is screwed down to the top of the bedside table."

"Funny what they think people will and won't take off with," Daniel smirked.

"I sneaked down to the second floor when the police officers were doing some earlier searches just to see how thorough they were being with their practices, just so I would know what to expect."

"How thorough *were* they being?" Watkins asked.

"Not very. They'd be lucky to find ants at a picnic at the rate they were going. Hang on," Merc said to her teammates.

"Alright, ladies," they heard the doctor say. "Time to get into place. I'll have you in and out of there in a jiff."

Mercedes helped the elder Dorothy down onto the floor first. She was surprised by how limber the octogenarian was. Melissa watched as her grandmother crawled underneath the top of the bed and slithered her way back into the corner between the bed and hotel room wall, and she quickly followed suit. Once they were situated, Mercedes moved the bed back into place, rumpled the bedclothes, and scattered some women's undergarments onto the floor. She took Sam's suitcase, zipped it back up, and put it in the closet. Then, to be as off-putting as possible to the two male officers headed her way, she took off her shoes, socks, and pants, leaving herself in just her t-shirt and underwear.

Dr. Lara checked her look in the hotel room mirror.

Yes. Just right.

"Hello, boys," she said to her Dragon's Men partners, using a thick midwestern accent. "How does my Milwaukee timbre sound?"

"Oh, boy, ya got me in the mood for some brats and a cold one," Sloane said echoing her inflection.

When a Delta Force team member was dropped in-country somewhere in Spain, the last thing they needed blowing their cover was for their Spanish to sound like they were from south Barcelona when they were supposed to be from upper Madrid. Not only was their knowledge of particular languages intact, but their use of regional dialects and accents was tighter than a medical glove, as well.

All four of them heard the emphatic knock on the hotel door at the same time.

"Natchitoches Police! Could you open the door, please?"

The blond-haired bombshell opened the door slightly and revealed just enough of herself to get the policemen's attention.

"Oh, hello, officers," she said blithely. "How can I help ya tonight?"

"Good evening, ma'am," the first patrolman said. He produced two pictures, one of Melissa Thoreaux and the other of Dorothy Michaud. When he did, Mercedes opened the hotel room door wider to get a better look at the photos. This prompted the two men to get a better look at the doctor and lose focus on what they were saying.

"Um, yes, we're searching for these two women...the hotel for these two women, door-to-door–what I mean is, we're going to each room—"

"What my partner's trying to say, ma'am, is..." the second cop began to stammer, "is that we're...Uh, would you mind putting some pants on, ma'am?"

Merc heard Samuel and Daniel burst into laughter through her com.

"Oh, goodness gracious. I'm so sorry," Dr. Lara feigned shyness. "Please, come in, fellas. Ya caught me right in the middle of putting on my PJs for the night."

Mercedes motioned for the officers to enter the room.

"I saw those two ladies earlier on the nighttime news," she said as she grabbed a pair of pajama pants from her suitcase, sat down on the bed closest to the hotel room door, and pulled them, slowly, on over her long, tan legs. "That's really somethin', but if ya want my opinion, those two are about as gone as a couple o' girls can get. If I can ask, whaddyoo two fellas think? Ya think those two ladies are still in town?"

"That accent of yours," the second patrolman, whose name tag said *Shelby*, said. "I have a sister-in-law that lives in Appleton, Wisconsin. You sound just like her."

"I used to work in Appleton," Mercedes smiled. "Before I got transferred to Milwaukee."

"Well, as far as these two ladies are concerned...it's like the news report said. The younger woman is the wife of a police sergeant in a neighboring town, and the older lady is her grandmother," Shelby confirmed. "Earlier, you said you thought that these ladies weren't around here anymore. Mind if we ask you why you said that? Why do you think that?"

"Lord knows that you boys in blue–or in your case, you boys in olive green–get a bad rap from all those crooked politicians. Still, it goes without saying that there are dirty policemen. My gut feeling is that this woman was married to one, and, sad as it may be, dirty cops have a much longer reach than law-abiding officers do. My feeling is that this woman was married to one, and she needed to get as far away from his dirty cop reach as she could get."

Well, just between you and me and my partner here, we've worked with Sergeant Briggs before, and he seems...well...the word *corrupt* comes to mind. Still, we've got to do the footwork."

"Well, officers"—Dr. Lara gave a sparkling smile— "as you can see, there's no one here but me. You're welcome to look around if you'd like."

Shelby checked the closet, and then looked in the bathroom really quick.

"Looks good here, Tim," he said to his partner. Then he turned to Mercedes. "We appreciate your time, ma'am."

"You have a good night."

Tim gave her a friendly smile, trying unsuccessfully not to ogle Merc's body as he and Shelby walked out of the hotel room.

"Be safe, officers," she said, shutting the door behind the two patrolmen.

Mercedes listened patiently for them to knock on the door and enter the next room before retrieving Melissa and Dorothy from under the bed.

"Nice work, Merc," Hawk said poetically.

"We're at the Waffle House across the street from the

hotel," Watkins said. "We're just going to hang out here until the officers leave."

"And the three of us are going to hang out here in the room," Lara stated.

"Keep the lights off until the officers vacate the premises," John instructed. "We don't want to tempt the officers to come back for a second look at you on their way out."

44

A Gathering in Natchitoches

John had caught Jake Ritter when he was just about ten minutes from the Best Western and told him to meet them across the street at the Waffle House.

When Jake walked into the restaurant, he spotted Watkins and company sitting at a booth just off to his left.

John spotted his friend and waved to him.

As Ritter got closer to the booth, Watkins stood up and gave his friend a quick hug.

"What's goin' on, Shaky Jake?"

"Do me a favor and try not to get me killed tomorrow night, baby," Ritter began as he slid into the booth. "I'm down here on my own dime. I buy the farm, and my wife and kids don't get my pension or my wonderful life insurance policy."

It was Jake Ritter's thing to call everybody 'baby.'

"Well, then you may not want to come with us tomorrow night."

"Let me guess, we're no longer going to just take pictures of Mr. Lazarus and his merry band of bandits?"

"No," John said flatly.

"Aw, come on, Johnny baby. You could've told me that before I came all the way down here. You're killin' me here."

"Well, *I'm* not killing you, but if you come with us tomorrow night...that might get you killed."

"What are you plannin', Johnny?"

"We're here on a job to get a woman away from her raping, abusing husband. If we don't get these guys tomorrow night, we're going to have to find her and her grandmother—"

"And my grandmother, for that matter," Hawk interrupted.

"And his grandmother, for that matter...a new location to live. So, we have a plan to get both the cops and Lazarus. Although, if you want to be of some help to us without coming along tomorrow night—"

"Yeah, baby? Don't cut out on me now."

"Part of our plan calls for us to contact the Coast Guard in New Orleans. They would probably take it a lot better coming from an ATF agent as opposed to hearing it coming from a group of retired military types."

"Your plan calls for the Coast Guard in New Orleans? Yeah, then maybe going down there wouldn't be such a bad idea. Not a bad idea at all, baby," Agent Ritter said obnoxiously.

"Yeah, I'm liking this plan of yours more and more all the time."

"You just heard the plan," Sloane smiled.

"If it's a 'John Watkins Plan', then I don't need to hear it any longer. It's platinum, baby."

"The man obviously knows Johnny," Sam said.

"Wanna stay here tonight?" Watkins asked.

"Here I am in Louisiana, and I could stay in New Orleans or– what's the name of this town again? Natchitoches?"

"Yes."

"Hmm, let's see, New Orleans or Natchitoches? I'm going to New Orleans, baby, and I'm going now," Agent Ritter said. "I'll give you a call when I get there to hear what the good word is."

A Waffle House waitress came by the table. "Hello, sir, I didn't see you come in. May I get you a menu?"

"No, ma'am, baby. I'm headed to New Orleans," Ritter said. "Now, I know you may hear that a lot, but I surely don't get to say it nearly enough." He stood up. "I hope to see you guys on Sunday." He turned to the waitress. "I probably won't see you on Sunday, so... have a good weekend."

With that, Jake shook John's hand, gave a formal salute to Hawkins and Sloane, said "Godspeed tomorrow night, men," and left the restaurant.

John's cell phone went off. It was Latin.

"What's up, Jax?"

"Yeah, are you guys listed under your own names in the hotel?"

"No. How far out are you?"

"We're actually in the parking lot, but I've worked with you all enough to know that when you're on a job, you rarely use your real names in a public setting outside of town."

"Really? You guys are here already?" John was surprised. "You and Lieutenant Jack?"

"He had never ridden in a Ferrari before, and he asked me what it could do. So, I showed him...the whole way down. I guess once he realized I knew what I was doin', and the novelty of being in one of the world's finest automobiles had worn off, he climbed into the back seat with Lou and took a nap for a while. And let me tell ya, when he did, I really took off. So, where are you guys at?"

"Do you see the Waffle House across the street?"

"Yes, I do."

"Mercedes is inside the hotel under an assumed name. Samuel, Daniel, and I are here, if you'd care to come join us."

"Ya know, as much as I like looking at Mercedes, it's not lost on me that, out of the four of you, you're my only friend. So, we'll come over and break bread with you boys for a bit."

"Come on over, brother. We can break some waffles together."

"I'll be there in two minutes," Latin laughed.

Latin had money and he did not mind flashing it around. He put that on full display when he did a few donuts in the white Ferrari he was driving in the relatively empty parking lot of the Best Western.

"I really wish he wouldn't do that," Sloane griped. "We're trying to keep a low profile here, and things like that don't really do us any favors."

"I'm speaking strictly on a personal basis here and not making excuses for Latin, but if I were driving that car, I might feel compelled to show it off a little, too."

"Yeah, but I'm pretty sure that if you did, you'd choose a better time and place to do it."

Latin and Jack Thompson entered the restaurant.

Latin, much like John Watkins, had a strong sense of personal style. He almost always wore a gray fedora, a power tie of orange or red, with a white button-down shirt, black suspenders, and matching trousers. Latin's stride also had a certain style. It was as if entrance music was playing in his head while he walked–bouncing rhythmically with every step he took.

Jack was right behind him in his usual black tee, blue jeans, cowboy hat on top, snakeskin boots on the bottom. The only thing missing was his brown leather duster, but the weather was just a hair too warm for that.

"What's the good word, fellas?" Latin asked happily.

"The good word is maple syrup on blueberry waffles," Hawk chimed in.

Jack slid into the booth directly behind John, Daniel, and Samuel. He leaned back against the wall, his legs stretched out on the seat.

"Did you leave Lou in the car?"

"I did. Wasn't really sure what the Waffle House policy was on four-legged creatures," Latin answered. "Besides, he is out like a light–all nestled up in his pillows. Did I ever tell you that he likes to be nestled?"

"Can't say that you have."

"Oh, yeah. Every night when he gets in his dog bed, he arranges two pillows on each side of it, and there's a space in between the pillows just big enough for him to lay down. Nestles himself in between the pillows and sleeps the whole night away."

Latin slid into the booth next to John. He made an odd face.

"Something wrong?" Hawk asked from across the table.

"Why does it feel like someone has been sitting here already?"

"There was. ATF Agent Jake Ritter just left for New Orleans," Sloane informed him.

"Hmm, I think I like this guy already. Anyone smart enough to leave the company of the likes of you must have some good sense about him." Thompson chuckled from behind them. "Why did he leave?"

"Our plan for tomorrow evening, it's going to require someone to contact the Coast Guard in New Orleans. And we figured we'd get more movement out of them if they were getting their marching orders from a decorated ATF agent instead of four retired military has-beens."

"I wish all has-beens were as tight as you guys and Doc are," Latin commented.

The same server that had come around earlier made another appearance. "Hello, sir, May I get you a menu and something to drink?"

"Did you guys order food?" Latin asked.

"We did…about twenty-five minutes ago," Sloane complained. "You didn't forget about us, did ya, lady?"

"Oh, no, sir," the waitress said apologetically. "We only have one cook tonight, so things are a little backed up back there. It won't be long now."

"If I wanted excuses I'd go to Juan Epstein and ask him why he was late for class," Daniel smarted off with the antiquated reference.

"I'm afraid I don't know who that is, sir," the waitress said meekly.

"Oh, don't worry about him, ma'am," Latin consoled the worker. "That guy was born in an anger management class. Hey, I'll take a Diet Coke and a patty melt."

The waitress looked at Jack Thompson. "Are you with them, sir?"

"I like to think of it as *them* being with *me*, but no need getting caught up in a syntax discrepancy when all I want is coffee. Black with two sugars."

"Coming right up, and again I apologize for the lateness of your food."

When the waitress walked away, John said, "Jack, why don't you and Sam change spots, and I'll go over the plan with you and Latin."

"Yeah, I saw this sketch in an earlier episode. Then, in a later episode, I spent about two hours prepping the location for tomorrow night."

As the two passed each other on the way to swapping seats, Hawk patted Thompson on the shoulder. "Good to see you, Jack. Glad you're here."

"Thanks, Sam," Jack said as he moved in next to Daniel Sloane.

"Dan."

"Lieutenant."

John flipped over one of the paper placemats, pulled out a pen and began to draw the setting at Pier 51.

"Okay, so, there are trees on either side of the grassy entrance to Pier 51. We've got surveillance cameras posted here, here, here, and here," John said, pointing to the four trees on which Daniel and Samuel had placed cameras. "These two cameras here and here are aimed at the front. And in these front two trees, we have the cams aimed at the river. This way there's no blind spots."

"Are you going to be recording this?" Thompson asked.

"Yes. That's why we're going to be wearing masks and gloves. We plan on turning this over to the F.B.I., anonymously. This way, if there's any killing by us, we'll be covered."

"Plus, the weather tomorrow night gives us a good news-bad news scenario. The good news is that it's going to be raining incredibly hard, so it will wash away any kind of forensic evidence. The bad news is that it's going to be raining extremely hard which will make it hard to see, make it hard to shoot." Daniel informed Jack and Latin.

"We're going to post Samuel in this tree here because it will give him his best line of sight for taking out the crooked cops. We're hoping the element of surprise gives us a hand up in this little shootout." John took a swallow of his drink before continuing. "Alright, now from here, we're thinking that the crooked cops will have their backs to the river. Mercedes and I will be in the water, flanking these dopes. If they don't drop their weapons, or they make any threatening moves, we will put them down like the dogs that they are."

"Okay, so you take out the cops, then what's the plan to get your gun runners?" Latin asked. "Also, any idea how many cops we'll be dealing with?"

"My first answer will be to your second question. One of the local cops has given us some inside information, so we have it on good authority that there will be between fifteen and twenty people associated with or belonging to the Natchez Police Department. Now to answer your first question. After we deal with the police, we're going to use some of that illegal merch and, once we see the gunrunner's boats coming around the bend, we will begin firing on them in hopes that they will realize that their load has been hijacked and turn tail 'n' run."

"That's when you call your guy from the ATF?"

"Is the plan."

"What if the boats don't turn around?" Jack Thompson asked.

"Then they're going to drown," was Sloane's answer.

"We'll fill 'em so full o' lead," Sam said, doing his best Chicago mobster impersonation, "they'll be using their boat for an anchor."

"Here we go, gentlemen." The waitress had returned with two trays of Waffle House food which she divvied up to each individual according to their order.

The men were about halfway through devouring their chosen meals when a female voice came through the ear coms of John, Sam, Daniel, and Mercedes. "Hey, who's on with me?"

"Solange, are you just getting out of the shower?" asked a surprised Hawk. "Dang, girl, that was over two hours ago!"

"Goodness, no," the officer laughed. "I just pulled into the parking lot at work. I got the ear com on, and I just put on the lapel camera. Can you see if it's working?"

"Solange, this is Daniel Sloane. Give me a few seconds to open up the program on my phone." Sloane grabbed his mobile device from off his hip and took a few seconds to pull up the surveillance program. Within moments he was able to see through the fiber optic lens of the lapel pin on Solange's collar. "Oh, yeah. This is coming in nice and clear. Okay, I see that you're in your car. Let's take a walk real quick to make sure that the video reception doesn't go in and out when you're moving around."

"10-4," Leblanc replied. "I'm heading inside now."

Daniel watched as the video played through his phone. The feed was perfect.

"Officer Leblanc," John spoke up, "the Natchitoches police are here at the Best Western."

"What? I thought we were going to be coordinating our efforts to find the sarge's wife. I guess they decided to move ahead without us. I'm sure we'll get filled in at roll call. How long have they been there?" Solange asked just before she entered the station.

"Going on two hours," John riposted. "They've already talked to our team member, Dr. Lara, and were convinced that she knew nothing of the whereabouts of your sergeant's wife nor her grandmother, even though both of them were hidden inside of Dr. Lara's bedroom."

Through the movement of the lapel pin, Daniel could see that Officer Leblanc was looking around her immediate area to make sure she was alone. She then said in a low register, "Alright, y'all, this is where my talking to you ends for now. Hopefully, you'll be able to see and hear everything I do."

"Sounds good, Solange," Daniel said. "You'll be able to hear us talking to you and each other. If we do have any questions, we'll try to make them yes or no questions, so that way you can respond with a cough or by clearing your throat. Other than that, be safe and be cool."

45

'Twas the Night Before an Arms Deal

Food eaten, check paid, and cops gone, the troop wrapped things up at Waffle House and were now back at the hotel. Jack, Latin, and Louie exited the Ferrari, while John, Daniel, and Samuel hopped out of the company SUV. As they crossed the well-lit parking lot, Daniel used Samuel Hawkins' cell phone to sync up video from the flag pin on Solange Leblanc's lapel.

Sloane handed the phone back to Hawk. "Now you can see what she sees."

"Samuel," John said, "you keep your earpiece in. The rest of us are going off the air so that we can recharge ourselves. Solange, you'll be one on one with Samuel the rest of the night. Have a good shift and remain just the way you always are...alive."

They heard her clear her throat in acknowledgement of John's directive.

The Dragon's Men crew entered the Best Western around 2 a.m., just as Jack and Latin were registering for their rooms. Jack was getting his own room, while Latin and Louie were bunking together.

The two young women working the front desk were swooning over the furry cuteness that was the Chocolate Labrador. Being a natural entertainer, Louie loved the spotlight. The only one loving the attention as much as Louie was Latin Jackson. He thrived on answering questions about Louie and himself, especially questions coming from the fairer sex. And tonight was no exception. The stout computer hacker was soaking it all in, so much so that it caused Daniel to lean over to Jack and whisper, "And now we see why dogs are man's best friends."

"Got that right they are," Jack replied.

It being a slow Thursday night in Natchitoches, everyone was able to get a room on the third floor so that they could be in the vicinity of each other, as well as Melissa Thoreaux and her Grandma Dot.

Within twenty minutes they had all dropped their bags and gotten acquainted with their rooms. Then Jack, Latin and Louie, John, Daniel, and Samuel all met in the hallway and headed to Melissa and Dot's larger suite.

Upon entering their quarters, Hawkins was surprised to find Grandma Dot wide awake and chattering away with her granddaughter and Dr. Mercedes Lara. The other four men and Louie quickly filed in behind Sam and found a place to sit down. Mercedes performed the obligatory introductions before suggesting that it might be a good time for everyone to retire for the night and get some sleep.

"Here's how we'll mind Pier 51 and Solange Leblanc's lapel pin on the laptop to make sure no one from the Natchez Police does any kind of pre-dawn preparation down by the river. We can watch from right here," John suggested, generalizing the den area of the hotel suite. "That way if anything unforeseen occurs here or there, someone will be here to protect our clients while they alert the rest of us."

"Is it okay for me to volunteer to take the first shift?" Jack Thompson asked.

"Perfect. Sam, why don't you leave your earpiece here for whomever is on computer duty. That way they'll have sight *and* sound for the lapel."

"Did you hear that, Solange? You'll have multiple friends to hang out with tonight," Hawk said.

"Mm-hmm," she said quietly.

"Jack, hang out here for the next two hours. Mercedes will relieve you at 0430 hours. I'll take the last shift at 0630 hours, for however long that may be," John summarized.

Daniel pulled one of the agency's laptops out of a bag and opened the program that let them observe the entrance of Pier 51 from the vantage point of all four surveillance cameras.

The lieutenant took the computer from Daniel and began looking at the four split screens.

"So, two hours of staring into the black abyss," Jack Thompson was bored already.

"You sure you're up for this?" Melissa asked him.

"Up? Yes. Am I excited about it?" Jack sighed. "Not even close."

"That's the kind of can-do attitude that I've come to expect and appreciate from you, Lieutenant Thompson," Mercedes gave a wide smile.

"Alright, we're going to go for the night," Watkins announced. He turned to Melissa and Dorothy. "If anything spooks you during the night, no matter how trivial you may think it is, call out. Someone will be here on guard throughout the night. I assure you that this is strictly a gratuitous measure. The Natchez police are desperate to find you, and they've already looked here. They've got a lot of territory to cover, so doubling back to look through this hotel again would be an ineffective and inefficient measure on their part. I know you might be getting a little stir crazy being stuck inside here for hours on end, but that's what's necessary to make sure that absolutely no one sees or recognizes you."

"Stir crazy?" Dorothy Michaud laughed. "Sweetheart, I've lived in the same place for the last forty years. It's about half the size of this, and it hasn't seen any kind of improvements in the decade since my beloved Lionel passed on to his eternal reward. If I didn't have a friend at the housing authority, my little homestead woulda been bulldozed long ago. So, being stuck here is like Père Noël being stuck on the beach in the Bahamas."

Laughter, whether real or polite, filled the room.

John, Daniel, Samuel, and Latin stood up and headed for the door, while Mercedes walked over to hug Melissa and Grandma Dot.

"You ladies just stay calm," Daniel said over his shoulder, "and we'll see you in the morning."

Latin Jackson bid Mercedes and Samuel a fond goodnight from the door to his room directly across the hall. He laughed quietly as he watched Louie sprawl out on the bed closest to the air conditioner, let out a long yawn, and lay his head down to begin his slumber.

"I'm right behind you, buddy," Jackson said, tossing his signature fedora onto a nearby table before loosening and removing his tie. Within a few seconds he had kicked off his shoes, flopped onto his bed, and drifted off to sleep.

Meanwhile, across the hallway, Dr. Mercedes Lara and Samuel Hawkins were all tucked into their separate beds–and talking.

"You worried about your meemaw through all of this?" Merc asked.

"Not really. The way I figure, these dudes know if they mess with my meemaw and word gets to us, we'll be hightailing it up here pronto. The last thing Chief Briggs wants is for us to be poking around while he and his people are trying to pull off his gun exchange with Mr. Lazarus."

"Good point," Dr. Lara nodded, flipping aimlessly through the channels in search of anything that might be worth watching.

* * *

The night went according to plan. Mercedes arrived right on time to relieve Jack Thompson. She sat down next to the lieutenant and put her hand on his right leg.

"I am so glad you're here, Jack," she said to him.

"Are...are ya?" he stammered. "You know I'm a happily married man, Dr. Lara. Right?"

"It's not like that!" she whispered loudly, grabbing a throw pillow and hitting him across the stomach with it.

"Well, gee whiz, what'd you expect me to think?" he asked defensively. "It's late at night, and you're in here touching my leg—"

"Good gosh. I touch John and Samuel and Daniel like that all the time, and you don't see me sacking up with them, do ya?"

"I don't know. I don't live with you guys," he leaned forward. "I live with my wife...who I love very much."

"I just meant that I'm glad you're here to have our backs tomorrow night. There's no one we trust more."

"Is everything okay over there?" Solange Leblanc asked into Lieutenant Thompson's earpiece.

"Everything's fine, officer. I'm going to turn you over to the very capable Dr. Mercedes Lara for the next little while. I hope to see you later on tonight. Have a good rest of your shift."

Jack took the earpiece out, wiped it off with his shirt tail, and handed it to Dr. Lara. "Good night, Mercedes."

Merc took the com from Jack and put it in her ear.

"Good morning, Officer Leblanc," the doctor said pleasantly. She waved good night to Jack before asking Leblanc, "I trust it's okay for you to talk for a little bit?"

"I am outside of the station, having a cigarette."

"I didn't get an update from Jack. Did you talk to him much? Has anything changed over the last couple of hours?" Mercedes asked.

"I really didn't get freed up to talk until just now," Solange answered. "My partner and I have been out most of the night. We've either been answering calls or looking for Melissa."

"Did you find her?" Mercedes joked.

"Oddly enough, no," the officer laughed.

"Anything I need to know about?" Merc asked.

"My partner and I went to Dorothy Michaud's house during the night to give it another good goin' over just to see if we could find anything that we may have missed. We didn't find anything new."

"As far as the combined efforts with other law enforcement in the area, did any new clues to Melissa Thoreaux's whereabouts come to light?"

"Not unless they're keeping secrets from us. I've heard everything that's come over the wire last night, and there has been nothing new that has shown up."

"And what's the overall attitude of the officers there at your house?"

"Basically, Sarge is losing his mind because he can't get clue number one as to where his wife is, and since no one has called making any ransom demands, he's thinking the worst."

"Which is what exactly?"

"That she's either dead, or she set the whole thing up and is long gone, never to be seen or heard from again," Solange explained. "Everybody else is losing *their* minds because Sarge is so off focus. Chief is thinking about pulling him off the detail tomorrow night because, at this point, he's nothing more than a huge distraction."

"That might be the best thing," Mercedes agreed.

"The thing about that is Sarge is the point man for these gun deals with Mr. Lazarus," Leblanc said. "Sarge has told me that on more than one occasion Lazarus has offered him a position with his outfit. The offer was pretty lucrative, but Sarge turned it down. He may be a wife beating, abusive piece of garbage, but he does seem to have some semblance of a moral compass."

"Yeah," Mercedes smirked. "I'll be sure to nominate him for a global humanitarian award tomorrow night when he's being led away in handcuffs."

Officer Leblanc tried to stifle a laugh as she took one last drag on her cigarette. "Okay, Mercedes, I need to head back inside. It was good talking to you."

"Same. I'll be here if you need me."

The rest of Mercedes' time on computer and com duty was uneventful.

At 6:30 a.m., Watkins came into the hotel suite to relieve her.

"Anything to report?" he asked her.

"Not really. No movement down by the pier, and I talked to our new friend for a little bit, but her shift has been relatively humdrum and unremarkable."

Mercedes said goodbye to Officer Leblanc and turned the earpiece over to John.

"Wake me up when we're ready to get things rolling," Merc said as she walked out the door and headed back to her bed.

A little past seven a.m., Officer Leblanc was on her way back to her locker to change out of her uniform when she was stopped by fellow female officer Anais Arceneaux.

"Chief's called an emergency meeting in the break room," Arceneaux informed her.

"Can I get changed, at least?"

"No, Chief said now. So let's go."

"Alright," Solange let out a tired and frustrated sigh.

Then she heard John Watkins say through her ear com, "Well, this promises to be interesting."

46

THE CHIEF'S BIG FAT LIE

Solange and Anais were the last to arrive at the break room. Solange noticed that Sergeant Clinton Thoreaux was conspicuously absent from the meeting.

"Alright," Chief Briggs bellowed, "I know some of you are just coming off shift, so I'll try to make this as quick as possible." He took a moment's pause before beginning again. "First off, let me update you on the search for Sergeant Thoreaux's wife. We have received good intel that she is with Sandrine Benoit's grandson and his friends. Whether she went with them willingly or not is still uncertain at this point. However, we do know that they are in Miami and preparing to head down to the Keys, so we have turned over the search and investigation to the Miami-Dade Sheriff's office. From what I understand, they will be calling in the FBI to assist with all of that."

"Oh, now that's rich," John Watkins said on the other end of Officer Leblanc's com. "There's only one reason he did that, and that's to keep the feds and any other outside law enforcement away from the area so there's no interference with the gun deal. Hey, Solange, I need you to ask him if anyone has brought in Sandrine Benoit for questioning. Will you do that for me?"

"Excuse me, Chief," Solange called out. "Has Sandrine Benoit been brought in for questioning? I mean, how did we get the intel that Sarge's wife was with Sandrine's grandson?"

"Yes, we did question her at her home," Briggs lied. "That is how we got the information about Melissa Thoreaux."

"Has Ms. Benoit been arrested?" Solange asked a follow-up question.

"Not as of right now," the chief answered. "Because she was forthcoming with the information, we have not as of yet taken her into custody."

John Watkins was already out into the hotel hallway and headed to Sam and Mercedes' room. He cracked the door open ever so slightly and asked, "Merc, are you decent? I need Sam."

"It's cool. Come in," she answered.

John stuck his head into the room and called out, "Sam. Wake up."

Hawk opened his eyes, lifted his head a little, and answered groggily, "Yeah? What's up?"

"I need you to call your meemaw and find out if anyone from the police came to see her last night."

While John waited for Sam to make the call, he tuned back in to what Chief Briggs was telling his troops.

"...the sergeant will wait until we hear from the authorities down in Miami before he decides his next move. That being said, our last point of business is tonight's meeting with Mr. Lazarus and his crew. The truck with the payload will be arriving at the pier tonight at 9 p.m. We'll need all hands on deck to get things unloaded and staged for Lazarus and his men to take possession of it all between ten-thirty and eleven-thirty tonight. We'll meet here at 8 p.m. sharp and go up together.

"Now, I'm sure all of you have seen the forecast for tonight," Briggs continued. "It's supposed to get pretty hairy, but we've all dealt with this kind of weather before. Ain't nothin' new. We'll deal with it like we always do. Tonight's shipment is one of the biggest we've ever had, so it's going to take everyone's A-game to make sure there are no hiccups in the process. That being said, once we pull this off, we're all going to be a lot richer for having done so."

"No, Boss," Sam called out after having talked to his meemaw, "she said ain't no one been there, policemen or otherwise."

"That's what I figured," John replied.

"What's going on?" Hawk inquired. "Why'd you want me to ask her that?"

"Chief Briggs is holding a meeting with his officers. He told them that Sandrine had been questioned at her house, and she told them that Melissa Thoreaux was with us heading to the Keys. He told them that the investigation had been turned over to the Miami-Dade Sheriff's office, and that they were probably going to call in the feds."

"Well, isn't that clever," Mercedes said dryly. "What did Clint have to say about that?"

"I don't know," John shook his head. "I don't think he's even there."

John asked, "Hey, Officer Leblanc, is Sergeant Thoreaux there in the meeting? Cough if he is, clear your throat if he isn't."

Solange cleared her throat.

"No," John shook his head to Sam and Merc, "he's not there."

"Well, where is he?" Dr. Lara asked.

John stayed quiet and listened to see if he could hear whether Chief Briggs was finished speaking.

He did not hear Chief Briggs talking, but he did hear a lot of other people talking in the background.

"Solange, is the meeting over? Can you talk?"

"Hang on," she said, barely loud enough for Watkins to hear her. He then heard her say, "Chief. Chief Briggs."

"Yes, my dear," the chief smiled at Solange.

"You said that you were waiting to hear from the Miami-Dade Sheriff's Office. When do you think that will be?"

"According to Ms. Benoit, her grandson and his friends left yesterday around noon. She called him last night while we were questioning her, and he told her that Melissa was with them, and that they were going to get to Miami around noon or so today. I called the sheriff's office down there, and they will be awaiting their arrival."

"So, they didn't say if Sarge's wife was with them against her will or not?"

"They didn't say," Briggs shrugged.

Leblanc could not believe her chief was stone-cold lying straight to her face. Not that she should be too surprised. Since Briggs had the entire Natchez police force neck deep in a gun running operation, lying seemed like such a lesser offense. Still, she was now beginning to wonder what else he had been lying to her about.

Solange did not like being lied to, and now that she knew Chief Briggs was lying to her–and probably had been for some time–the fact that he would be receiving his comeuppance tonight at Pier 51 seemed all the more justified to her.

"Very good," Solange nodded her head. "See you tonight."

She left the precinct's break room and went directly to her locker. After doing a quick check of the locker room and shower stalls to be sure she was alone, she spoke quietly to John. "I'm going to change out real quick and head home. Once I get to my car, we can talk at length. I never know when someone's going to come busting in here, and I'd rather not take any chances this close to the finish line."

"I understand. Just make sure you don't lose that lapel cam. Things like that cost a lot of money," John instructed her.

Still in Sam and Mercedes' room, John advised Sam, "I think it's a good idea if you ask your meemaw to go someplace else for the next twenty-four hours. Perhaps a friend from church or something like that. Just make sure she doesn't come here. She may have eyes on her."

"Copy that, Boss."

Watkins made his way back to the hotel suite to keep an eye on the cameras down by Pier 51 and to wait for Solange Leblanc to make communication with him again. When he entered the suite, he was greeted by Grandma Dot.

"Well, good morning to you, Mr. Watkins. Everything go okay last night?"

"Yes, ma'am, it did."

"So, we're safe here for another day?"

"Absolutely," John answered. "If things go according to plan, the Natchez police will be in custody by the end of the night, and you and your granddaughter can return to a much more peaceful life."

"I certainly haven't minded the change in routine these last couple of days, that's for sure," Dorothy smiled. "You hit a certain age, and you find that all your days start to run together because all your days are pretty much the same. But I know my Melissa will finally have the peace and happiness she so muchly deserves, and I cannot thank you enough for that."

"Of course. You're both very welcome," John said, taking a seat back on the couch to resume looking at the monitors. "Another good thing to come out of all this, I suppose, is that you and Melissa can start spending more time together without fear of Clint taking it out on her in an abusive nature."

"He does do that," Dot said, a somber look overtaking her face. "She said to me that he doesn't, but I know that he do. And it keeps me away from her, too. I hate that."

"Well, after tonight, you can see her and spend as much time with her as you'd like without fear of any repercussions at all."

"That sure will be a nice day, Mr. Watkins."

"The best day ever," John smiled warmly.

Through his com, he heard the sound of Solange Leblanc's car door shut.

"Okay," the officer said. "I can talk now."

John made some hand gestures to Dorothy Michaud to let her know that he was going to be talking to someone else on the communication device he had in his ear.

"So, I take it that the sergeant is M.I.A.?"

"He wasn't around for that meeting this morning," Solange said, pulling out of the station's parking lot. "Chief said Clint was waiting to hear from the Sheriff's office before he went down to Miami."

"Since we know that your chief lied about talking to Sandrine Benoit, I have to figure he lied about talking to the Sheriff's office, too."

"Why?" Solange asked, shaking her head completely befuddled. "Why do you think he did that?"

"He needed to shift the investigation away from this area before someone called in the feds. He lied to your sergeant to get his attention off his missing wife and back onto tonight's operation."

"I'll just be glad once all this is over."

"You know, Solange, with you being the one good cop on the whole force, you're probably going to be the one that gets put in charge of bringing in a new company of cops. Think you'll be up for that?"

"Me? But I'm just a patrol officer," Solange said with some trepidation in her voice. "I mean, I've been thinking about taking the sergeant's exam, but that's all that it's been…a thought."

"Well, given the circumstances, I'm sure they'll make some kind of special dispensation for you. How long have you been with the Natchez Police?"

"Seven years."

"Seven years is a long time to be a police officer in a small parish like yours," John said. "You know the people. You know the inner workings of the parish. You know the laws, the by-laws, the in-laws, and the outlaws. You'll be a natural fit."

"We'll see how things go, I guess."

"Yeah, let's focus on getting through tonight in one piece. The rest of the stuff will take care of itself."

47

THE MOST IMPORTANT MEAL OF THE DAY

Friday's sunrise came with little fanfare as patchy clouds moved in from the southwest. A wave of haze and humidity made the early morning Louisiana temperature feel more like 86 instead of the thermometer reading of 79 degrees,

Inside the deluxe accommodations of the Natchitoches Best Western, however, the temp was a pleasant, air-conditioned 70 degrees.

The entire group was assembled in Melissa and Dot's suite where they were listening intently to the meteorologists' reports on tonight's impending storm.

The forecast was not good. Some places were expected to see as much as two inches of rain an hour, with winds as high as 70 miles per hour.

"Yeah, tonight seems like a real swell night to go playing around in a river," Mercedes' words dripped with sarcasm.

"The wetsuits we'll be wearing aren't just shark- and alligator-bite resistant," John said. "They are also made to resist temperatures over twenty-seven thousand degrees Celsius. Unless the lightning hits us just as we're emerging from the water, we'll be relatively impervious to lightning strikes."

"You're kidding," Sloane furrowed his brow. "Where'd you get those?"

"Patagonia."

"Wow," Melissa expressed. "How much does something like that even cost?"

"About the same as a Mercedes S-Class."

Grandma Dot let out a whistle and exclaimed, "Now, that's a lot of clams."

"Speaking of clams," Mercedes commented, "I am more than just a little bit hungry."

Louie, who was laying at Mercedes' feet, lifted his head and looked at her in agreement.

"Aww, does my little buddy want some breakfast?" Merc asked softly.

"Where do you want to go?" John asked.

"I want to go to Waffle House," the doctor answered.

"We just went to Waffle House last night," Sloane griped.

"Correction: *You* went to Waffle House last night," Mercedes pointed out. "I was here with the ladies. Now, I don't really care where the rest of you go to eat, but as for me and my mouth, we will be at Waffle House."

"I'm down for some waffles," Hawk said. "If you give me that deserted island scenario, and I could only eat one food for the rest of my life, it would be waffles. As long as there was the caveat that I could have the different flavors of waffles–chocolate chip, blueberry, buttermilk, etc. And different toppings like whipped cream one day, syrup the next, butter for another, hot sauce. Yeah, waffles for me."

"My deserted island food would be country fried steak with white gravy," John admitted. "I ordered a box of country fried steaks wholesale one time. I ate country fried steak every day for three weeks straight, and twice a day a couple of times."

"What ran out first?" Grandma Dot asked. "Your desire to eat country fried steak or the number of steaks in the box you ordered?"

"The box of steaks."

"Anybody else wanna play 'Let's see how boring we can make our lives'?" Sloane asked.

"I can't imagine being stuck on an island with just one thing to eat for the rest of my life. Unless it was fish. I'd probably be okay with that," Latin laughed.

"With everything that's going to happen," Melissa said, "you all just don't seem worried at all. I'm sitting over here worried to death."

"We've dealt with worse," John said evenly. "You don't have to worry about anything. Enjoy your day and night. We'll worry about whatever comes next."

"I don't know what you charge," Dorothy said worriedly, "but I know we don't have it to pay you."

"Dot? May I call you Dot?" Latin asked.

"Of course, sweetie," Dorothy answered.

"I'm already knee-deep into the Natchez Police Department's banking accounts. Whatever the tab is for this job, the Natchez Police will have it more than covered."

48

Preparation

After breakfast, Jack Thompson, Latin Jackson, Daniel Sloane, Samuel Hawkins, and Dr. Mercedes Lara were in Latin and Louie's hotel room going through the plan of exactly how they were going to take down the evildoers that were the Natchez Police Department–and simultaneously foil the villain that was Josiah Lazarus.

John Watkins spent the day with the ladies.

He, Melissa, and Grandma Dot passed the time telling jokes and sharing stories of their past. It was important to Watkins that these two women, who had been through so much already, feel as at ease as possible.

"You'll be okay," John said to them on no uncertain terms. "If you don't hear from us by sunrise tomorrow morning"—John produced a red satchel and laid it in Melissa's lap— "there's new identities and enough money in here for you to go wherever you want to, and you can start a new life together. The most important thing is that you can do it together. You will always have each other."

"You know we'll never be able to thank you enough," Dot said.

"Good news: you won't ever have to," John assured them. "We work in the richest town in America. We do jobs for them and make more money from them than we'll ever need. That way we can do jobs for folks like you that can't afford us."

"Will you kill them? The Natchez Police?" Melissa asked.

"We'll give them a chance to come peacefully," John responded. "However, if they don't, we'll do what we must."

"God bless you and your people, John Watkins," Dorothy Michaud said.

"God already has," John said solemnly.

There was a knock at the hotel door.

"Come on in, Jack," John said.

Jack Thompson stuck his head in the door. "How'd you know it was me?"

"Because everyone else knows the secret knock," John smirked.

"Aw, man," Jack moaned. "I wanna know the secret knock."

"I wish I could tell you, but…it's a secret."

"Ha, ha," Jack said dryly. "You're 'bout as funny as a broken blender on Daiquiri Day."

"I'm guessing you are here to tell me something. Or did you just want to come hang out with the ladies and me?"

"Yes, we've got the plan together for tonight. We just need you to come back here to the room and give it your okay."

Watkins stood up and looked at Melissa and Dorothy.

"I need you two to promise me one thing," he said.

"Whatever you want," Dot said.

"We'll be back in a few hours, but…like I said, just for some outside reason we aren't" — John smiled at them reassuringly — "you have everything you'll need in that bag. So, enjoy the day; watch some movies, pig out on whatever you want, and lean on each other."

"God is with you. We promise. We'll see you in a few hours," Dorothy looked at him warmly.

※ ※ ※

Watkins entered Latin and Louie's hotel room and took a seat next to Dr. Lara on one of the beds. Jack Thompson stood in the front of the room and began articulating the fine tuning that the group had done to the plan that John had laid out earlier. He went through the movements, the placement, and the expectation of each person. Once he had finished, he looked at Watkins.

"Well?"

"Impressive," John said, nodding his head. "You guys took a premise–an idea of attack–and you turned it into a clear-cut, faultless machination that will, no doubt, be a complete success."

Jack laughed. "I'm not sure that I've ever received such high praise before. Your elocution of the English language is second to none, my friend."

"The plan is great, and you explained it wonderfully," John said. "What we need to do now is get down to the SUVs, take them someplace isolated–which around here, should be easier to find than marshmallows in a mug of hot cocoa–and go through the ordnance of weapons that we brought down. Get them out, load them with bullets, find whatever else you'll need–bullet-resistant garb, any other accessories you might want."

"You have some of those night vision goggles?"

"We do," John answered, "but in a thunderstorm—"

"Oh, no, no, no," Sloane interrupted. "If you're wearing those night vision goggles and lightning strikes, it's like staring into the flashbulb of a Polaroid camera. It *will* make you temporarily blind."

"Then how are we supposed to see out there?" Jack asked in a bit of a panic.

"Well," John began, "I'm hoping our good friends at the Natchez Police Department will have some kind of illumination rigging set up when they're unloading the truck full of weapons. If not, we have a plethora of flashlights and lighting implements that will both shed light on the ground in front of you as well as keep your location hidden."

"The skies are starting to turn," Mercedes said, looking out across the room's balcony. "We should probably take the SUVs someplace view-inaccessible and get them readied for tonight's festivities right away."

"Sounds good," John answered. "Let's get ready to load them up and move them out, gang."

※ ※ ※

The view-inaccessible place that the group found turned out to be a vacant cinderblock body shop just a few miles outside Natchitoches parish limits. The building backed up to within a few yards of a thick line of trees. It was here, as opposed to inside the emptied-out body shop, that they chose to park the two black vehicles and perform their preparatory duties.

"Watch for snakes and spiders, and more than anything else… fire ants," Sam warned.

"Why are we even out here?" Daniel questioned. "Wouldn't we be safer inside this joint?"

"Because inside this joint there are a plethora of other varmints, critters, and things that go bump inna night. Out here, it's a nice breeze blowing, and it doesn't smell" — Sam drew in a deep breath and his face soured a bit — "as much."

"This is a good spot," John announced, opening the hatch and tailgate on the rear of the first SUV. He started sliding out large canvas bags of weapons, ammunition, lights, bullet-resistant apparel, and much, much more.

Daniel Sloane went to the back of the other SUV and began performing the same task. Everyone else began separating the bags and going through them to see what they would need for tonight's job.

"Strictly asking for a friend," Jack Thompson started, "is all of this stuff legal?"

"Strictly askin' for a dude that don't wanna land his ass in jail later on down the road, is my answer something that can and will be used against me in a court of law?"

"Aww, come on, Sam," Jack smiled. "I wouldn't do that to ya. You know that."

"Then as far as you know, all of this stuff is legal." Sam hesitated. In most countries."

"Wow, you've got some new toys in here since the last time I worked with you," Latin said excitedly.

"We've got a few new things, Jax," Mercedes affirmed.

"Like what?" the lieutenant asked.

"Well, Jack, like...a new sign language translator gizmo. Hawk got a new spotting tool for when he's sniper shooting by himself. I got a device that will locate a bullet inside of a gunshot patient, and it will show me the path of least resistance to extract it from inside of them."

"Don't they already have that?"

"Sure they do, if you're doing surgery in a high-end surgery center. But if you're out in the field trying to perform the same surgery? They don't have that there."

"That thing's going to save a lot of lives for you, Merc," John Watkins said.

"Hopefully not tonight, though," Sam said.

Everyone turned to look at Hawkins in disbelief.

"What?"

"Oh, no, people. Come o-o-on. You know good and well that that's not what I meant. I meant that I hope no one gets shot tonight. Is all I was saying."

Because there were so many different kinds of weapons, ammunition, safety wear, gadgets, and so much more, it took nearly two hours for everyone to decide what kind of equipment and accoutrements they wanted to use for tonight's mission.

And they were sweating. Sweat was dripping off them like a leaky faucet and their clothes were drenched.

Latin Jackson looked around at the others. The tall, lean Watkins; musclebound Sloane; athletic Hawkins; the incredibly beautiful Dr. Mercedes Lara; the well-put-together Jack Thompson.

"Well, this is fair," he said.

"What are you talking about?" Sloane asked as he zipped his bag of paraphernalia shut.

"The five of you look like you're ready to be the cover models for the next issue of Maxim magazine. And I look like the poster boy for a 'Don't Eat Too Much Bacon' poster."

"First of all, you look fine. Trust me," Sloane said. "Women love a little extra padding on their men. I know this is true because I read it on the internet. Secondly, and perhaps most importantly... there's no such thing as too much bacon."

"Here, here," Lieutenant Thompson said.

Everyone stood with their hands on their knees–hot, tired, and worn out.

"You all feel like you've got what you need?" John asked.

The entire group answered in the affirmative.

"You got any words of wisdom for us before we head into this mess tonight, John?" Thompson asked.

"I was going to save this for later, but I'm pretty sure it's going to be raining like crazy, and you wouldn't care if I was giving you the Martin Luther King, Jr. 'I Have a Dream' speech. So, I'll just go ahead now and say what's on my mind."

John took a moment to wipe the sweat from his brow. He unbuttoned the top button on his white button-down shirt, rolled up his sleeves, and began to talk.

"There isn't a lot left to say. Most of you have already heard all my motivational speeches about faith and encouragement, my speeches about having a proper mindset and being reasonable with our actions, my speeches about having a fire in your belly but also having ice in your veins. So, no speeches this time. But I will send up a quick prayer."

John bowed his head and began. "Lord, give all of us the strength to do the right thing and the ambition to do it well. Amen."

"Amen," they all answered in unison.

"Hey, John," Jack said, holding up some garments that looked like insulated underwear. "You sure these long johns are bulletproof?"

"Yes, I promise you that they take a bullet better than Kevlar... just like I promised you the first hundred times you asked."

"I just ain't never seen anything like this before," Jack scowled.

"That's because they're prototypes. In a few years they'll be mass produced, and every police squad in the country will be using them."

Daniel Sloane looked over at Hawkins, who was looking up at the skies.

"You doin' some more praying, Sam?" Daniel asked.

"No, just looking at those clouds moving in. Since we've been here, the winds have picked up a good ten miles per hour." Hawk looked at Sloane. "We've had some fire fights in bad weather before, but I have a feeling tonight's job is going to be one for the books, baby."

"Tell ya what, that lightning starts getting close, you better be moving your ass down to the ground really quick. Do you know about lightning?" Sloane asked.

"I know about lightning. I know about weather," Sam answered emphatically. "Being a pilot as well as a sniper, the weather is the *first* thing you factor into your approach."

"Okay, gang," John said, "if everyone has what they need in their packs, then let's load them all into this Escalade." John touched the SUV to his right. "I'll drive this one back; everyone else will ride in the other Escalade with Daniel driving. We'll get back to the hotel and take an hour to pack up our gear and get washed up or whatever. Let's meet down in the hotel lobby around six o'clock. Then we'll check out and hit the road."

"And we'll let the fun begin," Merc added.

49

ON THE ROAD AGAIN

Once the group had packed up and checked out, they were greeted outside by the most menacing sky any of them had ever seen. Charcoal-gray clouds spread in every direction and the wind was blowing so hard it was difficult to even hold onto their bags.

"Good mighty!" John exclaimed. "We are going to get pounded."

"*And we're gonna love it!*" Hawk said, raising his fist into the air.

Everyone looked at him like he was a crazy man. He sheepishly said, "And we're gonna love it."

Jack Thompson and Latin Jackson tossed their bags into the trunk of Latin's Ferrari for later, while the Dragon's Men crew put all their gear in the Escalade that John Watkins would be driving. Then everyone took their seats in the Escalade that Daniel Sloane was driving.

Daniel pulled out of the hotel parking lot first, with John Watkins following a safe distance behind. They spoke freely through the coms they were all wearing.

"I love these Escalades, Johnny. This wind is blowing like crazy, but these crafts of fine American workmanship are holding the road just fine," Sloane said.

"I did my homework on the safest SUVs available, and these were the hands down winners. But, yeah, you aren't kidding. They're holding the road like nobody's business. Of course, I have a lot more weight in mine with all this gunnery and munitions in the back."

"Hey, I have a question...and maybe a bit of a confession," Jack Thompson spoke up from the passenger seat. "Let's just say that these crooked clowns do surrender and come peacefully. Who is going to arrest them?"

"We've performed citizen's arrests before," Dr. Mercedes Lara said as she looked out the window, cringing at all the dust and debris being kicked around by the high winds.

"Yeah, well, you might be able to pull a citizen's arrest on some yahoo up in White Pines, but trying to pull a citizen's arrest on a bunch of dirty cops probably isn't going to fly. And that's okay. I gotcha covered."

"How are you going to arrest them, Lieutenant?" John asked. "You're a little bit out of your jurisdiction, aren't you?"

"Well, that's where the confession part comes in. Have you noticed how I've disappeared from time to time over the last few months? Thompson asked.

"Yeah," Hawk answered. "I just figured you were in and out of rehab."

"I thought it was marital issues," Merc put in.

"I just figured you had logged a lot of leave time that you were going to lose unless you took it before a certain timeframe ended," was Sloane's guess.

"Good Lord, people!" Thompson said. "Is that what you all really think about me?"

"No, no, of course not," Hawk said, shaking his head.

"Yes," Mercedes said unabashedly. "Maybe not you, specifically, but law enforcement types, in general. Which would be you, so, yes."

From the back of the SUV, Louie barked twice.

"What does two barks mean?" Sloane asked. "Yes or no?"

"Two barks let me know that there is imminent danger," Latin informed them. "Lou's back here looking at the clouds, the wind, the debris flying all over the place...he knows we're heading into a real mess."

"Um, I'd like a chance to explain to you people just what it is that I've been doing with my time. And take a minute to let y'all know that I'm not some sort of narcotics addict that's been shackin' up with some college coed at her dorm room whenever I have some leave to burn."

"Sure thing, baby," Hawk patted him on the shoulder. "Whatcha been up to?"

"Remember last fall when we had that manhunt in White Pines, and there was a slew of U.S. Marshalls in town?" Jack asked. Without waiting for an answer, because he knew that all of them recalled what he was mentioning, he continued. "Well, it turns out that they were rather taken with the way I handled myself during that particular crisis, and they offered me a position. So, for the last few months, I have been going to training courses to get my Marshall's certification. I graduated two weeks ago."

The gang, including John from the other SUV, let out a round of cheers for their friend.

"Impressive work, Lieutenant," Sloane smiled and gave a nod of approval.

"That's great, Jack," Mercedes reached forward and shook his hand.

"That's quite the achievement," Latin chimed in.

"So, will you be leaving the department?" John asked.

"Oh, goodness, no. Helen would have a fit if we were to ever move from White Pines. No, no. This is just going to be a part-time thing where, should the situation fit, I would be called in to lend a hand."

"So, if our police friends and their crew do decide to come along quietly tonight, you can arrest them under your Marshall's purview?"

"I can. I've already called Bill Whittenburg–he's the head of the Marshall's service out of Baton Rouge–to let him know that I may have stumbled on to something down here."

"What'd he say?" John asked.

"He told me if I needed anything to let him know."

"Wait a second," Dr. Lara said, "you mean we could have had more people to help us out tonight?"

"Well...I mean—" Thompson stammered.

"It's fine," John came to his rescue. "We've got enough people to get this done. Everybody knows their role."

Suddenly, a sustained heavy wind began blowing things around. And around. And around.

"John, I know this is the right road," Daniel said, squinting to see the road through the gusts, "but I can't see the cutout where we're supposed to pull off. Heck, at this point, the daggone cutout might be completely blown away."

"Check your map on your dashboard. I put a pin in the sight when we were out here yesterday. We passed the Pier 51 pull-in about five hundred yards ago. We're just about right on top of the cutout now."

"Yeah, yeah, yeah, brother! I see it!"

"Pull on through. I'll come up alongside you," John said evenly.

Sloane pulled into the cutout. Watkins drove past, then circled back around so that John's passenger door matched up next to Sloane's.

"Hey, mind if I ask you a question?" Thompson shouted over the noise of the battering winds. "With these crazy winds, what's going to keep these vehicles upright?"

"Probably the anchors I'm getting ready to drop," Daniel answered.

"I didn't know Escalades came with anchors," Jack was surprised.

"Oh, they don't. But I installed them on both vehicles about two months ago," he said. "Suckers will keep us grounded in up to one hundred-fifty-mile winds."

Daniel reached down and pressed a button on the vehicle's console marked with a decorative picture of a ship's anchor.

John did the same.

"I guess you'll have to leave Louie in here tonight?" Mercedes turned around and asked Latin.

"Oh, no. I've got a harness that will attach him across my upper body. I'll put a poncho over the two of us, and we'll keep each other protected till we get to our destination. Once there, we'll hunker down and try to stay safe and dry until showtime. I mean, you all are highly proficient in firearms and hand-to-hand combat. Louie's my weapon of choice when things start to get hectic out there tonight."

"You want one of us to carry him for you, Latin?" John asked.

"No, he stays real still. I've carried him like that before. He's very docile."

"It's a pretty decent stretch that we'll be walking in high winds," John pointed out. "Are you *sure* you're going to be able to carry him for that long, buddy?"

"Are you volunteering, John?" Watkins' hacker friend asked.

"Who wants to carry the dog?" John asked.

It was silent for a moment before Daniel, Jack Thompson, Sam Hawkins, and Mercedes all spoke up at once.

"I don't mind."

"I'll do it."

"If nobody else wants to...sure."

"No."

Everyone looked at the lieutenant.

"Did you say *no*, Jack?" Sloane looked over at Thompson in disbelief.

"Yeah, I'm just not a dog guy, and I'm especially not a dog *harnessed to me in high winds* guy."

"But I've been to your house, Jack," Watkins said. "You have a dog."

"Correction: Helen has a dog. I just live with it."

An incredibly high gust of wind blew two large chunks of tree bark against the side of Sloane's Escalade, startling its occupants.

"Alright, now that we've come to that quick understanding, perhaps we should get ready for the job," Latin suggested.

"Okay," John said from his vehicle, "here's what we're going to do: one by one, come over here through the front passenger's side door, climb in, climb back, gear up, get out. From there, it will probably be best to stand against the passenger's side of my vehicle since that will offer the most protection from the wind until we're all ready to start hoofing it up the road to the pier. Daniel, you'll carry Louie in, so wait for me to get prepared before you head over. Understood?"

"Copy that," Sloane answered back.

"Let's not waste any more time then."

Jack Thompson kicked off the proceedings, and seventeen minutes and forty-three seconds later, everyone in the group was girded up and ready to go. John and Mercedes were each shod in a wetsuit and a small air tank. John carried a black duffel that contained the duo's flippers, masks, and other necessary scuba equipment, plus their assorted weapons and ammo.

The two walked down the road with the rest of the cast for a few hundred yards until John said to Dr. Lara, "This is us down this way."

"You two going to be able to hear us while you're under the water?" Latin asked loudly enough to be heard over the wind.

"Yes, once we pull our wetsuit hoods up into place, it will keep any water from flushing in and compromising our earpieces."

"Nice," Latin said as he moved in and gave his best friend a hug. "You guys be safe, and we'll see you when you come out of the water."

"We'll keep you alerted to everything that's happening on the surface," Hawk said.

John and Mercedes each gave Louie a quick scratch behind the ears and an assured nod to everyone else before heading off through the woods and toward the river.

"Keep your head up for any falling branches," Mercedes warned John.

"Roger that," John replied. "Your feet feeling okay in those shoes?"

"Not too bad for a pair of rubber pool shoes."

The ground under the couple was quite soft and boggy, and with every step they took, they seemed to sink a little further into the ground.

"Feel the coolness in the air, Doc?" John asked.

"It's sticky, humid, and uncomfortable," Merc wiped her matted hair from her sweaty brow. "And we're walking through a jungle here. Isn't there a clear path to the river?"

"This is the shortcut to the path," John told her.

"Why couldn't we have just started on the path? This brush is thicker than Madonna's head."

"Because to hit the beginning of the path, we would have had to backtrack about a quarter mile. We're almost to the clearing. Just follow me."

"I always do," Merc smiled somewhat begrudgingly.

The wind blew cold against John and Mercedes' wetsuits.

"We'll hit the path, and that will take us to the river."

"Okay, David Byrne," Mercedes shivered, "take me to the river."

And then, as if of one mind, they began to sing:

> *Take me to the river, drop me in the water.*
> *Take me to the river, dip me in the water.*
> *Wash with me now, washing me now.*

50

The Arrival

Jack, Latin, Daniel, and Samuel made their way through the wind and toward Pier 51. Hearing John and Doc singing through their coms, the four of them began singing along for a few moments.

Everyone was checking the weather on their phones. Despite the heavy cloud cover, radar showed that the rain was still a ways off to the south.

"The clouds are so dark it feels like it's nine o'clock out here," Jack said to Latin.

"Speaking of *out here*, I know why I'm out here. Why are you out here?" Latin asked the lieutenant.

"John called me, asked me to show up…so I did."

"What would you be doing otherwise?"

"Yeah," Daniel chimed in, "what *would* you be doing… *otherwise?*"

"I'd be at home with the missus, sewing my wild oats."

"Ha!" Daniel laughed out loud. "It's more like you'd just be at home with the missus sewing, period. Your wild oats turned into Cream of Wheat a few years ago."

"So, it's not like you'd be busy anyway, then."

"Yeah," Jack nodded, "it's not like we were busy anyway."

"Is she mad that you're down here?" Samuel asked through the gusting wind.

"Tell ya what, Sam, I've got one huge aspect going for me: my wife's understanding of my job's importance knows no limits," Jack explained. "She knows that if I'm down here with you guys instead of being with her, my being here is of the *utmost* importance."

"You definitely got your *one*," Latin said, pulling up the collar on his coat.

"Yep, and she's been my *one* for thirty-three years."

With that, the quartet arrived at the entrance to Pier 51.

"I guess this is where we part ways, fellas," Hawk said. "This is my tree right here."

"Looks like a heckuva climb, Sam-well."

"I'll let you know when I make it to the top, boys."

After first making sure his backpack and rifle bag were secure to his person, Hawk began his ascent.

"Look at 'im go, Jack," Sloane said in awe. "The way he goes up that tree–looks just like a—"

Hawkins stopped his climb on the spot. "Sloane, so help me dawg, if you say that I look like a monkey climbing this tree, I will drop straight down on that retractable dome of yours, and I will beat you senseless."

"What?" Sloane said, moderately offended. "I was gonna say *champ*. You're climbing up that tree like a champ. It's a compliment."

"Tell him you were joking," Latin requested. "It's not that I care whether you were or not, but with this wind blowing like it is, he's more than likely to drop down with all the best intentions of landing on you and end up getting blown right on top of me."

"Can I put your dog down yet?" Danny asked with an expressionless look.

"C'mere, Lou," Latin wrapped his arms around the Chocolate Lab.

Sloane turned his eyes upward toward Sam. "It was a compliment, Hawk."

Sam resumed his climb up the tree. "Compliment, my *dèyè*," he muttered to himself.

Hawk finished his ascension to the top of the tree, crawled out onto a thick branch, and got himself comfortable.

"You good, Sam?" Jack Thompson asked.

"It's a tad bit breezy up here, but I'm taking to it like a bird to its nest," Hawk laughed. "My com is picking you up just fine."

"Can you see us down here?" Latin asked.

"I sure can."

"That's good because we can't see you at all," Jack Thompson commented.

"Holy Malone," Hawk said, sounding a bit surprised, "I can see forever from where I am up here. And you all need to get to steppin'. I can see the weapons truck, and it's not that far from being here."

Sloane, Latin, Louie, and the lieutenant scurried toward the river. Jack and Daniel broke off and into the woods to their left, taking cover in some heavy brush. Latin and Louie moved to their right, back into the wooded area until they felt they were safely out of sight.

"Solange? Are you with us?" Sam asked from his hide near the top of the tree.

"I am," everyone heard her through their coms, though her voice was barely audible.

"There's a truck getting ready to get to Pier 51. Are you with them?" Sam inquired of her once again.

Radio silence filled everyone's coms.

Finally, she responded in a whisper, "No. We're all still back at HQ. Not sure who's on the truck, but we cops are still back here at base."

"Any idea on when you'll be headed this way?"

"Less than thirty," Solange said, again barely loud enough to be heard over the high winds at Pier 51.

"Confirm with a sniff...less than thirty minutes before you head this way?"

The female cop sniffed discreetly.

"Copy that," Jack said.

"Hawk, can you see me and Lou?" Latin asked.

"From up here I can see the hairline of a bald eagle."

"Do you think we're out of sight enough?" asked a nervous Latin Jackson.

"You're fine," Sam answered.

"Doc and I have reached the river," Watkins came through on everyone's coms. "We're going to hold. Sam, you're everyone's eyes and ears for the next hour or so."

"If you have to pee," Sloane said, "now's the time to do it."

"Eyes on the delivery truck," Sam said calmly. "ETA is roughly forty-five to fifty seconds. Everyone get ready to hunker down for a while."

"Is that military speak?" Thompson laughed. "*Hunker down?*"

"Stay chilly, everybody," Hawk smiled as he began to line up the sights on his scope.

Everyone hunkered down. Show time was at hand.

51

SHOW TIME

The members of the Natchez Police Department sat in the break room listening to their chief talk on the phone. They heard Chief Briggs and Mr. Lazarus speaking to each other for one last time, confirming plans for the night.

"Very good," Chief Briggs said. "We'll see you in just a couple of hours then."

The chief hung up the phone and looked at his team.

"Everything's a go," he said. "In just a few short hours, we'll be richer than any of us ever thought possible when we signed up for this stupid off-the-grid assignment."

"Even I never thought we'd see this day," came a voice from the back of the room.

It was Clinton Thoreaux.

"Sergeant," the chief smiled, "I was hoping you'd make it."

"That makes two of us," Clint smirked. "I was sitting at home driving myself crazy, feeling sorry for myself over Melissa, and I just figured…why not go do something that'll take my mind off things and make a bit of coin while I'm at it?"

"Alright, people," Officer Guillory rallied the troops. "I just got word that the merchandise is already at the Pier. Let's move out and get this show started."

"Chief," Solange called out.

"What's up, Leblanc?"

"I need to swing by my place for a minute. Okay to catch up with y'all on site?"

"Sure, but don't screw around. With the weather being what it is, I don't want to take any chances. Things have to go just perfect for this to work, and in order for things to work perfectly, preparation is key."

"I won't be long at all."

Solange made her way out of the building, and as soon as she was sure she was out of earshot of all the other officers she asked, "Can you guys hear me?"

"We read you five-by-five," Hawk answered.

"Were you able to hear what was being said at the meeting I was just in?"

"Yeah, the truck is already here," Jack Thompson answered.

"We are all in position," Hawk told Solange. "I am up in a tree, hanging on for dear life. The rest of the crew are spread out in the woods by the river. Since you've been here before, I'll take it that you understand about where I'm talking. The truck is here, and I have counted nine targets working on unloading the weapons."

"That sounds about right," Solange said as she pulled her car out of the police station's driveway. "We'll be bringing twelve, not counting me. I am stopping by my house real quick. I'm going to pick up a few back-up pieces, and I'm also going to pick up a red stocking cap. I'll be wearing that so that I'll stand out from the rest of the officers, so if things should go sideways, and you guys start shooting, you'll be able to know which one I am, and you won't shoot me."

"Copy that," Hawk confirmed. "Everyone hear that?"

"Ten-four," Thompson said.

"Got it," Latin replied.

"Roger that," Sloane muttered.

"We read you down here by the river," Merc said.

52

River Talk

John Watkins and Mercedes Lara were not romantically involved. They never had been, and they never would be.

For one, Mercedes had her own thing going on with Harper Rowe, a government assassin.

For two, John Watkins was part of the one percent of humanity that was attracted to neither men nor women. Even though the members of the Dragon's Men Protection Agency knew this, it still didn't stop them from trying to set him up with woman after woman. Even Dr. Mercedes Lara had run test after test. But to no avail.

However, at the moment, the two of them lay on their sides facing each other in the tall weeds on the bank of the Cane River. Between the howling wind and dark clouds, the sunset was completely blocked. Electric spider webs of white lightning filled the air.

Noting the lag time between the lightning and the rolling thunder, Sloane spoke up through the coms. "That storm's about twenty minutes away."

"How far away from the pier do you think we are?" Mercedes asked John.

"When we were down here yesterday, I put a beacon underneath it." He patted the chest of his wetsuit. "I have the beacon locator right here. The communications com is in my right ear, and the beacon signal is here in my left. When we get close to the pier, I'll signal you. Then we wait for Hawk to give us the signal to surface."

"I have the spear gun just in case we encounter some of the friendly neighborhood wildlife. You be the lookout. I'll be the shooter."

"How many spears do you have in your quiver?"

"Four," Mercedes answered. "I've got a bowie knife attached to my ankle, too."

"With the river running as strong as it is, most of the amphibious creatures will be taking to the land. It's good to be prepared, but I don't think there's any chance of us running afoul of dangerous beasts during our subaquatic journey."

"Since I know you've done your research, how deep is this river?" Dr. Lara asked.

"According to the internet, the river is close to nine feet deep. We'll want to stay as close to the bottom as we can to avoid getting caught up in the current."

"I'm guessing this is the part of the job where swimming all those laps at the White Pines Y will finally pay off." Mercedes lifted her head above the weeds for a quick glance at the raging river. "Yeah, I'm a strong swimmer, but even I'm a little apprehensive about this particular task at hand."

Reaching into his bag of gear, John pulled out two three-pronged garden cultivator tools. He handed one to Mercedes and said, "When we dive in, use this to keep yourself anchored to the floor of the river until you can get out deep enough that the current lets up."

Mercedes took the tool and smiled. "Now, John Watkins, I know you're always telling us that you're not the leader of this team, and how that all ended when we became civilians, but it's genius ideas like this that *make* you the leader of this team."

"Eh, anybody else would have thought of this," John deflected.

"Um, I would've never thought of that," Hawk said from his spot in the tree.

"Yeah, me either," Sloane said.

"You know how I know that you're the only one who would think to do that, Johnny?" Latin asked rhetorically. "It's because you're the only one who thought to do that."

"Okay, gang," Samuel Hawkins said, "I've got a convoy of six, seven, eight...yes, eight cars headed this way. Starting to get serious now."

John put the gear bag between him and Mercedes. "Time to strap up and get ready to move."

"Just a reminder," Officer Solange Leblanc came through the coms. "I am about five minutes behind that convoy."

"We got you, officer," Watkins replied.

Mercedes pulled up the hood of her wetsuit and strapped an underwater light around her head. Next, she strapped the spear gun to the outside of her right leg and a Heckler & Koch P11–a handgun that would fire underwater–to the inside. An ADS amphibious rifle went across her back. Inside her wetsuit, her usual handgun was holstered on her hip. With her flippers over her beach shoes, she finally readied her air tank and mouthpiece.

John Watkins strapped only an SPP-1 underwater pistol to the outside of his right leg. In one hand he carried the cultivating tool that would keep him grounded to the riverbed. In the other, he held an underwater spotlight that would help them find their way to Pier 51.

However, under his wetsuit John was wearing a double shoulder holster. In one holster, he had "The Cannon"–his Glock 20 that would knock a Sumo wrestler on his fat butt from a block away. The other holster held a Glock 17 Gen4, the most reliable, lightweight, and easy to use handgun ever made. Lastly, John's hip holster held his Glock G43x MOS, the gun that he usually used as his back-up piece. With his wetsuit keeping the guns dry, he would be ready to fire when the time came for him and Mercedes to come up out of the water.

"Okay, you guys, Merc and I are going into the river. We're counting on you to let us know what's going on, and when we're to come out of the water."

"You got it, Johnny," Sam answered. "But I gotta tell ya, they's gotta lotta people here. I'm counting twenty-three. Normally, I could take out a lot of 'em, but this wind…man, it's unforgiving."

"You just get their attention. Merc and I will flank them from the river. They won't know what hit them."

"You two be ultra careful, Boss," Sam pleaded. "From here, that river looks angrier than an alcoholic at an intervention."

53

Underwater Disaster

John readied his air tank, then checked his mouthpiece and inserted it properly.

He looked at Mercedes, held up the cultivating tool, nodded to her, and the duo took off on a dead sprint toward the river. Two steps into the water, they both took a powerful dive to attempt to get below the current.

John swung with all his might, smashing the cultivating tool through the rapids and into the floor of the riverbed. It grabbed perfectly, and he lifted and slammed it again and again to pull himself out of the rapids.

Once in the calm, John turned the spotlight to find Mercedes. He expected her to be on his right side, but she was not there.

He shined the light to his left. No Mercedes.

He looked behind himself. Nothing.

Watkins frantically started searching the water for his partner. He did an entire three-sixty only to find that Mercedes was nowhere in sight. He finally looked up toward the surface to see Merc some twenty yards upriver, desperately flailing around in the strong rapids.

Ah, Huck...Finn! John thought. He used the cultivating tool to try to move toward her.

It did not work. Actually, the harder he tried to move toward her, the further away she seemed to get.

He tried not to panic, knowing that he and Mercedes had been through worse situations before. But he also knew that all good things must come to an end.

No. He refused to believe that this was that time for them. He readied himself for whatever her move would be.

John turned off the spotlight and released it. He knew he would need both hands free to, hopefully, grab Mercedes and pull her to safety.

54

The Lineup

Hawk drew in a deep breath and began to rattle off the following: "Alright, boys and girls, I am your eyes and ears, so ready your ears because this is what my eyes are seeing. The truck is unloaded and moving out. At the end of the pier, running parallel to the river are six crates, stacked three on three, underbarrel grenade launchers. Stacked likewise behind them, we have four crates, eight to a crate, of SCAR assault rifles. Then, we have running longways, thirty-six to a crate, four crates of AR-15 assault rifles. After that, we have some shoddy workmanship of stacked, sorta-stacked SIG SG 550s and Heckler & Koch G-136 rifles.

"Now, as far as personnel, I know we want to give our local law enforcement folk a chance to give themselves up, but if they don't give themselves up…we have a group of eight standing down by the river, looking like they cannot *wait* to get back to the nearest vehicle that has a well-working A/C unit. John, Merc–they're all yours. Next, we have another group of six on Latin and Louie's side of the pier, lookin' like they's already countin' their money before the ink's even dried.

"From there, we have seven more on the lieutenant's and Danny's side o' the pier, waiting for someone to tell them that Simon 'n' Garfunkel are no longer together. And, lastly, I got a pretty young thang in a red stocking cap standing next to the fat tub o' lard they call *Chief* around these here parts. Solange, if he doesn't give himself up when the time comes…feel free to shoot that S.O.B. right square in his hangin' chads."

"Whenever you're ready for me to politely ask them to give themselves up," Jack Thompson said, "you let me know."

"Roger that, Lieutenant," Hawk replied.

Everyone took a moment to collect themselves.

55

THE ART OF USING ADRENALINE

TO DO THE IMPOSSIBLE

Mercedes heard everything through her ear com.

Dr. Lara did not need anyone to tell her that the plan was going to go off with or without her being there. She knew that her teammates were good enough to pull off the job at hand whether she was there or not. But, by golly, she wanted to be there.

However, given her current situation, if she did not find a way to quickly get out of these rapids, life as she knew it would soon be over.

Merc removed the spear gun from the outside of her right leg and fired the spear into the floor of the riverbed.

It stuck firmly.

Next, she grabbed the rope attached to the end of the spear and began to pull herself, hand over hand, down and out of the Cane River rapids.

Watkins was waiting for her to make a move. When she did, he grabbed her by the arm and assisted her down to the floor of the river.

Using sign language, Mercedes signed, "Thank you."

John gave her the corresponding hand signal to carry on with the operation. He then signed what would literally be translated as, "Follow me two surface."

Mercedes removed the light fastened around her forehead and handed it to Watkins so he could guide them to the pier. Grabbing onto John's leg, she held on tightly as he led her along the riverbed floor to the embankment. He then floated up to the surface, letting the rapids carry them downriver toward the pier. He finally let go of the gardening tool, freeing both of his hands to grab onto the edge of the wooden dock.

While the rapids moved them downriver at a rate of twenty miles per hour, John fought to stay close to the bank.

The team that had unloaded the weapons from the truck had also set up a light rigging that completely lit up the entire Pier 51 area. John yanked the light off his head, turned it off and chucked it into the water.

Now all that was left to do was to use his adrenaline to help him latch onto the dock and find a way to get Mercedes to safety.

Here we go, Johnny, Watkins said to himself. *Grab it. Grab it!*

As he reached his hands out to grab the end of the pier, the rapids sucked him under. Strangely, it worked to his advantage as he was now able to grab onto the wooden support leg of the pier. Holding on for all he was worth, he used the momentum of the river to swing his legs around and slingshot Mercedes up and onto the riverbank.

John then pulled himself out of the water and crept around the end of the dock, up the side, and toward the banks. Meanwhile, Mercedes had removed her breathing apparatus and stripped the air tank from her body. She kicked off her flippers and crawled along the embankment to help John from the river.

The roar of the rapids provided enough noise to drown out the sound of John and Mercedes coming out of the river, while the crates of weapons gave them visual cover as they prepared to attack.

56

IT ALWAYS RAINS WHEN YOU'RE HAVING FUN

The wind was blowing at an unforgiving rate, and now the rain finally began to fall.

"What do you think, Sam?" Jack Thompson asked.

"Do your thing, Lieutenant."

Seemingly from out of nowhere, Jack pulled a bullhorn and put it up to his mouth. "This is U.S. Marshal James Donovan McKnight Thompson. Members of the Natchez Police Department, we have you surrounded. There's no need for bloodshed or loss of life. Lay down your firearms and surrender peacefully."

"Is that really your name?" Sloane asked Thompson.

"Ha! Kiss my ass, Marshal!" Chief Briggs shouted back.

"I was afraid he was gonna say that," Jack Thompson said as he produced his U.S. Marshal card to Sloane. "You ever refer to me as *Donovan* or *McKnight*, and it will be the last thing you ever do."

Jack put the bullhorn back to his mouth. "This is your last chance, Chief…" Thompson turned his head away from the megaphone and asked Sloane, "What's this dude's last name?"

"Briggs," Sloane answered.

"…Chief Briggs. It's your life to lose."

"Come and get us, Marshal!" the chief yelled.

"Say goodnight, Chief." Sam took aim and gently squeezed the trigger on his sniper rifle. The bullet hit its mark, putting the chief down for permanent nighty-night.

"What the heck, Hawk?" Sloane asked through his com. "I thought we were shooting to maim?"

"Must've been the wind," Hawkins said with a sly smile.

Mortally wounded and on his back, Darryl Briggs looked up at Solange Leblanc. With his final breath he said, "Avenge me, Solange."

"Yeah, that's probably not going to happen, Boss," Leblanc said as she twisted her boot heel into the chief's hand. Then, in an effort to get her police contingent to engage Dragon's Men, she yipped, "Go get 'em, boys!"

In response, the Natchez Police Department members and the weapons crew began firing blindly into the night.

"Hey, Sam?" Jack asked. "Are we supposed to shoot these morons or just let them use up all their ammunition?"

"Lieutenant, it's these morons that've been keepin' my meemaw and her friends and the people of this town living in pure dread and fear for the better part of the last decade. *You* ain't gotta shoot 'em, but I sure as God's loving grace am. I got no quarter to give these jackals."

"Hawk's right," Sloane said. "If they could see you, Jack, they wouldn't hesitate to put you down. Me and you, we come from the land of the civilized…the land of rules. These people would call you Donovan McKnight just as soon as look at you."

"Well, since you put it that way—"

Lightning flashed, lighting up the targets.

Before the scene went black again, before Jack or Daniel could even get a shot off, Samuel Hawkins sniped down the bad actors.

"Dad burn, that kid's good," Thompson remarked.

"John, Merc," Hawk said. "We're ready for your close-up. As

for the rest of you, you're on your own. It's getting a bit breezy up here for my liking. I'm coming down."

Still in her wetsuit because of the rain, Merc took stock of her situation. She realized that when she had removed her air tank, the gun strapped to her thigh had been washed away in the river. And she had lost her spear gun when she'd used it to get out of trouble. That left her with no weapons.

She and John stayed low and tight against the pier, out of sight of the people right above them on the dock. They watched as some of the members of the Natchez Police Department worked open the crates of AR-15 rifles.

"Psst," Mercedes whispered into John's ear. "I lost my weapons in the river earlier. A guy like you wouldn't happen to have a spare gun that a pretty girl like me could use, would ya?"

"Yes," John said, unzipping his wetsuit and handing Mercedes the Glock17 Gen4. "And don't even think about asking me about there being a banana in my pocket."

"You're no fun, John Watkins," Mercedes tried not to laugh. "No fun at all."

"I'll have you know...I've been told the same thing by women that were a lot less attractive than you are."

Their witty banter drew the attention of the ne'er-do-wells that were fishing around for the AR-15s.

"Head's up, Merc," Watkins warned.

He shoulder-rolled on his right toward her as she simultaneously rolled over top of him, onto her left arm.

They commenced firing from the switchgrass.

Mercedes' shots were a bit more aggressive than John's, with her shooting to kill and Watkins merely kneecapping his targets. Although, with the amount of pain associated with being kneecapped, one could argue that Mercedes's kill shots were more merciful.

* * *

Louie and Latin were laying low and staying out of sight. "Stay down, Lou," Latin stroked the fur on his best four-legged friend. "This'll be over soon. Keep me safe, buddy."

The Chocolate Lab curled up next to his owner and licked Latin's face.

Suddenly they heard footsteps rushing toward them.

Latin apprehensively lifted his gun and was getting ready to fire until Louie put his big brown paws on his masters' arm.

A bolt of lightning lit up the scene, illuminating the red cap on the incomer.

"Sweet magnolias, child!" Latin let out. "Y'almost got yourself shot."

"Yeah," Solange laughed quietly. "Good thing the safety was on." Officer Leblanc slid in beside Latin and Louie. "You're kinda cute."

"Are you talking to my dog?"

"No, sweetie, I'm talking to you," Solange gushed.

"Well…good thing…because I don't let my dog date just anyone."

* * *

"Looks like Hawk was right," Jack said, moving around Daniel to get a better look at the members of the Natchez police department and the truck crew. "Seven of them jokers out there."

"Yeah, Hawk might be a bit of a jerk and a loudmouth sometimes, but he does know how to count," Daniel admitted.

"Coming from you, that's pretty high praise."

"Okay, look alive here, Lieutenant," Daniel said in a quiet voice. "Do you want the four on the right or the three on the left?"

"I'll take the four on the right."

"Wonderful. That works out great because I'm left-handed," Daniel checked the magazine in his Beretta, slapped it back in, and said, "Let's have some fun."

Daniel moved to Jack's left and began shooting wildly. His

first eight shots managed to hit one of their intended targets. Jack Thompson took care of his four targets then put down two of Daniel's guys. "Hey," he said, looking over at Sloane, "are you sure you're left-handed?"

John and Mercedes came up from the riverbank, kicking bodies aside as they went.

Daniel Sloane and Lieutenant Jack Thompson came in from the east, guns drawn, rain dripping down Danny's face and off Thompson's cowboy hat.

Samuel Hawkins slowly paced his way onto the scene, his rifle drawn, his gaucho dripping wet.

Leblanc, Latin, and Louie moved in from the west.

In the midst of them were four hired hands and one member of the Natchez Police Department: Sergeant Clinton Thoreaux.

Clint looked at John. "Do you know where my wife is?"

"I sure do."

"Where? I want to see her."

"Yeah. I bet you do," Watkins said.

"Will you take me to her?" Thoreaux pleaded.

"I've got a good mind to tell you that I'm not gonna do that, ya thunderdome mook." John had a cool blank look on his face. "How bad do you want to see her?"

"Please?" Clint begged. "I just want to tell her I'm sorry."

"Well, let me think," John said quietly amidst the pouring rain and howling winds. "All those nights when you were beating the ever-loving crap out of your wife, and she begged you *please...I'm sorry*, did it ever make a difference to you?"

Clinton Thoreaux bowed his head in apparent shame.

"That's what I thought." Watkins looked at Clint "But I might be able to help you. Of course, the final decision to see you is up to her. I can promise nothing. First, though, we're going to need you to do something for us."

"Gladly," Thoreaux said. "Whatever it takes."

"Josiah Lazarus...he trusts you?"

"Y-y-yes," Clint faltered, realizing what it was that they wanted him to do.

"Yes, that is exactly what we want you to do," Watkins smiled through the pouring rain.

"And if I don't?"

"You can kiss goodbye any chance of seeing your wife," John answered.

"*And* we will kill you," Mercedes added.

"I'll do it," agreed Thoreaux.

John looked at the other four men. "Officer Leblanc, would you mind escorting these guys to jail? Jack, you wanna go with her?"

"I'll go with her," Latin volunteered. "Me and Lou."

"Very good," John agreed.

"I'll go back with them," Jack said. "I think I've had just about all the rain I can take for one night. Mind if I take one of the SUVs?"

"Sure, but take these four men with you. And have Latin and Louie ride with Leblanc in her vehicle."

Latin could not help but ask, "Why?"

"Because your dog is soaking wet, and I really don't want wet-dog smell stinking up the SUV, is why," John answered.

"Louie is no wetter than Jack is."

"Well...you make a valid point. Let me reconsider my initial answer," John said, feigning reconsideration. "Um, the answer is still *no*."

"That is the best answer," Lieutenant Thompson said. "I like it."

"Thank you, Lew," John smiled once again, then addressed Sloane. "Daniel, take a ride with Officer Leblanc. Direct her to the SUVs and bring back the one you drove. Alright?"

"I'll do it as long as I can ride up front on the way to the SUVs," Sloane stipulated.

"That's fine," Latin said. "I don't mind riding with the boy."

"Hold up," Solange protested. "Do I get any kind of say in this matter?"

"Sure you do. It's your car." Watkins commented. "However, that being said, you, Daniel, Latin, and Louie can hash it out on the way to your car. You need to get moving. *We* need to get moving."

"We can figure this out right now," Leblanc said. "I'll let your man ride up front, but after that I think I'm going to take this boy and his dog back to town and see if I can't get them out of those wet clothes," she smiled.

"Take care of my friend," John Watkins said. "And starting tomorrow...take care of Natchez. I know you're going to be busy tonight, but if you don't mind, could you keep your ear com in just in case we get into any trouble??

"For you guys, I definitely will. If you need anything–*anything*–don't hesitate, okay?" Solange looked at Daniel and Latin. "Let's go, boys. Like the man said, there's a lot to get to."

Jack Thompson walked up to the four men and said to them, "I realize that things are happening kinda fast, and you're probably thinking, 'What the Sam Hill just happened?' It's like this: you've played things pretty smart so far, which is why you're still alive and not lying dead in the rain like a lot of your colleagues here. So, let's just keep the good times rolling, and you fellas keep playing it smart. You cooperate with me, I keep you boys local with the whole arrest scenario. You give me grief, things will end one of two ways, and neither one will be good for any of you You'll either be shot dead by me, and if you're fortunate enough to *not* be shot dead by me, you'll be arrested by me and given over to the Marshal's Service on federal charges. At that point, you will wish you had been shot dead by me because your lives, for all intents and purposes, will be over. I trust we have an understanding?"

All four of them nodded like bobble head dolls in an earthquake.

"Wonderful." Jack turned in the pouring rain and said to John, "We're gonna go on and start heading toward the road. You sure you got this from here?"

"We got it," Watkins answered.

The lieutenant pulled his gun and motioned for the four men to start walking. As they made their way away from the light and into the darkness of the night, Jack hollered, "How 'bout this weather, huh?"

Within a few minutes, Daniel Sloane returned with the black Escalade. He parked out in the road and left the engine running.

"Latin's driving the other SUV back. He'll be here in a minute. Officer Leblanc is following him."

"Much obliged," Jack shook Daniel's hand as the two men passed through the vehicle's headlights. "You guys be safe."

Sloane zipped up the hoodie he had grabbed from the SUV. "I'm not really sure how this is going to go. I guess we'll figure it out when the time comes."

With Latin behind the wheel, the second black Escalade pulled past them and into the entrance for Pier 51. Solange Leblanc, with Louie already in the back seat, pulled her car in front of Thompson's SUV.

"Just follow me back to HQ!" she yelled out to Thompson once Latin had opened the passenger side door and climbed into her car.

Face down in the wind, Sloane double-timed it back toward the river.

57

THE FINAL CHORE

Wind and rain.
Thunder and lightning.
John Watkins and Daniel Sloane.
Samuel Hawkins and Dr. Mercedes Lara.
These eight forces of nature were gathered in one place: Pier 51.
And they were waiting for one thing to happen: the arrival of Josiah Lazarus.
Sergeant Clinton Thoreaux walked off the pier and over to where the body of Chief Briggs lay. He reached down and removed the radio attached to the chief's waistband–the same radio that Josiah Lazarus had been using to communicate with Briggs. Sergeant Thoreaux carried the device back to the dock and knelt beside some crates to shelter himself from the wind. John stood next to him, making sure that the sergeant did not convey a warning to Lazarus.
"Tall Boy to Shot Caller. Over," Clint said into the radio.
After a few seconds, Lazarus' voice chirped over the radio. "Tall Boy? I had been told earlier that you might not make it tonight."
Watkins heard a very distinct Syrian accent in Lazarus' voice.
"Yeah, things looked a little iffy for a while," Thoreaux replied, "but I'm here now. Here with a new crew."

"A new crew? I was not told anything about a new crew. Please explain."

As Clinton was getting ready to respond, John leaned over and put his hand over the radio. "I don't want to put any undue pressure on you, but what you say next will probably determine whether or not you ever see your wife again, so…make it count."

Clint put the radio back up to his mouth, holding it face down so that the heavy rain would not interfere with the transmission. "With all the times that we have done business, I don't think we've ever had to deal with weather like this before."

"No, never weather like this, my friend."

"Well, the chief was out here earlier–I think you spoke with him–but this weather has caused him and the rest of the gang to head back to Natchez. Car accidents, wind damage, power outages. They've got a lot of fires to deal with, some literal, some figurative. Anyway, we had to call in the back-up crew."

"I understand." The Damascus native chuckled, "I was not aware that there was a back-up crew."

"We've always had a back-up crew standing by; it's just that we've never needed them until tonight. No worries, they're a good bunch. We'll have you loaded up and on your way in no time." Clint took a deep breath. "Any idea on your ETA?"

"We are coming up on the final bend in the river before we arrive. You should see us within the next few minutes. I have my usual accompaniment of people with me. Two smaller boats and the tugboat."

"And you'll see *us*. We have the lighting rig in place."

Watkins tapped Clinton Thoreaux on the head and signaled him to wrap things up.

"All right, Shot Caller, we'll see you in just a few minutes. We'll be ready to get things moving upon your arrival," Thoreaux said.

John reached down and helped Clinton stand up.

"We need to hustle," he said. "CRD, gang."

"Ah, dang it!" Hawk said in a not-too-happy tone.

"CRD? What's CRD?" Clint asked.

"Corpse Removal Detail," John answered. "You might be able to convince Mr. Lazarus that we're the second-string gunrunners, but if he sees all these stiffs laying around, it's going to make that argument a lot harder to sell."

Mercedes moved to the feet of one of the dead bodies and asked, "Where do you want to put them, Boss?"

"Let's move them to the trees," John answered, moving to help Mercedes. "Over there," he nodded in the corresponding direction.

And move them to the trees they did.

They finished the task just as Josiah Lazarus and his crew came into sight.

In his ignorance, Lazarus thought he, his two speed boats, and his small tugger had been let through the delta at Lake Pontchartrain because he was playing it cool–proper paperwork signed, sealed, and in order–like countless times before. Never a bother, never been bothered. Why would this time be any different? He was just on his way up to see his good friends at the Natchez Police Department.

Why would it be different this time? Because this time, one little old lady's love for her granddaughter was going to get in the way.

So, the second Josiah Lazarus had been given the go-ahead by the New Orleans Coast Guard, ATF Agent Jake Ritter had put in a call to John Watkins. That call had taken place just under two hours ago.

In fair weather, the trip from New Orleans up to Pier 51 would have been a two-hour float. But given tonight's weather conditions, the trip would be noticeably longer.

John looked at his watch. "Two hours and twenty-five...*ish* minutes. Not bad."

"Ya know," Mercedes began, "we've been standing out here so

long, I can hardly tell it's raining anymore."

"Ya know," Hawk started his own smart-alec remark, "you've been lying so long, I can hardly tell when you're doing it anymore."

"Well," Merc smiled, "I guess game recognizes game."

"Alright, Sergeant Thoreaux," John said, wiping the rain from his face, "I'm giving you the lead here. You do the talking, and we'll do the loading. But we'll also be listening. So, please…don't foul this up. If we go down, we'll take you down with us. That's a promise."

"Let's just get this over with as fast as we can," Thoreaux answered.

"Merc," John said, "stay out of sight and keep your gun aimed toward the boat. Anything seems like it's going sideways, open up on them."

Merc moved out of sight, leaving John, Daniel, Sam, and Clint standing on the dock, watching as Josiah Lazarus' boats moved in toward the pier.

Lazarus maneuvered his tugger up to the dock, and within moments he had placed a mobile ramp connecting it to the dock. Two speed boats, each containing two men and one woman, pulled gently up to the shore nearby.

The six occupants, covered in various types of foul weather gear and boots, leapt onto the shore. As they moved to join the others at the end of the pier, a triple strike of lightning crackled around them.

"Let's move it, my compadres!" Mr. Lazarus hollered. "I don't want any of this merchandise getting wet."

Lazarus and Clinton Thoreaux stood off to the left of the pier while the group began loading the tugger. John and Daniel were the first to haul a box down into the ship's hold.

"Do you hear that?" John asked.

"You mean that slightly muffled sound in our ear coms?"

"Yes," Watkins whispered. "Jack gave me his com before he left. I sneaked it into the lip of Clint's stocking cap while he was kneeling down talking to Lazarus earlier, so if he decides to try to get the drop on us while we're loading these weapons into the boat..." John's sentence trailed as he and Sloane lowered the wooden crate to the lower deck.

"Beauty, baby," Sloane felt under his hoodie for his shoulder-holstered gun. "Beauty."

* * *

"This weather is unfathomable, isn't it, my friend?" Josiah Lazarus said under the umbrella that he was holding over his and Thoreaux's heads. "You don't know how much I appreciate your being here to help me tonight."

"I don't mind at all," Clint said, smiling at the heavyset man. "But it wasn't all my doing."

From there, Clint detailed the whole story of Dragon's Men and what they had done to him and the chief. He described all that they had done regarding his wife, plus, everything else up to and including tonight.

"And they even have one of them over there in the trees."

Josiah turned to look over Clint's shoulder.

Unbeknownst to them, Mercedes was standing behind and to the left of the two men–with two guns trained on their heads.

"When it rains, it pours, doesn't it, fellas?" she asked.

"Son of a bitch," Clinton said under his breath.

"Yeah, it is," Merc laughed.

Looking up, she saw that Hawk also held two of the speedboat men at gunpoint. "Let's keep it down out here, boys." Hawk politely requested.

"How are you and Danny doing in there, Boss?" Dr. Lara asked.

Just then, four men came up from the hold of the tugger with their hands high in the air. John and Daniel followed close behind.

"Good." John replied to Merc's question. "Danny and I are doing really well."

"Let's round 'em up and move 'em out, boys," Sam said.

"And get back home to where the weather is a little more humane," Danny quipped.

58

A JOB WELL DONE

Within less than an hour of his arrival, the four members of Dragon's Men had Josiah Lazarus and his entire crew, as well as Clinton Thoreaux, tied up, gagged, and back in Lazarus's tugboat. Daniel had gone to the ship's cockpit and set its automatic steering mechanism to return down the river toward the gulf. For their part, the Dragon's Men quartet was happy to return to the dryness of the company SUV.

John was on the phone with Agent Ritter letting him know what was coming his way.

"Well, I've already sent out two teams to apprehend Mr. Lazarus, John," Ritter informed him. "I'll radio out to tell them what to look for."

"Very good," John answered. "The boat is on auto-pilot, but it's moving at the speed of a tired turtle. I'm sure your team will be able to board it with little trouble. They'll find Lazarus and his cabal bound and gagged and relatively scratch-free."

"Although, for the record," Sloane said loudly from the passenger's seat, "I wanted to at least shoot 'em in the shoulder. I mean, sure, we zip-tied them and put some rags real tight in their mouths, but you know a decent henchman could get through those in twenty-five, thirty minutes."

"Did you guys put them in separate cabins?" Jake asked.

"Of course we put them in separate cabins. We're not amateurs," John said. He then pulled the phone away from his face and whispered to Daniel, "You did put them in separate cabins, didn't you?"

"Of course, I did," Sloane whispered back.

John put the phone back to his ear.

"Definitely ready to be picked up," Watkins said, attempting to ease Agent Ritter's mind.

"That may be so, but do you guarantee your work?" Jake inquired.

"Come on, Jake, you've worked with us before. You know we've always, *always*, come through for you in the clutch."

"That you have," the ATF agent agreed, "however those situations were *those* situations, and this situation is tonight's situation."

"We've come through before, and we came through tonight. I guarantee it," John reassured him. "As a matter of fact, the tugboat that your assailants are on just went out of sight, so they should be to your crew anytime now."

"Okay, but I do have one last question," Agent Ritter took a deep breath. "When Lazarus and his squad came through, I counted three boats. Two speed boats and his tugboat. You're sending down just his tugboat. Where are the two speed boats that I saw earlier?"

"I have them right on the shore next to the crates of illegal guns. Plus, once this rain lets up, my team will be safeguarding the weapons and the boats until someone gets here." It was John's turn to take a deep breath before relaying news he knew would upset the agent. "However, I do need to inform you that the U.S. Marshals Service are on their way here to seize both the guns and the boats."

"What?" The news did, indeed, upset Agent Ritter. "John, you can't do this to me, brother. I'm an ATF agent. You do remember what the *F* stands for, right?"

"I do, but the Marshals have jurisdiction here," John informed Ritter. "They call it 'managing assets seized from any criminal enterprises.' And that's just what they're going to do. Besides," John continued, "you are getting to arrest Josiah Lazarus, one of the biggest fish in the sea of illegal weapons. You'll be remembered for this long after those guns and such are yesterday's news. Also, just think about all the paperwork you won't have to do because the weapons are elsewhere."

"Yeah," Ritter said, quickly regaining his good mood. "You make two excellent points. Ya know, John, the ATF could always use a good man like you."

"I'm fine where I'm at with the team, but I do appreciate the offer."

"It never hurts to ask," Jake said. "Okay, Johnny, I've got to go. The teams just radioed that they are alongside the tugboat and are getting ready to board."

"All right, Jake, godspeed, buddy."

Watkins ended the call.

Just as John ended his phone call, the rain suddenly ended, almost like a spigot being turned off.

"Thank you, Lord," Watkins said.

"I'll stay and chaperone these weapons," Sloane volunteered.

"Now that the rain has stopped, let's get out of these wet clothes and get someplace a wee bit drier," Hawk suggested.

The quartet rallied at the back of the SUV. As John opened the hatch, Sloane commented, "I must say, kids, this op was just about flawless. None of us even got so much as a scratch."

John gave Mercedes a quick look before saying, "Yes, it was absolutely flawless."

They each grabbed their corresponding suitcases, undressed, then redressed into dry clothes. By the time they were presentable, a crew of U.S. Marshals pulled up to the scene. The passenger's side window came down, and one of the marshals hollered out to them. "We have been told there's a cache of illegal weapons around here. You four know anything about that?

"Yes, sir," John answered, pointing toward Pier 51. "Follow this dirt road here all the way down to the water. You'll see what you're looking for sitting at the end of the pier. The boats are on either side of them."

"Much obliged, son," waved the clearly Cajun lawman.

As the marshals pulled down the muddy path, Sloane said with a smile, "Looks like we're all going to get outta here."

"Sam, do you want to call your meemaw and tell her we're on our way?"

"You know it," Hawk replied.

"I will be so glad to get back home," Dr. Lara said. "This weather is just stupid. It's almost midnight, and it's still 96 degrees out."

"We'll head home soon," Watkins said, climbing into the front passenger's seat.

Daniel got behind the wheel, Sam and Mercedes hopped into the back.

"Gotta tell ya," Sam started up, "that wind was blowing so hard tonight…I had myself tied to that tree limb, but man, baby, that limb in that wind, it was like I was riding a bull."

"How'd you manage to hit all your targets with it being like that?" Mercedes asked.

"Cos I'm good, baby. I…am…good."

"That was theater out there tonight," John smiled, "and everyone played their part to perfection. Thank the good Lord, Melissa and her grandma can stay in Natchez, and Hawk's meemaw won't have to tremble with fear every time a car drives past her house."

"I can't thank you guys enough," said a relieved Hawkins. "I know we do a ton of jobs for other folks, but when it's personal like this, there's always that added touch of pressure to get it right. We hit this one dead, solid perfect."

"Got that right, we did."

Sloane started up the Escalade, and they drove off into the night.

59

THE CLEAN-UP

When the sun rose over the parish of Natchez, Louisiana the following morning, it found John Watkins, Daniel Sloane, and Dr. Mercedes Lara lending a hand to the citizens of Natchez as they went about the task of cleaning up the mess that was left in the wake of Friday night's gulf storm.

Fallen tree branches, window shutters, pieces of roofs that had been blown off, and massive amounts of debris littered the yards and streets of the small parish.

"This is gonna take a while, brother," Daniel Sloane said to John and Mercedes as the three of them surveyed the damage.

"We've got time," was Watkins' solemn response.

"I know it looks like an unconquerable mess," Merc said, "but with everyone chipping in and doing their part, it won't take very long."

"Whatever the case may be, we'll be here till the end," John told them.

"Well," Sloane clapped his hands together, "let's get at it then."

* * *

Sam Hawkins was back at his meemaw's house, helping her with the clean-up around her property. Helping Sam was Latin Jackson's

Chocolate Lab, Louie. Hawk had gotten a wheelbarrow and a metal rake from underneath his meemaw's house. While he raked up the rubble and refuse and deposited it into the wheelbarrow, Louie picked up branches, brought them over to the wheelbarrow, and dropped them in. Meemaw stood next to her grandson, just talk, talk, talking away.

"Now, Sambo, who is going to be the police now that the police are all arrested or dead?"

"Our man, Jack Thompson–he's a lieutenant for the police department where we live–he also does some work with the U.S. Marshal Service. Now, the Marshals are sending a few folks down here to fill in as law officers until they can get a permanent crew together."

"Well, how long ya think that'll take?"

"I'm not one-hundred percent sure, Meemaw." Sam used the rake and his free hand to pick up a pile of twigs and leaves and put them into the wheelbarrow. He stood up straight, then leaned against the rake. "If I had to make an educated guess, I'd say that within six to eight months, Natchez will have its new police department in place, and life as you knew it will be back in style."

"Six to eight months? Goodness, Sambo, I may not even be around by then."

"You won't be around? Where you gonna go, Meemaw?" Sam asked.

"I don't know if you've noticed or not, honey bear, but I ain't exactly no spring chicken anymore."

"You're talking about dying?"

"I sho nuff ain't talkin' 'bout a vacation in Fiji," Sandrine snapped at her grandson. "I'm ninety-eight years old, Sambo. I could go anytime now."

"We could all go at any time, Meemaw, but look at yourself. You're not sick, you're active, you live in a town where everyone loves you and wants to see you be around for a long time. People your age pass away because they're lonely, and they just give up hope. They have nothing left to look forward to, so they just sit around waiting to die."

"Did your doctor friend tell you that?"

"She sure did."

"I like your little friends, Sambo. You've surrounded yourself with good people. And if your parents were still alive, they would be so proud of you," Sandrine said, her eyes misting up. "And you already know how I feel. Plus, Dot and Melissa will be forever grateful to y'all for everything you did for them this week. They were scared. Scared for their safety. Scared that the only answer was to relocate to someplace where they wouldn't know no one and have to say goodbye to everyone and everything that they did know."

"Well, I'm just glad the good Lord saw fit to work it out for them to be able to stay put right here where they belong," Hawk said, getting back to raking the cluttered yard.

"Jesus always takes care of His own," Sandrine said reverently.

"Amen to that, Meemaw."

"I have to say, it will be nice to have proper law enforcement types around here again. You don't know what it's been like, Sambo, always havin' to be lookin' over your shoulder all the time, wonderin' who the police is going to hassle and hound next. You see them being combative with someone on your street, and you feel bad cos of what they's havin' to go through, but at the same time, you feel relief cos it ain't you that's bein' harassed."

Sandrine's emotions began to overcome her once again.

"Aww, Meemaw." Sam let the rake fall to the ground as he moved to put his grandmother in a comforting embrace. "You don't have to worry about that anymore. The nightmare is over."

Sandrine basked in the hug for a good while before releasing her grandson. "So, when will the new police get here?"

"It will be sometime tomorrow."

"Tomorrow? Well, who's gonna be the police till they get here?"

"You remember Officer Leblanc, right?"

"Oh, yes, that sweet little colored girl. Mm-hmm."

"Yeah," Hawk answered slowly. "Some people might call her that. Actually–check that–*you* would call her that."

Sam raked a bit more before continuing. "Anyway, she was the one good apple in the whole bunch. She came through like a champ, and she really helped us seal the deal as far as taking down all those dirty cops. She is now the acting chief. Plus, we'll be sticking around for another day or two to help out however we can."

"God bless you, boy." Sandrine started to tear up again.

"Geez, Meemaw, you about the cryin'est woman that I ever did see. What's wrong now?"

"Aww, Sambo, I should have called you and your friends a long time ago," she whimpered. "We all been livin' in this utter turmoil for so long now, I just figured that this was the way life was gonna be. I kinda surrendered myself to it. But the whole time, the answer was just a phone call away."

Samuel put his hand on his grandmother's shoulder. "Meemaw, I'm going to tell you something that I learned in the military: *What's done is done; now let's move on.* What that means is that you can't dwell on the past or past mistakes. All you can do is your best in the present to make your future as good as it can be." Sam locked eyes with his Meemaw. "No one really knows what tomorrow will bring, but I can tell you this: Your tomorrows are going to be a lot better from here on out. And I, for one, will sleep a lot better knowing that."

"Looks like he will, too," Meemaw nodded in Louie's direction.

The brown dog had decided it was time to take a break and was now sprawled out underneath a nearby shade tree.

"Good ol' Lou," Hawk smiled. "There's a dog that knows the secret to life: Work hard, play hard, and never miss a chance to take a nap."

* * *

Lieutenant Jack Thompson, Latin Jackson, and Solange Leblanc were in what used to be Chief Darryl Briggs' office at the Natchez Police Department. The lieutenant and Latin were helping Solange get settled into her new position.

Latin was at the computer setting up a new operating system that would help Solange with the transition to the department.

Solange was standing behind Latin, listening intently to everything he was teaching her about the new computer system and how it worked.

Wearing his signature cowboy hat and snakeskin boots, Jack was tipped back in a wooden chair, propped against a wall in the corner.

"I have to imagine, Chief Leblanc," Thompson said, "that you must be excited, happy, and scared to death all at the same time."

Solange flashed a wide smile. "I am so glad that someone else knows what I'm feeling. I mean, I know I'm up for the challenge, and things are going to get a lot better around here now. But still, I am definitely apprehensive about being in charge of a whole new team."

"Solange," Jack said, "I can assure you that the men and women that are coming here are the top of the line. Professional, through and through. You'll be teaching them about the area, the people—"

"The weather," Latin cut in.

"Yes," Jack agreed, "and they'll be teaching you about procedure and helping you turn this department into a finely run machine."

"I just hope it goes smoothly, is all," Solange commented.

"Don't you fret nothing about that, Chief. We're the U.S. Marshals Service. We only do smooth transitions."

Latin was typing furiously. "Just…about…got it."

He stretched his arms up over his head and cracked his knuckles. Then the stout fellow stood up. "Alright, Chief, she's all yours. I wrote down all your passwords, and every account is double verified–which means you're the only one that can access anything on here. Just don't lose your cell phone," Latin warned. "Now, just go ahead, have a seat, and let's take her for a test drive."

As Chief Leblanc sat down in the chair, she smiled first at Jack, then over her shoulder at Latin. She put her hands on the keyboard, drew in a deep breath and said, "Okay…here we go."

EPILOGUE

Four days had passed since the dangerous and damaging Gulf storm had nearly devastated Natchez, Louisiana. However, thanks to Dragon's Men, Jack Thompson, Latin Jackson, Louie, and all the folks from the parish, Natchez was well on its way back.

It was time for the heroes to be on their way home, but there was one last thing left to do.

Sam Hawkins, Dr. Mercedes Lara, and Louie were in the first black SUV that pulled into the parking lot of the Natchez Police Department. In the other SUV, Daniel Sloane and John Watkins sat up front while Melissa Thoreaux rode in the middle seat behind them. As Daniel parked the ride, John turned around to address Melissa. "Are you sure you're up for this?"

"Of course," she answered. "You promised him that you would let him see me, and I certainly don't want to make a liar out of you."

"I hope that's not the only reason you're doing this," John said.

"Definitely not," Melissa smiled. "I have more than a few things to say to Clint before he starts the rest of his life without me."

The three of them got out of the Escalade just as Latin and Jack pulled up in Latin's Ferrari.

"Coming to say one last goodbye to your lady friend?" John asked his portly buddy.

"Afraid so," Latin lamented. "She's the one. Sadly, she's also the one that is probably going to be the busiest person in the country with all the new responsibility she's undertaking. Plus, she's about ten hours away from White Pines, and while I'm sure that these are all obstacles that love could conquer, I feel certain that I'm not the tango partner that *love* would need in order to get this particular dance done."

"So close, yet so far away," Sloane said, walking around the front of the Escalade.

"I couldn't have said it better myself." Latin gave a bitter smile. "So I'm not even going to try."

The six of them and Louie walked out of the blazing Louisiana heat and into the air-conditioned coolness of the police department building. One of the new temps was standing behind the Plexiglas window in the lobby.

"Good afternoon," the officer greeted them.

"Is the Chief in?" Latin asked.

"Yes, sir. Chief Leblanc is back in her office. You can go on back, Mr. Jackson."

"Thank you, kind sir," Latin waved as he headed back to Solange's office.

"Is Clinton Thoreaux still here?" Melissa asked.

"Yes, ma'am, he sure is," the officer answered. "After the whole lot of them were denied bail at their arraignment yesterday, they were moved to the state pen. But Mr. Thoreaux was kept here under the orders of Chief Leblanc."

"May I go back to see him?"

"Yes, ma'am. I'll take you back."

* * *

Latin knocked on the door to Solange's office.

"Come in," she invited.

Latin turned the knob and pushed the door open just enough to stick his head in.

"Hey!" she exclaimed with genuine delight.

He entered her office and shut the door quietly behind himself. He watched as Solange moved from behind her desk to come and throw her arms around him. She planted a kiss on his lips–a big, sweeping, Hollywood romance kiss that, literally, took his breath away.

"Wow," the computer geek said. "I'm going to go out on a limb and say that you've missed me just a little."

"It's just been crazy," Solange said. "Seems the world is moving around me at a dizzying speed, and you're the first thing I've seen all day that's helped me catch my balance."

"Well, I'm glad I could be of service," Latin smiled.

Solange moved back to her chair and sat down while Latin planted himself in a chair on the other side of her desk. They looked lovingly at each other for a few moments before Solange broke the silence. "Is Louie here?"

"Yeah, he's out front with John and them."

"Aw, I want to see 'im," Solange said.

"Sure." Latin stood up, opened the office door, and whistled softly. Within seconds, the brown Lab came trotting into the chief's office.

"Louie," she said to the dog playfully.

Lou moved around the desk and took a seat at Leblanc's feet, resting his head in her lap.

"Oh, you're such a lovable boy," she said as she scratched Lou's furry head. "Just like your daddy."

"Alright, Lou, let's let the lady get back to work." Latin smacked his hand against his hip and said, "Heel, boy."

The Chocolate Lab came around the desk and sat obediently next to his master.

"So, if I asked you to *heel*, would you come be by me?" Solange asked.

"I would love that," Latin answered.

"But...?"

"But reality being what it is, I have a life to get back to in White Pines. So, while you are definitely someone that I'd give everything up for, I'm not so sure my lifestyle and yours are two types that can coexist together. Besides...John, Daniel, Sam, and Doc...they're my people, and they need me."

They each exchanged a sad smile.

"I knew it was too much to wish for," Leblanc said. "And I'll have my hands full for the next little while getting law and order rectified around here again. Probably won't have much time for eating and sleeping, much less trying to nurture a new relationship. Still..."

"Yeah, still."

Louie let out a long yawn.

"Oh, I'm sorry, Mr. Lou. Are we keeping you awake?" Latin playfully chided his dog. He then walked over to Solange's desk, leaned over it and gave her one last kiss. "Well, if you ever do find that you have some time on your hands, I'd love to show you around my town someday."

"Hmmm," Solange sighed, "I'd say you've got yourself a deal, Mr. Latin Jackson."

She walked around her desk, put her arms around Latin's neck, and gave him one long, last kiss goodbye.

* * *

Clinton Thoreaux was resting on the cot in his jail cell when he heard her approach. He sat up on the side of the bed and rubbed the blurriness out of his eyes.

"I see Mr. Watkins kept his promise," Clint said.

"He said that you might have something to say to me," Melissa replied.

"Look, baby, I know I screwed up, and words can't—"

"Aw, gee whiz, Clint, if all you're going to say is the same ol'

BS lines that you've been saying for the last five years, then just shut your hole up. I actually came here because I have something to say to you."

"O-o-okay," Clint stammered in surprise.

"Y'ain't nothin' but a coward, Clint, and the only coward bigger than you...is me. I shoulda left yer lyin', abusive ass years ago. But I was too scared. Too scared and too dumb to know any better," Melissa said in shame. "But you know what? I have people that love me and care for me–the two things you were supposed to do for me. But you didn't because *you* were too stupid to know any better."

"Now, look here, Mel—"

"Shut up, Clint!" Melissa yelled. "You've had five years to talk. Now, it's time for you to listen. You had it all, you know that? A loving wife, a house, a great job, a child that would have loved you as much as I did. But that's over now. We're over. You're over. I'm going to have this baby, and he will be loved more than any child ever could be. But don't you worry–I'm going to tell him all about you. I'm going to tell him how you abused me, how you beat me, how you tortured me. And I'll be sure that he knows that when I was pregnant with him you made sure that you didn't miss a single day of beating me and him. I'm going to make sure that he becomes the complete opposite of what you are: a complete piece of trash."

Melissa took a moment to breathe and then said, "Goodbye, Clint."

She began to walk away but then stopped. "Oh, one last thing. Don't drop the soap."

A WORD FROM DOC

Thank you for reading *Dragon's Men: Swamp Covered Shields*. I hope you enjoyed it.

I occasionally send newsletters with details on new releases, special offers, Christmas stories, and other bits of news relating to all of my characters.

If you would like to sign up to the mailing list, please go to:

www.goldenalleypress.com/doc-ephraim-bates

(Please know that I hate spam as much as you do. Your email will never be shared.)

I love hearing from my readers. Here's my email address: doc@docephraimbates.com.

You can make a difference . . .

Reviews are the most powerful weapon I have when it comes to getting my books noticed. Your honest review will help bring them to the attention of other readers. If you've enjoyed this book, please consider leaving a review online.

Doc

ACKNOWLEDGEMENTS

I would like to thank the following people for their contributions and motivation during the writing of *Swamp Covered Shields*: Logger, William Jenkins, PJ Steelman, Misty Van Arsdale, Bob Shackleford, and Alene Fast.

For all the research assistance on this project, I send a big-time "Couldn't have done it without you, Gaylord!" to my great friend Bo "Bosef" Powell.

I would also like to extend my great appreciation to Jordan Donaldson, Chuck Purnell, Mike Ford, April Ussery-Millward, and Michael J Hoffman.

And I could never be grateful enough to Nancy Sayre–publisher, editor, and most of all, friend.

※ ※ ※

And now a bit of explanation about my dedication of this book to Angela Leone.

Angela and I met through a mutual friend, Thomas Kane, right after I graduated high school. She and I dated briefly until one day her father decided that I was no good for his daughter.

About a decade later, I ran into Angela at a restaurant in Aberdeen, Maryland. As we quickly became tight friends once again, I came to see that Angela had a thirst for knowledge. She loved listening to my stories, she loved asking me questions, and she loved researching ideas.

I was dating a woman named Jessica at the time, and I knew that I was going to marry one of them: Jess or Angie.

I chose to marry Jess.

Sadly, in one of those circumstances where a person finds himself asking God why He did what He did, Angela died just a few months later from a rare form of blood poisoning. She had been admitted to the hospital on a Thursday, and she was gone before Saturday night.

Angela was only 26 years old.

For a long time after that, I would play the *What If?* game. What if I had married Angela instead? Would circumstances have turned out differently? Eventually, I had to make myself stop thinking about her that way because I was driving myself mad. Certainly, there are no winners in a game of *What If?* Rest in peace, Angela. You are not forgotten.

SOUNDTRACK

https://bit.ly/swamp-covered-shields-soundtrack

1. **Riversilvers** - "Dreams" 4:25
   (to be listened to while reading the Prologue)

2. **CHVRCHES** - "Over" 3:44
   (to be listened to while reading Chapter 4: Road Chatter)

3. **Kari Kimmel** - "Cruel Summer" 2:27
   (to be listened to while reading Chapter 5: Home Again)

4. **Michael FK & Faodail** - "Holding Back" 4:04
   (to be read during Chapter 15: The Operation Begins)

5. **Keep Shelley In Athens** - "Don't Fear The Reaper" 3:24
   (to be read during Chapter 30: The Old Bus And Switch Routine)

6. **The Midnight** - "Sunset" 5:27
   (to be read during Chapter 56: It Always Rains When You're Having Fun)

7. **Marvel '83** - 'Remember When' 5:58
   (to be read during Chapter 59: The Clean Up)

ABOUT THE AUTHOR

Doc Ephraim Bates is the author of the popular Boom!!...Killers. and Dragon's Men series.

He has been writing comedic action thrillers since age fourteen. The youngest of seven sons, Doc mastered the three skills most valuable to his characters: maintaining a sense of humor, learning how to take a beating, and the art of not getting caught.

Doc makes his online home at
www.docephraimbates.com.

Connect with Doc on Facebook at
www.facebook.com/DocEphraimBates.

If the mood strikes you, send him an email at
doc@docephraimbates.com

Sign up for his occasional
and always-entertaining newsletter at
www.goldenalleypress.com/doc-ephraim-bates

Made in the USA
Middletown, DE
05 May 2024